# DARK WATERS RISING

# DARK WATERS RISING

## Cassandra Clark

**SEVERN
HOUSE**

First world edition published in Great Britain and the USA in 2022
by Severn House, an imprint of Canongate Books Ltd,
14 High Street, Edinburgh EH1 1TE.

Trade paperback edition first published in Great Britain and the USA in 2023
by Severn House, an imprint of Canongate Books Ltd.

severnhouse.com

*British Library Cataloguing-in-Publication Data*
A CIP catalogue record for this title is available from the British Library.

ISBN-13: 978-1-4483-0665-7 (cased)
ISBN-13: 978-1-4483-0670-1 (trade paper)
ISBN-13: 978-1-4483-0669-5 (e-book)

*All Severn House titles are printed on acid-free paper.*

Typeset by Palimpsest Book Production Ltd.,
Falkirk, Stirlingshire, Scotland.
Printed and bound in Great Britain by
TJ Books, Padstow, Cornwall.

# PROLOGUE

*Autumn 1394*

A man was watching from the trees. He was waiting his chance. As soon as one of the fishermen brought his boat to shore he would take it. He fingered his knife.

Behind the trees a puddled lane emerged from between the cottages round a green. It wound down to the bank of the estuary where a few boats lay above the tideline. The man concealed among the trees guessed this was where the villagers did their fishing, either sitting on the bank with a line in the water or by sculling their makeshift boats into the deeper channel further off to drop a net over the side. Their boats were little more than coracles, unseaworthy in his estimation and he didn't want to take any more chances. A boat already in use would be safest. He fingered the knife again.

It was foul weather. Nobody was about but for one man on the water, whistling through his teeth while he waited for a fish to bite. Suddenly a flash of silver broke the surface. Moments later he turned for home at last. Hold back, the man with the knife warned himself. Hold back. Wait until the luckless fool comes ashore. Wait for it.

He melted further in amongst the wet branches as the craft forced a way through the swollen waters. The tide looked full enough to break its banks. It was already flooding the path from the village. The knife-man frowned with impatience. He had to get across to the other side before dark. His life would be nothing if he was stopped now.

The Humber estuary was wide here, narrowing upriver to where they said there was a Roman ford and beyond that was a bridge near a small town whose name he didn't know. This was the last place where he could risk the crossing.

What he would find on the other bank he had no idea beyond the vague knowledge that not far off would be the Abbey of

Meaux, a priory of nuns at somewhere called Swyne, and a house of Austin canons hidden in the woods. He grimaced and, rubbing the back of a travel-stained hand across his face, he narrowed his eyes as the fisherman at last beached the coracle and jumped ashore.

The grip on his knife tightened and he wondered if he would have to use it.

# ONE

When Hildegard entered the Prioress's private chapel she found her sitting in a wooden chair, boots resting on a stool and her cat lying across her knees. This was unusual enough to drag a remark from her after her usual obeisance. The Prioress gave her a resigned glance and allowed her gaze to drift towards her altar with its single icon and the candle burning in front of it.

'*Vita brevis*, my dear. None of us live for ever. It is for this reason I want to speak to you. You will know my mind. I wish you to take my place when the time comes for me to resign—'

Hildegard's comment that, God willing, it would be years yet before such an event took place was scarcely uttered before the Prioress put up a hand.

'It's the way of the world, Hildegard. It's no good pretending. When the time comes I'm sure you'll enjoy staying in one place and not being sent hither and yon. But my point is this. I do not intend to leave you with a priory of disobedient and irreligious nuns. It has come to my notice of late that there is dissension among them, about what I have no idea.' She raised her eyebrows to invite a comment.

Hildegard hesitated. 'A feeling of unkindness seems to have arisen among the novices. I've noticed it too. It's a sort of malice, whispering behind hands, that sort of thing.'

'What do they have to be malicious about? Are they not happy, doing God's work?'

'They seem to be taking sides over something. I can see no reason for it.'

'As in the outside world, so here.' She sighed. 'The Schism caused by two men claiming to be the true pope is a contagion. And even our own realm is riven in twain. At least two of our barons see themselves as king in place of their young nephew. Ever since Richard was crowned and conducted himself with such impressive regality – astonishing for a ten-year-old –

they've hated him because of the malice deep within their own hearts.'

'He didn't endear himself when he behaved so generously and courageously during the Great Revolt either,' Hildegard added. 'Offering to free the peasants from bonded labour showed the barons up for what they are.'

'No good will come of their greed. We must be vigilant—' She broke off. 'To the point, Hildegard. Search out the dissent here in our small corner and let's put a stop to it.'

'Very well, my lady.'

She moved towards the door but the Prioress leaned back in her chair, closed her eyes and gave one long impatient sigh. 'Why does this current crop of novices prefer petty jealousy and spite? Do they not prefer peace and harmony? Are we not all living in the hope of the same thing – a useful and contented life followed when the time comes by God's grace to bless our endeavours?'

As it was a question that did not require an answer Hildegard made none and after a pause the Prioress continued. 'I've been thinking it might be to do with those twins, Bella and Rogella. They prefer secrecy to openness. Dark to light. Or am I too harsh?' She opened her eyes and fixed a questioning glance on Hildegard to invite an answer.

'I believe they resent what they see as restrictions on their freedom.'

'Don't they understand, we work for the good of everyone, not just for ourselves? They have no vocation. I regret taking them in. Their father sent them here because his heir persuaded him they wouldn't get husbands with such small dowries. In his view there was not enough to divide between three. Do you remember that inundation near Withernsea two years ago?'

Hildegard said she did.

'The old fellow lost much of his land to it. The manor would not be viable if it were split between his three children. The girls do not like being cut out. He told me he could do nothing with them after their mother died.'

'They're fond of boasting about their run of nursemaids who could do nothing with them either.'

'Bella and Rogella.' She sighed again. 'Yes, I remember their mother, so sad. I believe her husband drove her to her death.

He's a harsh fellow, Sir Roger. It's ironic that one of the twins should have been named after him. Rogella – what vanity!' She gave a wan smile. 'In some respects he's not much different to our dear Lord Roger up at Castle Hutton – both men vain and over-sure of themselves, Roger's philandering now severely curtailed by young lady Melisen, of course.' In an aside she added, 'Who would have thought that preening child-wife should be the one to bring the old rogue to heel!' She frowned. 'But Roger de Campany is a different kettle of fish, as cold as an eel in my opinion, and those two girls of his are well out of it. I'm surprised they don't see it and welcome the chance to make a good life for themselves.'

'They do complain a lot and it sets the other novices off in a search for imperfections in their own lives—'

'Which in this weather are no doubt many!' She gave Hildegard one of the sudden warm smiles that softened her features with a thousand wrinkles. 'Do what you can, my dear. Offer them consolation. If there are any real complaints we will deal with them at once. Meanwhile I hope the new young priest from Meaux will instil in them a greater sense of obedience to the Rule. I hear he's quite a zealot. Hubert is watching him carefully to make sure he doesn't overstep the mark.'

Dismissed, Hildegard went out into the garth. It was raining. No summer to speak of, ruined harvests, a bleak winter ahead, and everything already perpetually damp with the dreary drip of rain falling steadily from the eaves. She pulled a greased cape over her head.

The Prioress's mention of Hubert, lord abbot of Meaux, made her brush thoughts of the weather aside and dwell instead on pleasanter speculations about when she might next see him.

# TWO

I t was still pouring with rain when she crossed over to the cloister later on. Her boots were beginning to let in water, and she stepped round puddles with a muttered curse. Quickly crossing herself, she reached the north cloister where a handful of nuns were copying letters.

Sister Josiana was surrounded by an interested group while she explained the working of an astrolabe. No ill-will there, she noticed, the three young women looked equally fascinated by the workings of the brass instrument, said to be a model of the universe that would allow them to predict the whereabouts of the planets and fix the time of the tides. She went over to have a look.

Just then the Prioress, holding a cover over her head, made a sudden appearance. 'It's Tierce, everyone! Did you not hear the bell?' She began to shoo them out onto the garth.

'But, my lady, it's bucketing down!' It was one of the twins.

'It's only wetness!' The Prioress was sharp. 'You're not made of salt, are you? Get away with you into church. And later,' she added, 'I'll need somebody to go down to see those canons at Haltemprice Priory to find out how they're preparing themselves in case the river really does break its banks as we're being warned.'

'I'll go,' Josiana said at once before the Prioress could ask.

'If you're going in this,' indicating the lashing rain, 'you must take someone with you. But be careful. Astrolabes aside, I doubt whether the river will hold its banks much longer.'

Josiana, an ethereal young woman, short-sighted from too much bending over books, cradled the brass astrolabe in her arms now it was folded shut and gave a nod. 'I'll go straight after Tierce, my lady. I need to check a few figures with their astronomer. I can't believe what they're telling me. I must have got it wrong. All I can say is, praise God our priory is on higher ground! We should be safe enough here when the flood sweeps up.'

'If that's your view, make sure we have everything we need to help sit it out.'

'Are we ever caught out, my lady?' Hildegard smiled.

'There's always a first time, Hildegard. Let it not be under my jurisdiction!'

As everyone prepared to make a dash across the garth one of the twins made a sarcastic remark about it being more useful to build an ark if it was going to be as bad as they were being warned.

'Prayers aren't going to do us much good when we're waist deep in flood water, are they?' She tossed her head with derision.

One or two others tittered but several of the older nuns looked askance and Hildegard followed them across the rain-swept garth feeling thoughtful.

# THREE

The new priest gave a short, sharp sermon about obedience to the Rule of St Benedict, 'Now reformed and clarified by the writings of Bernard of Clairvaux – bless his soul,' he added, making Hildegard purse her lips.

She had a soft spot for the famed lovers – the nun Eloise and the monk Abelard – how could she not with Hubert de Courcy just down the lane? She considered Bernard's treatment of the renegade monk barbaric – castration? For falling in love with a soul-mate? – but her wandering thoughts returned to the young priest as he continued, unaware how his words were being received.

He was at pains, no doubt after the Prioress's instructions, to point out that it behoved them to carry out their duties to their Order, to their Prioress, to their fellow companions, nuns, novices and secular workers alike, and to the lord of all whom they served – with no complaints and good hearts. He glared round at everyone as if searching out any hint of dissent.

With his unruly black curls frilling round his tonsure belying the expression in his eyes of unbending reproof – eyes which were darkly piercing and seemed to probe deep into the souls of his listeners in a most intimate manner – he launched deeper and more vigorously into the realms of rhetoric with further probings into their purpose here on earth and whether they were intended for any other reason than to submit— She jerked awake. *Submit?* She picked up the thread and forced herself to listen more carefully to the very end.

Afterwards the fourteen nuns and an assortment of novices filed out in a strangely chastened manner like women shaken to the core except for Bella or was it Rogella? Whichever one it was she gave a swift glance at her twin under her eyelids and bit her bottom lip as if to suppress a gale of mirth and when she noticed Hildegard catch this glance she bent her head, pulled up her hood in as demure a manner as possible and mingled in among the others to seek cover.

\*    \*    \*

Later, noticing Hildegard heaving a few logs out of the basket into the stove in the warming room, one of the twins went to help.

'That poor young monk,' she murmured in a syrupy tone. 'Imagine being a priest here. Is he going to have to ride back alone through the woods to Meaux in all this rain?'

'I expect he's used to it by now.' Hildegard shrugged and wiped her hands on a cloth. 'No doubt he'd stay here if he could.'

'What? Have a man in the priory! Whatever next, domina!' She gave a tinkling laugh as if shocked by such a thought. 'I see Josiana doesn't care about the threat of floods.' She added on a note of longing, 'She's already left for Haltemprice Priory to see those Austin friars.'

'Did she take anyone with her?'

'One of the lay-sisters, I believe.' She paused and added, scarcely audibly, 'Being obedient as she is, would she do otherwise?'

'Rogella—' began Hildegard but the girl giggled. 'I'm not Rogella, domina. I'm Bella.'

'Forgive me—'

'It's always happening.'

Hildegard noticed the way she exchanged glances with her twin on the other side of the chamber as if some thought had flashed between them.

'It must be strange to see someone identical to yourself, like looking into a mirror,' she remarked, thinking, there is a difference – is it the shape of their eyebrows? – though it doesn't help in deciding who is who. And they also walk slightly differently, Bella, or was it Rogella, being lighter on her feet – but how could she really tell which was which – this one could be Rogella, having a laugh. No wonder they drove their nursemaids away.

'You must have had a lot of fun swapping places when you were children?' she remarked.

'That'd be telling, domina. Would we seek to deceive? Us?'

Hildegard couldn't help smiling.

# FOUR

Later, as she splashed through the puddles in the dark on her way back to bed after Matins, she couldn't help sympathizing with the novices. No wonder they found it irksome to join the strict Cistercian Rule at Swyne. Having to get up out of a warm bed at midnight to stand in a draughty church to sing antiphons was enough to make anyone rebel, especially if they had ever had dreams of being the chatelaine of a fine manor house.

With the melancholy drip of rainwater sliding off her cloak to the stone floor she got into bed and pulled the blanket over her head. But before she could fall asleep a sound came that made her freeze in alarm. It was a shout, violent and demanding, followed by the thumping of fists on the door of the lodge.

Her bed chamber was in the wall of the priory defences and the sound could not be ignored. When it came again, even more insistently, she sat up. Something must be wrong. Reluctantly sliding her legs over the edge of the bed she rammed her feet back inside her damp boots and groped towards the door in the thick dark.

Rain was still falling when she went outside. Pulling her cloak over her head, she hurried towards the light above the gatehouse. There was definitely something up. Shivering with cold, and suddenly apprehensive about what could be afoot, she pressed a shoulder against the door and, blinking at the sudden garish light from a flambeau, stepped inside.

The porteress, Blanche, was leaning against the outer doors with the peephole open so she could peer outside but, startled, she glanced up when Hildegard suddenly appeared.

'Praise God, you're here, domina. There's someone outside in the lane demanding to be let inside. At this time of night! What shall I do?'

Hildegard joined her at the little flap but could see nothing. It was pitch black out there. Both women listened for a moment. There was no need to ask whether it was man or woman, a man's hoarse voice renewed its demands to be admitted. Fists hammered again on the doors.

Hildegard took charge. 'He's going to wake the entire priory. Keep the beam in place.'

Speaking through the peephole she demanded, 'Who's there?'

From the lane a voice gasped something and Hildegard had to ask again, 'Who is it? Declare yourself.'

'I beg you – please, sister, for the love of God, let me in – I beg you, let me inside or I'm a dead man!'

'Your name, sir?'

'Master Leonin, King's musician, and I beg entry to your convent. Sister, I mean you no harm – I am alone. One man only. Help me!'

'Are you armed?'

A pause followed.

Hildegard repeated the question. Eventually a hesitant voice replied, 'Only with my one knife, for eating and practical purposes while travelling.'

'That could mean anything,' whispered Blanche the porteress.

Hildegard whispered back. 'Fear not. I have my own knife, equally practical.'

She gave a glance towards several nuns who, roused from their beds, had crowded into the lodge. She noticed one or two looking as formidable as ever and decided to take a risk.

Peering back through the peephole she could just about discern a hooded figure move into view. Behind him was the short bridge over the moat and beyond that only the dense black of the thicket at the edge of the woods. Apart from this one fellow battering at the door there was no sign of anyone else, no band of cut-throats, nothing but the swish of rain and the gurgling in the gutters as it spewed down through the waste pipes.

She whispered to Blanche, 'Go on. Open it slowly.' She gave a last hurried glance outside before stepping back as the bar slid out, the door flew open, and the stranger fell inside.

He was clawing for breath and gasping, 'I thank you with all my heart, dear sisters! Thank you, thank you!'

His hood fell back and they saw he had black hair plastered to his skull and a clean-shaven face washed by rain.

Kneeling in the puddle he brought in he seemed incapable of

rising to his feet. With hands clasped he lifted his face to them, eyes stark with something like terror. He was no more than a boy, a very handsome, exotic-looking boy, wearing filthy but expensive velvet and worn-out embroidered Spanish-leather boots.

'My blessed saviours – my dear angels of mercy,' he whispered in a strange accent, then he astonished them all by leaning forward to kiss the flagstones in front of them.

'Can you stand on your feet, young fellow?' Hildegard demanded. 'Come, get up. You're safe from whatever threatens you outside our precinct.'

'A moment.' He was gasping for air. With what seemed like fear, head bent over his clasped hands as a prayer issued from his lips, he broke off with a sob then took another gulping breath before slowly subsiding to the floor in a dead faint.

# FIVE

'So what do you advise?' Blanche asked Hildegard as the most senior nun present. 'I can't imagine what we're supposed to do with him. This has never happened before.'

Hildegard was bending down to take the fellow's pulse. She lifted his eyelids one by one to reveal the whites. He didn't stir. With her head against his chest she paused, listening for a heart-beat, hesitated for a moment, then a look of relief crossed her face. 'He lives. I thought for a moment that he—' She sat back on her heels. 'We'll have to find a bed for him until he recovers. He's rather too heavy to carry across to the hospitium and in this rain—'

'What about that little chamber at the top of the tower?' Blanche indicated with her thumb. 'He'll be safe up there.' Her meaning became clearer when she added, 'I have a key for it.' Groping through the ones on her belt she quickly detached one and held it out. 'Shall we try to get him up those steps somehow? We ought to be able to manage it between us.' She glanced round.

One or two nuns stepped forward, the twins being first, and with some puffing and confusion they managed to drag and half carry him to the stone steps that led to the upper floor. Narrow and spiralled, there were only a dozen or so, and all the while the stranger remained oblivious to their efforts as they tugged and lifted and finally reached the upper chamber and dropped him onto a hay-sack against the wall. He lay on his back without moving, both arms out-flung, eyes shut, limbs sprawling, dead to the world.

Someone had brought up the flambeau and they stood round and stared.

After a moment one of the twins murmured, 'He's even more good-looking than the priest from Meaux.'

'He's just a boy,' Hildegard pointed out. 'How old do you think he is? Eighteen, something like that?'

'Such black hair, his skin like dark gold, he's certainly not from round these parts, that's for sure. He's like a pagan god.' It was one of the twins again.

'Is someone going to offer to sit with him?' Blanche asked somewhat briskly. 'I'm to keep the doors. Someone has to make sure nobody else turns up else we'll have an army in here and then what? I'll be the one to get the blame. And quite right too. Come on, sisters, who's going to volunteer? It'll only be till Lauds then somebody else can take over.'

Hildegard grimaced. She felt dog-tired. Reluctantly she said, 'I suppose I'd better do it. Will somebody fetch the infirmarer? Say it's urgent. If the Prioress is awake perhaps she might be informed?'

Someone left for the hospitium and another to the Prioress's lodging on the far side of the range of buildings inside the purlieu while Hildegard considered whether it was appropriate for them to try to get him out of his wet clothes. He looked as if he'd been swimming in the river but it would be the rain, falling without let, that had given him a drenching. He should have had a waxed cape with him. It was folly to be out in this weather and be so unprepared. She wondered where he was from. The poor lad looked as if he had been travelling for some time.

The porteress brought Hildegard a drink when the others left. As she handed her the mug she asked, 'What's a king's minstrel doing in this part of the world, I wonder? It's certainly going to give everybody something to chit-chat over in that warming room. Mayhap something serious has happened down south? I heard King Richard was still at Eltham, grieving for the death of his beloved Anne—' Her eyes suddenly widened in alarm. 'Oh, I've just had the most fearful thought, Hildegard!' Her hand flew to her mouth. 'Do you think it's something to do with the barons?' Hardly daring to speak she whispered, 'Might they be arming themselves against the king again? Can poor, dear Richard be in danger from them?' She bit her lip until it bled and added with great vehemence, 'He needs his own army if he's to survive. Why cannot he see that a reverence for peace will not protect him from those men bent on war?'

Hildegard felt herself freeze. 'Pray you're wrong. This young fellow will tell us when he wakes. We should not try to second-guess him. We must pray for the best.'

'I have no faith in anything going on in London while Gaunt

and his brother Woodstock are throwing their weight around,' Blanche said rapidly. 'I tell you, Hildegard, I can do naught but fear for the king with those two ambitious devils snapping at his heels.'

'We're so isolated here, all we can do is pray the dear young king is safe from harm,' she repeated.

Blanche indicated the sleeping stranger. 'Call me when he wakes.'

Revealing the key in her hand she placed it in the lock outside. 'If you have to leave at any point, give it a turn. For his sake, maybe, as well as our own.'

# SIX

I t was still dark after Lauds when Hildegard wearily made her way down the steps to the lodge. The infirmarer and two stalwarts had turned up in order to shuffle the stranger out of his sodden garments and cover him decently with a clean sheet. Later the two appointed to keep watch returned.

She left them sitting side by side on a bench drawn up to the patient with a candle burning nearby, alert for anything to cause alarm. After doing what they could the stranger, waking for a few moments, had gone back to sleep and was expected to slumber peacefully into the late morning. Until then they would have to curb their impatience about what had brought him here.

Blanche thrust something into Hildegard's hands when she appeared.

'Before you leave, look at this.'

'Where's it from?' It was a leather bag of some kind, shiny with use, and was not as heavy as its bulk suggested.

'It must have been left by that young fellow up there,' Blanche replied, indicating the upper chamber. 'He was in such a state he must have forgotten about it when he fell in through the door. It was just left there in the porch. Are you going to open it?'

The infirmarer, about to leave after a final look at her patient, came over out of curiosity.

There were three or four knotted leather laces holding it shut but the rain had made the leather swell, and they were difficult to untie.

The infirmarer grimaced. 'Don't tell me it's his change of clothes after all our problems finding something decent in which to clothe him!'

'It's something hard,' Hildegard said, feeling again the shape of what was in the bag and trying to work out what it might be. 'Wait a moment.' She worked at the knots until eventually using her teeth she managed to loosen them. Pulling open the flap she felt inside. 'Heavens!' She withdrew her hand.

Forcing back the leather to open it out she revealed a stringed instrument made of polished elm. It was a beautiful and costly item. She ran her fingers over the silken curve of its body.

'So that part of his story seems true,' murmured Blanche.

'It's a vielle.'

Hildegard ran her fingers over the strings. They vibrated with plangent melancholy.

Now, instead of solving the mystery about their guest, the existence of something that might confirm his story only added another layer because it made it even more of a question as to why one of the king's musicians had travelled north of the Humber.

Fear flooded back. 'It looks as if you're right, Blanche. Something terrible must have happened in the south to make him flee this far north.'

The infirmarer folded her arms. 'If something has happened we'd be seeing men-at-arms strutting about by now, you can be sure of that. And our hospitium would be full of groaning wounded.' She was brisk.

'Is there anything else in the bag to enlighten us?' Blanche asked.

Holding the instrument by its neck Hildegard spread out what was little more than hide from the body of a small deer with the addition of leather loops and ties. Apart from a piece of vellum with what looked like a scribbled musical notation there was nothing to suggest a reason for the owner's arrival.

'Well, best be getting on. The day is nearly half-over and I've other patients to see to,' said the infirmarer, taking her leave. 'Keep me informed when he wakes up. I could find no obvious injury. No broken bones. It's my opinion he was merely exhausted – and took fright in the woods, being lost, like? Keep him calm and I'll come back and have another look at him later then maybe we'll get a few straight answers.' Before she closed the door behind her she added, 'Old as I am, I cannot deny the pleasure of dealing with a body like his. It makes a change from old women and their rheumatics!' With a dry chuckle she took her leave.

'She's droll,' sniffed Blanche without humour. 'She'll be on her knees muttering hail marys till kingdom come if she doesn't take care.'

'She won't be the only one,' Hildegard agreed, adding hurriedly,

'There was quite a flutter among the novices. I suppose you noticed? They'll no doubt need reining in.'

As she too turned to leave she remembered something. 'I didn't see Josiana during the night Office and she wasn't here just now. Did she return safely?'

Blanche looked alarmed. 'What, from Haltemprice?'

'Well there's been no sign of her—'

'I haven't seen her since she left to see those Austin canons yesterday. Wasn't she staying overnight in their guest house?'

'I suppose she must have done. It was nasty weather to travel in.'

'I'll let you know when she shows up. You look worried? I'm sure she'll have decided to stay over. She'll be riding back this morning when it's light.'

The rest of the day proceeded in its usual orderly fashion with the regular observance of the canonical hours but with a flurry of interest whenever the stranger was mentioned. A few comments were made when they were told he was in no danger and fared as well as could be expected after being out in the height of the storm. He was said to be too drowsy to talk.

The Prioress had already sent over to the guest-master at Meaux to ask him if he would take the fellow in, deeming it more appropriate that monks would attend to him in their own hospitium than in a priory of nuns. All they could do was wait for him to explain the mystery of his sudden appearance, then recover sufficiently to sit a horse and be escorted the few miles to the abbey.

Josiana's whereabouts were still a mystery. A servant was brought from the house of the conversi and questioned about the maid who had accompanied her but she had also failed to return. All anyone could do was practise the patience they were enjoined to exercise in their everyday lives and wait on events.

# SEVEN

What happened next shocked everyone. Hildegard was the first to be alerted.

Having gone down to the riverbank to discuss the fish supplied to the priory at one of the havens, she took the opportunity to gather the last of the brambles in the thicket outside the boundary wall and strayed as far as the lane that would eventually come out near Haltemprice Priory after several miles through uninhabited woodland. It was not a short distance, rather as much as a morning's ride, and she had no intention of going further than the lane end even though her basket was only half full. But then she heard a horse being ridden fast towards her and in a moment a cob appeared, blowing heavily, its rider whipping it to even greater exertion until he must have caught sight of white Cistercian robes bright against the backdrop of autumn leaves. He pulled his horse to a rearing halt.

'Domina! Domina! Quick! Fetch help!' He dismounted and ran towards her, gasping, 'There's a body down on the saltings!'

'Heavens, whereabouts?'

'Down by Hob's Creek.'

'Are you sure it's a body?'

'As sure as I stand here!'

'Then I'll tell you what,' she replied, thinking quickly, 'you ride on to the priory and inform them there. Tell them you come from me, Hildegard. Say we need some good strong lay-brothers, ropes, a ladder maybe, to spread across the mud, all that. I'll go down and see what I can do now—' She grasped the man by the arm before he could run over to his horse. 'Are you sure it's a body or is it somebody trapped?'

With the tide coming in if they were alive they would not have a chance unless they could be reached quickly. The lay-brothers would need time to gather the equipment and bring it down then drag someone, injured maybe, out of the mud to the safety of firm ground . . . Could they make it in time?

Already planning how she might get out to them she was dismayed when he shook his head. 'It was a body, domina. I saw no sign of life.'

With a chill, thinking of Josiana, she asked, 'And could you tell whether it was one of our nuns?'

He shook his head. 'It was just a washed-up bundle. Difficult to make out.'

'But it was a person? . . . Not just some weed shoaled up on a mud bank in human shape?'

He looked sombre. 'I'd bet on it,' he crossed himself. 'I saw what looked like a face, all puffy—' He waved an arm helplessly as if to describe the look of it by his gestures.

'Then hasten along to Swyne and rouse them to action! I'll go down and see what I can do.'

'Don't you go walking on them mudflats,' he warned as he threw a leg over the back of his valiant little mount. 'We don't want two of you copping it.'

# EIGHT

Hildegard left the lane and hurried down a narrow way, more rabbit-run than footpath, until, rounding the edge of a stand of trees, she could look out over the water from a slight rise in the ground. It was flat country here and there was no impediment to the sight that greeted her.

At the high-water mark where the marram grass gave way to a shelving sand strip a coloured band of stones and seashells with tresses of weed and bits of driftwood still glinted now and then after the last tide receded. Beyond that came the mudflats and, serene and now at a distance, the estuary itself withdrawn to a narrow, fast-flowing channel between the banks of mud.

Her glance travelled across the water to the opposite county, Lincolnshire, distantly visible as a thin line of smoky woodland with a few sheep dotted in a far meadow, then back again to the shelving sands where she stood, then further out to where the ground looked firm but was in fact treacherous marshland, and then she found it, caught on a mound of marram grass – a shape unlike any others.

If she had been close enough she guessed she could have made out the details of the body the horseman had seen, the mud-encrusted form, looking like little more than a shadow against the surrounding yellow-brown ooze.

Praying that it was not a human being, she made her way down the bank.

Once there it was clear there was nothing she could do. It would be foolish to try to set foot beyond the tidemark of cobbles where the mudflats began.

She walked about on the narrow beach where the sand had dried in patches but could find no way of crossing the mud and even as she waited for help to arrive she was conscious of the ever-increasing roar of the incoming tide.

If they do not come soon, she thought, it will be too late to bring the body back to shore. The tide will carry it out into the deep channels where the current is strongest. It will be swept out to sea and lost for ever.

Tears filled her eyes as she paced the shoreline.

Was it really a body? It was odd that Josiana had made no mention of staying over at Haltemprice.

She gave a start when the heap of what might be clothing seemed to move. Then she saw that it was only the wind, tuckering underneath a sleeve, pulling at the hem of a garment.

No amount of walking back and forth is any help, she fretted.

Why do they not come? She pulled up her hood as the tide brought a cold wind with it. Rain began to glimmer in the air.

# NINE

When at last a band of conversi arrived, led by their man Alaric and the one who had called the alarm, they were followed by several nuns and one or two novices. Alaric explained that they had decided to form a human chain to bring the poor wretch ashore.

When he had a proper look from the shingle where Hildegard was standing the folly of such a plan became obvious. In no time there would be half a dozen monastics and conversi struggling up to their waists in mud.

'I'm wondering if it might be best to get hold of a flat-bottomed boat and wait until the tide is high enough to allow a couple of men to scull out,' Hildegard suggested after some thought.

He frowned. 'They'd have to time it so they had enough water under them to reach the mound the body's on but not enough to sweep it out of reach.' He thought it over. 'I reckon we could do it.'

'Is there such a craft in the vicinity?'

'If there isn't one I'll make one with my bare hands,' he assured her. 'Jack!' He bellowed to one of the boys standing on the bank. 'You can run. Get up to Lig's shack and borrow his boat. Say the mistress of Meaux sends you.' He turned and gave Hildegard a glance. 'That should shift him.' When he turned back the lad had already reached the lane end.

More waiting followed. The nuns were praying in a huddle, kneeling on the cobbles, oblivious to pain.

Hildegard paced about keeping a close eye on what was now assumed most definitely to be a body caught on its islet of grass. The tide was already beginning to lap around it. To Alaric she said, 'It's going to be touch and go.'

'Fear not, domina. We'll do it. We'll make sure they get a decent burial. We won't let the river-serpents get a-hold of 'em.'

He fingered the wooden cross round his neck.

After what seemed a lifetime the lad returned with two men running at a trot with a flimsy boat between them. It was flat-

bottomed, narrow as the trunk of a tree, able to skim the water
with little draught and used for eel-catching in the shallows. They
dropped it into the water which was already lapping round the
feet of those standing on the shingle and the eel-catcher himself
stepped over the side and picked up the paddle.

To shouted instructions which he dismissed with a wave of a
hand the rest of the men heaved the boat off the mud and for
a few yards it ploughed through the shallows, stirring up swirls
of yellow mud as it scraped along. He nursed it into deeper water
until it was floating free on the tide.

Angling it until he was close enough to get a good look at what
was heaped up on the hillock of sand he glanced back at the
onlookers and gave a thumbs-down. Murmurs of dismay arose as
their fears were confirmed.

'Dead.'

'Is it Josiana?'

'Let's wait and see,' Alaric advised.

'Can Lig manage by himself?' Hildegard asked, referring to the
eel-catcher. Everyone was watching intently. He had paddled
slightly downstream of the body to let the tide drift his boat onto
the humped sand and then he leaned over the side and started to
drag the body closer. Soon he was able to heave it onboard.

'Good man,' Alaric murmured.

A small cheer arose and the eel-catcher set off back towards
the shore.

'He'll need to allow for drift,' somebody announced. He
shouted across the rising waters, 'Aim towards us, Lig!' As one,
the men began to run upstream to the place where they guessed
he'd fetch up.

Hildegard followed.

Behind her came the monastics from Swyne, silent now, focused
on only one thing.

As it neared the shore somebody asked, 'Who the hell is it?'

'Steady now,' the eel-man responded gruffly when offers of help
were shouted over.

As soon as the bow scraped onto the shingle willing hands
helped him out. They turned to stare at the body lying in the
bottom of the boat.

Somebody asked again, 'Who is it?'

'I think I may know.' Hildegard crunched down into the shallows and gazed at the body. It was caked in mud. Long hair had come loose from her coif and half-covered the bloated face. 'She must have been in the water since yesterday,' she surmised. Turning to the nuns who had followed she said, 'Will you help to lift her out? Maybe we can find a hurdle on which to carry her back to the priory?'

One of the women kitchen servants stumbled knee-deep into the water and reached out towards the body.

'No! It cannot be!'

The eel-man held her back before she could sink to her knees in the tide. 'Hold up, girl, she's out of it. She'll feel no pain ever more.'

'But she is gone!' The woman began to sob. 'We shall never hear her lovely laughter again. Oh, that it should come to this! How could it happen? Why?'

'We shall find out. I can promise you that.' Hildegard took hold of the woman gently by the other arm to steady her. 'Come now. Let's take her up to the priory and do what must be done.'

The woman sobbed without restraint. 'She was the one to enliven us on the darkest day! Things will never be the same without her.'

# TEN

I t was a grim-faced entourage that eventually reached the gatehouse and passed underneath the arch into the garth. The
porteress came out when she saw Hildegard following the hurdle
on which the body was lying.

'Josiana, domina?'

Hildegard stopped. She shook her head. 'It's one of the lay-
sisters from the kitchens but I believe she was the one to accompany
Josiana to Haltemprice Priory yesterday.'

Blanche frowned with foreboding. 'So where is Josiana, then?'

Hildegard's tone was sombre. 'We can only hope she hasn't
come to a similarly awful end.'

'Heaven forfend!' Blanche threw up her hands. 'Was it a spill
from a boat? Did they think it would be safer to leave their horses
with the Austins and return by water?'

'We shall endeavour to discover the truth. Be sure of that.'

'Amen to that, domina.' Blanche crossed herself. 'What is the
world coming to?'

The body was carried straightaway to the mortuary. The infirmarer
and her assistants were summoned. Hildegard stood by the door,
thanked the man on the cob who had noticed the body at the start
and had then ridden on to Swyne to fetch help, and now she gave
him instructions on how to find the bursar for some recompense.
She sent the eel-man along too in thanks for the use of his boat,
and the conversi who had carried the body back on a makeshift
hurdle were sent down to the kitchens for extra cheese and ale.
The novices who had come out to see what was happening were
instructed to make ready to attend the next Office of the day.

When they had all gone, Hildegard and a handful of nuns who
could be depended on went inside to see what the infirmarer had
been doing. Her assistants had removed the dead girl's garments
and covered her with a sheet.

'Domina, I think you should look at this.' Indicating that the body should be turned over Agnes tenderly pushed aside the hair on the back of the girl's head to reveal a massive bruise and some swelling. 'What do you think? Did she hit her head when she fell into the water? Or . . .?' She looked alarmed and tightened her lips.

Hildegard peered at the wound. Something had hit the girl with enough force to crack her skull. Tightening her jaw to stop herself from retching she bent to get a closer look at the pulpy mess. When she straightened she turned to the infirmarer. 'What do you think?'

'It could be a fall.' She wore a dubious expression.

'But you doubt it? . . . I feel the same way. It looks like a deliberate blow to the back of the head. Is that the only injury?' She and Josiana must have encountered someone in the woods.

'It's the only one I've found.'

Bracing herself Hildegard took a closer look. 'There seems to be something . . .' She asked, 'Are there any pincers here?'

'I have some.' Agnes reached inside the deep front pocket of her overalls and handed her a pair.

'Despite her immersion in the river there's still sediment or some other substance embedded—' Delicately picking amongst the fragments of bone and skin Hildegard started to probe until she could get a grip on a splinter of some kind. Believing it to be from out of the river she held it up. 'I think we might want to see more closely what this is,' she murmured. 'People don't usually fall backwards into rivers unless they're hovering about on the edge. To get into the river around here if you fell backwards you'd most likely fall into the mud.'

'She might have hit her head on a stone when she fell,' suggested Agnes, 'that is if for some reason she happened to fall backwards. But then . . .' She mused, 'I would think it unlikely that anyone would fall with such force as to stove their head in like that. She's lightly built,' she added turning to Hildegard. 'We seem to be in agreement, she was attacked by someone?'

'I don't know. It's too soon to come to any conclusion. We have no idea of her movements. Can you assess how long she's been in the water?'

'Several hours. Yesterday or early this morning?' She looked dissatisfied. 'If she fell in and drowned her lungs will be full of water. In fact there was relatively little. It suggests that she was already unconscious when she fell in.' Her glance narrowed. 'I don't like where this is leading, domina, I don't know about you. Where is Josiana, we might ask? She should be able to shed some light on the matter. What has happened to her? Is she safe some-where?' She lowered her voice. 'Did they have a quarrel? Is she afeared to return . . . knowing what she has done?' She hesitated. 'Heaven forfend I should imagine such a thing about one of our nuns, especially Josiana, the dear young thing, but the facts lead me to it.'

'I don't think we need to make any conclusive judgement yet,' Hildegard replied. She liked Josiana and could not believe that she would be capable of an act of violence. She was even-tempered, concerned more for scholarship than the jealousies that had recently sprung up. She would be puzzled by that sort of thing. But where was she?

'We must send someone to Haltemprice to find out when or if they arrived yesterday. We must also consider whether there have been any strangers in the woods at around the same time.'

The presence of one such glared between them but neither mentioned the royal minstrel.

She turned to Agnes. 'Do your best for Lydia. I must go to let the Prioress know what has so far transpired. Meanwhile,' she held out the shard of stone chipping, 'maybe this will give us a clue where she was when she met her nemesis.'

# ELEVEN

The Prioress was, unusually, sitting down again. In all the years Hildegard had known her their conversations had always been conducted while standing. The cat was lying on her lap, an indulgence in itself rare enough.

'So tell me about poor little Lydia,' she demanded as soon as Hildegard appeared.

'Agnes is taking a closer look at her. The only wound seems to be to her skull. We found a shard of some stone in amongst the broken bone. We're saying nothing definite yet. It's possible she might have fallen.'

'From a height, by the sound of it. Where are the heights in this part of the Riding?'

'Precisely.'

'Show me this stone, will you?'

Hildegard opened her palm.

'Clearly it's a shard of rock like the ones littering the river-bank,' said the Prioress slowly, 'but what I don't understand is what she was doing anywhere near the river. As I understand it she was simply asked to accompany Josiana to see the Austins at Haltemprice, they set off yesterday, through the woods and should have been nowhere near the river. Did they arrive at their destination or did this accident, as we must carry on calling it until evidence proves otherwise, occur on the way there, or on the way back?'

'We cannot tell—'

'I'll have someone sent over there at once. Let's hear what they have to say.'

'I'll attend to that, my lady. The conversi have been most helpful already. Let's find out how helpful the canons can be.'

'Lucky to have such help, are we not?' The Prioress stroked the cat and Hildegard realized that their interview was over.

# TWELVE

Crossing the garth she was stopped in her tracks by one of the twins. 'Domina, they would welcome your presence in the gatehouse at once.'

With an effort Hildegard brought her mind back to their midnight visitor. 'Is he awake now?'

'That's what I'm telling you.'

This must be Rogella, thought Hildegard, the one slightly rougher in manner than the other. 'My gratitude. Are you going into church now?'

'Unless I can be honoured with another errand?'

Grimacing at the girl's sarcasm Hildegard walked on, saying, 'I'm afraid I cannot oblige you.'

When she reached the gatehouse a couple of novices, apparently unaware of Lydia's fate, were giggling and nudging each other as they descended the tower staircase. When they noticed Hildegard they pulled themselves together, parting to allow her to pass, and she went on to the upper floor where one of the infirmarers appeared carrying a jug.

'Milord is awake,' she murmured with a glance over her shoulder to where a young man could be seen through the open door sitting up in bed. He was propped on pillows with a blanket round his shoulders and nursing a steaming mug of something that smelled of thyme. It appeared to be not to his liking.

'He has a case of the sniffles,' she added, 'a major reason for having everyone at his beck and call.'

'Has he said more about how he fetched up here?'

'Not a syllable beyond the fact that he comes from the royal household.' She pulled a face. 'Take that as you will.'

She raised her eyebrows and walked on.

Hildegard entered the chamber and the patient glanced up. His expression clearly said, not another nun. She went to sit on the bench beside his bed.

'How are you feeling this morning?'

He pulled a face. 'As you see, domina.' He closed his eyes with a sigh.

She felt she could understand the giggles of the young novices just now. A good-looking youth with glossy black hair and olive skin, he would be about their own age and not much older than her own son, a squire with the Bishop of Norwich, but unlike her son he looked sulky as if nothing much was going to please him. But not to be too harsh, she thought, he seems exhausted, maybe suffering the ill-effects of his trek through the woods during the storm. She asked him if there was anything she could do for him.

'I'm well looked after. I gather it's a special event to have a man within the priory precinct. I shall never want to leave if they continue to be so attentive.'

'We do have male guests but they stay in the guest house. You were only allowed in because we didn't want to wake the whole priory when everyone was so shortly abed after Matins. And of course,' she rattled on, hoping to put him at his ease, 'there was such a storm and your arrival in the middle of it took everyone by surprise. You sounded desperate. We couldn't work out whether you were the harbinger of a band of cut-throats or a lone traveller in genuine distress. Tell me,' she continued before he could interrupt, 'how is it you found us?'

'By God's good grace, I expect. I was lost and then I saw a light shining through the rain and headed for that.'

'But how is it you were in the woods in that vile weather anyway?'

He sat up a little straighter. 'I was hoping to find a place called Meaux. I have business there.'

'I see. Well, I'm sure we can guide you to your destination as soon as you're well enough to travel.' She watched him closely, determined to find out more, and spread her arms with an air of innocence, saying, 'I can't quite understand how on earth you came to be in the woods at all. We're off the beaten track here and quite isolated. Perchance you came from York?'

Deftly avoiding a straight answer, he replied, 'I've been travelling for ages. In fact I came from Sheen. You may have heard of it?'

Ignoring the fact that he was patronizing her she shammed ignorance and asked, 'Isn't that one of King Richard's palaces?' adding for good measure, 'Is there news?'

'I was forced to leave because . . .' His words tailed off and she only just managed to catch the phrase, 'a matter of life and death had arisen.' He closed his eyes as if too exhausted to continue.

'Heavens. Are you—' She gave a little gulp and leaned forward and whispered, 'Are you a wanted man?'

His eyes snapped open and, clearly insulted, he gave her a prolonged look then slowly shook his head. Unwilling to divulge his secret he seemed to be considering how to account for himself and eventually explained, 'I was in a special position at the king's court as one of his musicians. I believe I mentioned that last night?' When she nodded he said with boyish pride, 'I was in his personal entourage . . .'

'So is the king safe?'

He nodded.

When he paused again she prompted, 'He must trust you enormously . . .?'

He agreed. 'It's a dangerous position to be in – with you know who as his sworn enemies.'

She was unsure how to react. Was she supposed to know who the king's enemies were? Of course she knew. Only the most dull of dullards would be so out of touch as to be unaware of the threats hanging over King Richard and from whom they arose.

'I suppose you must mean,' lowering her voice, 'the Duke of Lancaster?'

'Him, yes. Who knows what goes on in his heart, if he's got one? But worse is his brother Woodstock. He even drew his sword on the king the other day. Only the fact that we were present made him give way. In my view that's treason. To draw on the anointed king?' His voice rose with incredulity.

Hildegard herself was genuinely shocked too. 'What drove him to do such a terrible thing?'

'The usual battle of wills over France. Woodstock's keen to get what pickings he can on chevauchée like Arundel. He seems to think if the Arundels can get rich by sending raiding parties into France why shouldn't he – but the king is of course totally against it – except that now dear Anne is dead . . . who knows what will happen?'

'The king must be distraught with grief even now.' She spoke with genuine sincerity.

His eyes clouded. 'The situation is worse than anyone can imagine. And I am the one with the key to it. I had to get out.'

Hildegard sat back.

When he did not enlarge on this she asked softly, 'I am remiss. I should have told you my name. I am Hildegard of Meaux – so called.'

He closed his eyes. 'Greetings, Hildegard.'

He really is too handsome for his own good, she thought, with time to study him – despite the sulky mouth he looked as if he might easily be encouraged to smile. Something about him seemed familiar, the turn of his head, a quickness of movement, something beguiling, with the charm of an attractive child. A weight seemed to be bearing down on him, however, and she feared to question him too far until he had more confidence in her.

She asked, 'And your own name, young master?'

'Leonin,' he replied shortly without opening his eyes.

His lashes curled long and black on prominent cheekbones. It was a face that might suggest wilfulness if not arrogance but it was that of a boy in desperate straits, not that of a man or what she would call a man. His feelings, although held back, swarmed across his face before he could stop them.

By closing his eyes he intended to erect shutters between them but too many questions remained unanswered to allow that. He had been in a state of terror when he tumbled in through their gates. Now in the safety of the lodge he was taking charge of himself again. The question remained, however, something had brought him to a state of stark fear last night.

'May I ask again, if this is not too personal a question, how you came to be lost in our woods? You maybe managed to cross the river somewhere nearby?'

With his eyes still shut he said, 'If you really want to know I paid a fellow to bring me across in his coracle from the Lincoln side of the estuary. I was told there was a ford but I couldn't find it.'

'The ford is long gone as a reliable way of crossing to the other side. I believe it may be accessible at very low water but I know of no one who has ever tried it.'

'My information was out of date, then.' He forestalled further questions by opening his eyes and asking, 'Will you guide me to Meaux, domina?'

'As soon as you can ride. It's not far. We might even walk it but I guess you'd rather get there sooner than later?'

His expression lit up for a moment. 'You guess right!'

# THIRTEEN

The Prioress sent for Hildegard. 'I'm told you've had words with our guest already?'

'He was not very forthcoming. He claims he comes from the king's court at Sheen. Such carrying-on down there, you wouldn't believe. Woodstock threatening King Richard with his sword!'

'Treason. He should not be allowed to get away with it. Still, that's men for you. What can we do about it?' The Prioress brushed this aside. 'Tell me, how is the king taking the death of Queen Anne? Most grievously, I hear. It was a true love match. They say he was quite beside himself?'

'It was very sudden—'

'Plague, they say. Nobody else had it. Contagious though it is.' The Prioress narrowed her glance. 'Was our young friend with the court at Sheen when she died?'

'I assume so.'

'And did he have anything to say about it?'

'Not much. Only that King Richard is still grieving.'

'Find out more if you can. I'm told our impetuous king dismantled his palace until nothing was left standing. Of course, they exaggerate as always. Some fools are even claiming he set a torch to the place in a fit of hysteria and burned it to the ground with his own hands! They'll say anything these days – whisper some outrageous story and in no time it's enshrined as fact, especially by the king's enemies, of whom he has quite a few in the phalanx of his egregious uncles, poor young fellow. How can we make up our minds about the truth of anything when people are happy to spread lies? Such vicious lack-wits! I despair!'

She spoke with unusual passion but then mentioned the incidence of plague in London and elsewhere and they both declared themselves relieved that York and Beverley had escaped the latest wave of infection. The Prioress turned the focus back to their visitor.

'Let's hope this so-called minstrel has not brought the plague with him.'

'He looked fit enough, a few sniffles after his previous night's drenching as you'd expect. Agnes did not seem perturbed.'

'Did he tell you how he got here?'

'I asked about the river crossing. He told me he paid a fellow to ferry him over.'

'I wonder who that was? I'll have it checked out.'

'I'm afraid – what I mean is – do you imagine he has anything to do with Lydia's murder? The timing fits.'

The Prioress looked grim. 'Poor child. I am at fault for not providing a safe haven for her. I cannot understand how those Austins were so lax. Do they treat all their guests with such disregard for their safety? And Josiana. Do we know where she is?'

Hildegard felt suddenly close to tears. 'I'm worried for her. I'd like to go over to Haltemprice, if I may have permission. Somebody needs to answer a few questions. They must know something. Where can she be?'

'I was about to suggest you got off there as soon as you've escorted our minstrel to Meaux. We'll have the woods searched.'

# FOURTEEN

Hildegard heard a commotion near the stables as she crossed the garth. She quickened her pace. Voices were raised and a horse was stamping about in the yard and steaming as if ridden in haste. A group of stable hands were milling around and nuns were appearing from all directions. From this distance she could only see their gesticulations and hear a babble of voices.

As she approached she saw a nun in the middle of this crowd. She was clinging to the bridle of the horse and looked as if she would never let go. With her head bowed she seemed utterly bewildered and when one of the novices, Bella or Rogella, shouted something she stumbled in horror as if struck.

Despite this Hildegard felt relief flooding over her. She pushed through the group and reached out. 'Josiana! You're safe! Thank heavens! Have they told you what happened?'

'I can't believe it!' Her face contorted with fear and confusion. 'Lydia? It cannot be! . . . Hildegard, I must speak to you in private.'

'Come with me.'

Josiana was still in a state of shock and Hildegard led her to a secluded place in the cloister where she could recover. They found an empty carrel and Josiana sank down onto the stone bench and leaned back against the wall with a face as white as chalk.

'So tell me what happened to her. They told me she's in the mortuary—'

'Did you reach Haltemprice Priory?' Hildegard asked.

'Of course. We didn't make very good time because of the torrential rain. I suppose I should have decided not to go but it was urgent and – and it was muddy and the horses kept stalling – but yes, although we arrived well after midday – can you believe it took so long? – and I decided to accept their invitation to stay overnight in the guest house as it was already getting dark, you know how short the days are now – and the canons insisted—'

'And Lydia?'

'The guest-master found her a place to sleep. I believe she spent the evening in the kitchens talking recipes with their cook. But then—'

'What happened?'

'It all went wrong.'

'Tell me—'

'I was irritated when I went to fetch her to escort me back this morning. She was nowhere to be found. Nobody seemed to have seen her after the guest-master went round dousing the lights after everyone turned in – a couple of pilgrims were staying overnight, going on to Beverley this morning they told me, so I decided to travel part of the way back with them.' She frowned. 'It's my fault. I should not have left without her. I was angry with the silly girl. It was urgent. I needed to get back as soon as possible. She knew that but she has no thoughts above the domestic . . . had . . . that is . . . I can't believe it . . .' She rubbed a hand over her face. 'What have I done? I abandoned her.'

'It's not your fault if – but I don't understand how she disappeared.'

'Nor do I, I mean, it was odd, there was no sign of her last night after Compline and I needed to instruct her to be ready to leave straight after Prime. It was annoying not to find her to tell her. I had to leave a message with the guest-master before I went to bed, telling her to be ready early as I had to leave first thing. It's to do with the floods—'

'And did you leave straightaway this morning?' Hildegard asked with a lift of her brow. 'You're late back.'

Josiana looked confused. 'Well, actually,' she admitted, 'no, I didn't. After hanging around waiting for her in the precinct and failing to find her I went down to the house where the lay-brothers live but it was a waste of time because nobody knew anything there either. They hadn't seen her. At least,' she added darkly, 'that's what they told me.'

'So you think they knew but did not want to tell you?'

'It looked like that. I don't know—' She gave an anguished moan. 'I should never have come away without her. I am too impatient. I needed to get back to correct my calculations after talking to the canon there, the one who knows how to use an astrolabe. It's urgent. I thought she was being – I don't know what I thought. It seemed to me that if she couldn't be bothered to be ready at Prime she could make her own way back . . . I'm at fault. I gave way to anger. I am at fault, Hildegard. I don't need a priest to tell me that. I will do penance. But how did she come to be in the river? It makes no sense.'

'Nobody knows how she got there. But we will find out. Are you sure you didn't see her on the way back?'

'How could I? I kept to the lane. And anyway I wasn't looking for her any longer. I had too much else to think about. The pilgrims weren't much use in that respect, only interested in visiting St John's shrine and saving their souls. They didn't seem to understand that the Austins are in grave peril. They should never have built a priory in such a dangerous location. It's a flood plain. Anybody can see that. Forgive me, a missing girl seemed like nothing compared to the threat of the many drownings we can expect if the Humber breaks its banks – if only I'd known she was— Oh, what a mess it all is!' She put her head in her hands and wept.

'Are these fears about an incipient flood well-founded?'

'Of course they are! The evidence tells us so.'

Hildegard left Josiana after reassuring her that everything would be done to find out what had happened to Lydia between reaching the priory at Haltemprice alive, and reappearing in the Humber, dead.

# FIFTEEN

'First,' the Prioress instructed, after she had been thoroughly informed of the latest, 'you must take our royal minstrel to Meaux. If he is in danger as he claims it's best that he finds sanctuary among those monks of Hubert's as soon as he can. They'll give short shrift to any threats. Or, if our suspicions prove correct, they can keep him in custody as necessary. You can ride over with a couple of men straightaway. Oh, and tell Matthew where you're going. He may as well ride with you.'

'I could take Josiana, if you agree, my lady. She's suffering terribly over Lydia. It will give her time to come to terms with things.'

'I expect she's blaming herself. Tell her it was not her fault. We do not blame her. The responsibility is mine.'

So it was, with everyone rounded up, two stout field-labourers, glad to be on horseback instead of digging ditches in the rain, the priest Matthew, rigid with general disapproval as usual, Josiana, dabbing eyes red-rimmed from weeping, and Hildegard, riding alongside Leonin, if indeed that was his real name, they rode out through the gatehouse into the woods towards Meaux.

One of the twins watched them leave. Standing under the arch of the gatehouse, her glance followed them, and when Hildegard glanced back she was still staring after them.

# SIXTEEN

The lane was so muddy the horses struggled up to their bellies in it but when they reached the well-trodden town road towards Beverley the going was easier.

'I would never have found this in the dark last night,' Leonin said after riding in silence for a while. 'I owe you and your sisters my gratitude, domina.'

'Our pleasure to help,' Hildegard answered.

He patted the leather bag containing the vielle and whistled a few bars of a tune. 'I shall compose a canzone praising the angels of Swyne Priory who saved my life.'

She gave him a curious glance. He seemed to have recovered from his terror but had still offered little explanation for it. Seeing a chance, she asked, 'So, Leonin, what made you imagine your life was in danger?'

He lowered his voice. 'I fear I know something that the king's enemies deem dangerous. I have been followed from the gates of Sheen Palace up the length of England to this very spot.'

He spoke so lightly she could not help thinking he was dramatizing his situation. Even so she allowed herself a quick glance into the woods. Nothing moved. Nothing, except the dripping of rain sliding from the leaves.

When they reached the new gatehouse at Meaux it appeared to Hildegard as always that it was designed to impress. She was used to it but its grandeur never failed. By the way Leonin's mouth fell open she saw he was taken by surprise too. The way he had spoken earlier about Sheen made her think he saw this part of the East Riding as a backwater and they themselves no more than country clods.

Wait until he meets Hubert, she thought grimly, our lord Abbot de Courcy will soon put him in his place.

As the conversi dismounted and one of them went to take Leonin's horse to the stables, she leaned over to Josiana before she could dismount.

'I've been thinking. Time is passing. What do you say to riding back to Swyne by way of Haltemprice?'

Josiana looked panicked. 'Why do you want to do that?'

'Naturally enough I want to know where Lydia went after leaving you.'

'But I don't have permission to go elsewhere. My instructions were—'

'I will give you permission and if there is a problem I will guarantee that I will square it with our lady Prioress.'

She looked doubtful but said, 'I can hardly refuse then, Hildegard, can I?'

'I hope not!'

Despite her agreement Josiana still wore a look of doubt, not to say alarm. She stayed in the saddle while Hildegard called the other escort over. 'Will you let the Prioress know that I'm following her instructions and riding on to Haltemprice Priory?'

'I certainly will, domina. But don't you want us to come with you?'

'I believe you might have to delay here until someone has explained to Abbot de Courcy who we've brought over for him.'

'Even so . . . Is it safe with a possible murderer at large?'

'So the rumour has grown into fact, has it?' She smiled to take any acid out of her words. 'It's broad daylight. I doubt whether anyone will harm us on the way.'

He grinned. 'I pity anyone who might try it. When shall I say you expect to return?'

'Depending on what happens at Haltemprice I'm sure we'll be back either around Vespers or first thing tomorrow morning.'

Leonin listened to this exchange but made no comment. Instead he pretended to fix some annoyance to the strap of one of his bags. She wondered if he was concocting another story for the abbot's benefit. If so, Hubert would soon drag the truth from him.

Their other escort, returning from the stables, had a brief word with Matthew then they watched him stalk beside the minstrel to the inner precinct.

Duty done the other converso, happening to catch what Hildegard had said earlier, strode over to them.

'I beg to suggest that we would be ten times at fault if we allowed you to travel on alone, domina.'

'But someone must inform the Prioress what we intend doing.'

'Then I suggest that one of us goes with you while the other heads back to Swyne? Will that solve the problem?'

'Very well indeed if it fits in with your other duties.'

With both men happy with this arrangement it took no time to decide who should return and who should ride on with the nuns as escort.

# SEVENTEEN

Haltemprice had enjoyed a colourful existence ever since its foundation by Lord Wake back in King Edward's day. He died before it was finished and it remained largely a building site even now nearly fifty years later. By marriage it had come into the possession of Princess Joan, King Richard's mother, but any royal connection was in little evidence these days.

When the two nuns approached there was an old fellow sitting on a bench in the doorway of the lodge with his feet up now the rain had stopped. He waved them through without moving.

In the garth a flock of hens were pecking at random and a nanny goat, tethered to a stake, was nuzzling at the lush grass, while one or two men in monastic robes were tossing a pig's bladder back and forth with cries of glee when one or other missed a catch.

From between the open shutters of a stone building to one side came an enticing aroma of cooking that made Hildegard think about the next hen destined for the pot. There was no sign of any activity that could be directly linked to the monastic life. Exchanging speaking looks the two nuns dismounted.

Alaric, their escort, took the reins of both horses and looked round for the stable lad but nobody seemed to have marked that strangers had arrived. He led them off himself.

'I can understand how Lydia's absence might have gone unnoticed.' Hildegard frowned. 'I had no idea it was like this.'

Josiana bit her lip. 'They do have a good fellow here. I'll see if I can find him.'

With long determined strides that showed she was familiar with the place, she went over to the kitchen and banged on the shutters. A head poked out and a moment later a roly-poly woman appeared in the doorway. She was wearing a large, bloodied apron, and wiped greasy hands down it as she came outside.

Noticing Hildegard she cried, 'My lady!' Looking flustered she glanced down at her apron. 'Do forgive me. I'm in the middle of preparations and the men do like their meat.' Bobbing a brief curtsey she hurried over. 'Is this about poor dear Lydia? Word came that she'd met with an accident.'

'Sadly so.'

'Let me call the Prior. He's at prayer, domina, but I'm sure he will not mind being disturbed when he knows how we are honoured.' Turning to Josiana she said, 'What an evil thing when a poor young servant girl can disappear from her very bed!'

With that she hurried off towards a small unfinished building across the garth.

Josiana noted Hildegard's bemused expression. 'They are somewhat more informal than we Cistercians. But the goodness of their hearts is not in doubt.' She added, 'They seem to have already heard that the body in the water was Lydia.'

She glanced after the cook where she was summoning a fellow loitering in the church porch, and said, 'I'd better go and find someone to fetch the guest-master.' She too hurried off.

The Prior himself emerged from the depths of the church soon afterwards. A large man with a large belly, he had evidently been gardening before attending to his prayers because grass stains marked his robe and he wore scuffed leather boots with mud still clinging to them. His manner, however, was genial.

After a friendly greeting he listened carefully to what Hildegard had to say then gave permission to question whomsoever she wished, adding, 'And pray join us in our midday repast before you leave.'

When he called a servant, Hildegard, with Alaric close at her heels, was conducted to the guest hall where Josiana eventually found them. Two friars followed her in and the guest-master introduced himself.

'After offering our condolences, there is nothing much to say, domina. The young maid spent the evening in the hall with other servants and then I presume she retired to the dortoir.'

'Did anyone see her later on? She must have provoked some interest as a relative stranger.'

He glanced hurriedly away and back. 'Would you like to ask them yourself?'

'If it is no trouble.'

He nodded and went out, followed by the friar.

Hildegard turned to Josiana. 'Is there any doubt over her whereabouts?'

Josiana pursed her lips.

Alaric was looking off to one side but caught Hildegard's eye and gave a slight nod. He glanced towards Josiana.

Hildegard frowned. 'Josiana, will you be kind enough to find someone to fetch us water after our ride?'

Without a word the nun hurried from the hall.

'What is it?'

Alaric bent his head. 'I think everyone knows more than they're telling us. When I was in the stable I heard a bit of a whisper going round.'

'What were they saying?'

'Let's ask for a fellow called Harry. He has his eye on the target. These friars are living in their own world and the conversi stick together.'

Shortly after Josiana returned with someone bearing a jug of water and some beakers a burly red-haired Saxon put in an appearance.

'Harry,' he introduced himself. 'What can I do for you, domina? I'll help you if I can.' He put his thumbs in his belt.

'If it's about Lydia, I can say this, she came into the hall after Compline with everybody else, asking for ale. They're a rowdy bunch but no harm in any of them. When she trotted off to bed that's the last we saw of her. Later next morning news come she's drowned.'

'How far is the river from here?'

'A way. But it's a draw, the foreshore, a haven, a sort of trysting place where the servants like to go for a bit of privacy on their evening walks, know what I mean?'

'So there were other servants down there the other night?'

'I doubt anybody much else was there. It was pissing down early on, pardon me. It didn't let up till after Compline so mayhap she decided to go for a walk by herself before turning in.'

Hildegard gave him a sceptical glance. 'Is that likely?'

His glance was unwavering. 'You'll have to prove otherwise.'

'I will do my best.'

He gave her a sardonic glance. 'I myself was in hall all evening and can guarantee the presence of my men.'

'Good. I'm glad to hear it.'

He left then with a sidelong glance at Josiana.

'So,' Hildegard sighed when he was out of earshot. 'What was he really saying?'

'She must have gone out for a breath of fresh air?'

'Alone?' She turned to Alaric. 'Is Harry noted first for his honesty or for his loyalty to his men?'

'He's honest and loyal enough, if lacking the usual courtesies.'

'I think it means we have to question everyone who was in hall that evening, don't you?' She sighed again. 'I cannot see us returning to Swyne tonight.'

It was a long day. Although the lay-brothers were not as numerous as they were at Swyne it took enough time to make a list and go through it only to find no discrepancies in their stories. It was the same with the small number of lay-sisters.

Everyone's presence was doubly witnessed by colleagues and without exception they expressed unequivocal horror when it was pointed out that Lydia's death could possibly be viewed as murder.

'But this is a peaceful part of the county, we never have anything untoward happening, not here, the friars are as much hermits as they can be while fulfilling their preaching and teaching duties.' The mistress of the female servants was flushed with a mixture of dismay and anger. 'How could anyone think it of us,' she demanded when she finished speaking, 'it's so outside our understanding.'

Hildegard found herself apologizing. 'It is not my intention to cast aspersions on you, mistress, nor on anyone else, but we assume that the poor girl was hit on the back of the head by human agency. We do not believe it was an accident.'

'Have you questioned other folk here or is it only we servants who are under suspicion?' Her lip curled.

'I wish to question anyone who was in the vicinity and who might have been with Lydia when and if she went down to this haven they mention.'

The woman looked thoughtful but took her leave with her head held rather high.

\*　　\*　　\*

The invitation to dine quickly followed and various friars strolled in from outlying buildings. The aged fellow who knew about astrolabes sat opposite Josiana and discussed numbers and declinations with her after briefly showing puzzlement when it was explained why she was back so soon. One or two other fellows, an anxious-mannered bursar, a sacristan, the sub-prior, and some other obedientiaries, were all present and accounted for on the evening in question. In fact it was unlikely that any of them would have bothered to mix with the servants once the final meal of the day was served. It was confirmed by one after another that they had retired as usual to their own cells for the night as soon as Compline was over.

'So we've drawn a blank,' Hildegard observed when the last one left.

'I told you the guest-master couldn't find her that evening to tell her what time I wanted to leave,' Josiana said. 'She must have gone off before he went looking. I spoke to him just before I retired for the night.'

Alaric entered from the direction of the servants' hall and hurried over when he caught sight of them. 'My lady,' he bowed. 'I can hear things that may not reach your ears. While it's true no one saw Lydia leaving, a stable lad has just mentioned that he thought he heard horses being taken out that night. He was about to climb out of his straw to see who it was when he realized it must be the pilgrims setting out so he decided not to bother as it was not his turn anyway.'

'And his bed was warmer than not.' Hildegard nodded in sympathy. 'Lydia could easily have gone down to this trysting place without being seen, but alone?'

'With one of the guests maybe?'

She turned to Josiana. 'Was she that sort of girl?'

Josiana bit her lip. 'I wouldn't know, domina.'

'Oh come on, you must have got some idea of what she was like. Did she obey rules or was she the sort to take the chance to flout them? Why did you bring her instead of one of the others with you?'

'I didn't choose her. She came to me when she knew I was coming over here and implored me to take her with me. She said she needed a change from being inside the enclave at Swyne.'

Alaric gave a snort and when Hildegard glanced at him, he said, 'We know what she meant by that, don't we?'

'What are you implying?'

'Well, domina, it's common knowledge—' He glanced hurriedly at Josiana. 'Come, tell her.'

'I don't know what you mean and that's the truth!'

Alaric looked askance and said, 'They all know – she herself talked about it often enough.' He turned to Hildegard. 'She said she wanted to be hand-fast to a fellow here and had to make up her mind – but I've no idea who it was before you ask.'

He glared from one to the other as if to say, This is women's business.

'That must be why she was so keen to come. What about you, Josiana. Do you know about this?'

'I might have overheard some tittle-tattle to that effect.'

'Josiana – you're not making this easy.'

'I really know no more than that, domina. I'm not— To be honest I'm not really interested. I know it's a terrible thing to say but I didn't care who rode over with me – they all chatter on about nothing anyway.' She gave Hildegard a despairing glance. 'I was more worried about the figures I'd gathered and how they didn't make sense, oh, and how much danger everyone is going to be in at next full moon with the big spring tide sweeping in and the danger of the waters surging through the flood defences.' Her hands twisted with anxiety. 'God willing it may be more like a slow seeping inundation over the low-lying land than a dramatic deluge.' She gave Hildegard a beseeching glance. 'How could I worry about the romantic hopes of one young girl with all that to think about? Even at its best it will still be an inundation covering miles of countryside. It will mean the drowning of cattle and sheep, the ruination of the cotters' wattle-and-daub dwellings. It'll result in hundreds of deaths, the young as well as the old, followed by starvation for those surviving . . . With all that to think about,' she broke out again, 'do you imagine I listened to gossip? They never have anything interesting to say about what faces us, it's all "she said, he said," without any rhyme or reason . . .'

After a pause Hildegard replied, 'I see.'

Turning to Alaric she asked, 'And this hand-fasting business. Do you know more about that?'

He looked grim. 'No more than I've told you, but I'll sure as the devil find out who this fellow is, if he exists.' Swivelling on his heel he strode from the hall.

Before Hildegard could call him back Josiana said in a small voice, 'I am abject, Hildegard. I do not pay attention to people and their little foibles. It is my besetting sin. If she mentioned wanting to be hand-fast I did not register it. I have no interest in such events – it is my great sin. I know it is. I acknowledge it. I find the magnificence of the skies overwhelms my interest with life on earth. Everything here seems so trivial by comparison. So fleeting. *Mea culpa*,' she finished. 'It is a form of pride, is it not?'

'I'm sure your confessor at Meaux will advise you.' Hildegard felt like shaking her.

It was some time before Alaric reappeared. Josiana had already gone to bed. Hildegard had been entertained by a couple of friars practising a song they had recently learned for St Augustine's day at the end of August.

'Who taught you that?' she asked when they paused to top up their ale mugs from the communal jug.

'Some fellow passing through to York Minster,' they told her. 'Pleasing, isn't it?'

Hildegard thought of the stranger who had turned up at Swyne and was now sitting safely at Meaux. Was it likely they were one and the same?

'He wasn't being pursued by enemies, was he?' she asked just to be sure.

Both friars laughed. 'I doubt whether he has an enemy in the world,' one of them replied. 'A good fellow all round. Why do you ask?'

She told him about their midnight visitor and he allayed her suspicion by telling her that this fellow was forty if he was a day and toothless, short and rotund into the bargain.

Alaric returned. His news was not much more helpful.

'I've found out who we need to talk to. Somebody by the name of Aethelburt. Not that it's much help. There's no sign of him. What is significant is that he hasn't been seen since the night

Josiana and Lydia were here.' He paused. 'They say he's gone
back to the manor where he was born to visit his sick grandma. It
might be Kirk Ella, Willerby or Cottingham. Nobody was quite
sure which.'

At Hildegard's exclamation of annoyance he added, 'They're
all in the domain of Haltemprice so he should be easy to track
down . . . The sub-prior will know where to find him – unless of
course he decided it's wiser to go into hiding.' His expression
darkened. Clearly he thought Aethelburt was the guilty man.

# EIGHTEEN

S o what have we got so far? Hildegard asked herself for the hundredth time as she tossed and turned in the small hours. At least there was no getting up in the middle of the night for Matins nor even, as it transpired, for Lauds. In the circumstances she might have welcomed the distraction.

She surveyed in her mind the likely events of the day ahead. They would find the lay-brother on his manor, wherever it was, he would confess all and that would be that. The fellow would be punished. And Lydia would still be dead. End of story. Another brief chapter in life here on earth. Maybe Josiana was right. Sometimes it was too bleak to bear.

Half-asleep, she went down to break her fast. The Prior would have to send men to the suspect's manor to fetch him back to face the judgement of the court. The Sheriff at York would be informed. It was out of her hands now. They might leave as soon as Josiana was ready and their horses could be saddled up.

The friars here kept the canonical hour of Prime at least, no doubt seeing it as a fitting start to any day, and Alaric was ready and leading their horses from the stables when Hildegard went out into the garth.

A little stable lad was running alongside him and Alaric announced, 'This is the lad who heard the horses leaving in the middle of the night.'

'It wasn't quite the middle,' the boy corrected.

After a greeting Hildegard asked, 'So if it wasn't the exact middle of the night how long was it after you crawled into your straw?'

'A while, the men were still carousing, one or two of them, so it was not too late.'

'And how many horses?' she asked. 'Could you tell?'

'Two. That's why I thought it might be the pilgrims who were heading for Beverley except that next morning they were still here and coming down yawning like everybody else and complaining of tiredness and how far was it to St John's shrine anyway, and then looking more cheerful after a few mugs of small beer and their pottage, saying how they were looking forward to it, despite the likelihood of more bucketing rain.'

'These are the pilgrims who accompanied Josiana part of the way back, are they?'

Alaric said they must have been as there were no others on the same pilgrimage, so far as he knew, and the little lad agreed.

'By the way, where is Josiana?' Hildegard asked, realizing they had reached a dead end, and now eager to leave. 'I thought she was already down?'

'I haven't seen her this morning, domina.'

Hildegard called a servant. 'Go up, if you will, and rouse my sister nun from Swyne, will you? It's time we left.'

The stable lad petted the horses and hung round as humbly as he could while Alaric kicked a stone with impatience, staring towards the guest house with a frown.

A stone bell tower had recently been erected near the church.

It was tall, too tall maybe, slender and as ephemeral as even Josiana might expect. Its shadow in the watery sun stretched from one side of the garth to the other, such was its height.

Eventually the servant reappeared. 'She's not there, domina, bed made, things gone. Anything else I may do for you?'

Hildegard rolled her eyes with impatience and, with brief thanks, returned indoors just as the elderly guest-mistress was coming out.

'I hear you're off back to Swyne, domina?'

'As soon as I can find Sister Josiana,' Hildegard replied. 'Is she within?'

'I'm afraid I haven't seen her. No doubt she's breaking her fast. Have you checked the guest dining hall?'

Taking the stairs two at a time Hildegard flung herself along the corridor until she came to the chamber Josiana had occupied but when she looked inside it was empty as they had said. This is too bad, she thought. A slow dread began to creep over her. It was too much like the events that had led to Lydia's murder.

Flying back down the steps into the yard she called to Alaric. 'Has she turned up?'

Looking worried he came over. 'You mean she's not there?'

'I'll have a look in the guest hall again.'

When she emerged shaking her head she said to him, 'Let's get over to this haven as quickly as we can.'

Following directions the reliable little stable lad had given them it took only a short while to canter down the lane to find themselves in an open grassy area that petered out on the foreshore. Surrounded by a thicket of hawthorns it was intimately screened from view by anyone passing.

The tide was in, sucking lazily at the shore as it seeped between clumps of grass. A bower, no more than a few wind-ravaged hawthorns, grew to one side of this trysting place and a small meadow studded with the dried heads of long-dead summer flowers lay on the other.

Hildegard dismounted. 'I don't know why I thought she might be here,' she said as she took in the details of the place.

The river was no more than a dull band of yellow-grey water in slow and perpetual motion a few yards out. As a haven it left much to be desired and was made more desolate by the constant shrieks of herring gulls in outrage at the presence of humans.

Alaric drove his horse towards the band of trees then splashed back along the water's edge to where Hildegard was standing.

He looked grim. 'No sign.'

'Is that good or not?'

'Doubtless she's stamping her feet back at the priory,' he suggested. He was still frowning, she noticed.

'What's the matter?'

'I don't know whether you can see it from where you are—'

'What is it?'

'Come and look here.'

Hildegard followed his glance. 'Something in the water, you mean?'

'Don't you see it? I think you may have to look from above. It's an imprint under a few inches of water. There, see it? Just visible where the mud hasn't been stirred up yet. It looks like the imprint of a boot made by someone dragging or pushing a heavy object?'

She bent to get a better look. After a while, as the ripples played tricks with the light, she imagined she could make out a shape. It was very like the print of a boot. Square-toed, quite large. Lifting the hem of her robe she stepped into the shallows, eyes searching, taking care where she put her feet so as not to disturb anything. Bending down she was able to make out more clearly what was there. Several inches further on was another, more difficult to see, grains of sand tumbling into nothing as the tide crept over them. They were definitely prints and once you could see them they looked clear enough. They could belong to anyone.

Straightening she glanced up at Alaric sitting astride his horse. 'What do you think?'

He slid down from the saddle and came to stand beside her. Water lapped at their feet, rising higher in tiny increments even as they stood. 'Somebody pushing a boat into the river . . .?' He glanced at her.

A cold hand gripped her throat. 'Like a repetition of what happened to Lydia?'

'Or a print from an earlier event, before the tide could reach so high? Look, there are footprints all along the strand where people have been strolling about.'

'I should think this footprint was made on the ebb, for it to remain.'

He nodded. 'We can go back along the shoreline to have a look further along, to see if there are any more—'

'Let's go.'

Haste sent them to their horses and soon they were riding at a trot above the waterline to make sure they missed nothing that might look out of the ordinary.

'Would Josiana get into a boat – without telling anybody?' Hildegard was speaking her thoughts aloud. It didn't make sense knowing what she did of her.

They rode as far downriver as a group of fishermen's huts, about a mile from where they started. Several people were about, an old fellow mending a net, some children playing with a puppy, two women sitting on a log chatting while they gutted fish into a bucket.

They had seen no one. No boats had been by this last hour or so, one of the women volunteered. Why would they? There might be one or two coming upriver now the tide was turning. There might even be the ferry from Wyke later on. Despite their help none of it told them whether Josiana had been this way.

'Better get back to the priory, otherwise they'll be sending out a search party for us as well,' observed Hildegard. Thanking the fisherfolk they turned back.

As soon as they reached the gatehouse they saw the old porter sitting there on his bench and as they clattered in a familiar figure emerged from the lodge. It was Josiana. A look of relief came over her face when she saw Hildegard and she ran to her and took her horse by the bridle.

'I feared you'd gone without me. It took longer than I expected but I had a whim to have a proper look round in daylight,' she explained in a rush. 'I hope you weren't worried. I only intended to venture down the lane but somehow I found myself going all the way to the haven. They said you'd been looking for me. I feel so bad. I hope you weren't worried?'

Hildegard pursed her lips. There was no point in showing anger. She was only relieved that the silly young woman was safe.

Behind her she heard a curse of exasperation pass Alaric's lips but did not react to it. 'What is that you have in your hand?' Her tone was clipped and she pointed to a blue kerchief Josiana was holding.

She thrust it towards Hildegard. 'I found it in the grass in that little meadow. I recognized it. It belonged to poor Lydia. I remember her wearing it on the way here. What it proves is that she was at the haven that night. Unless someone stole her scarf and dropped it there – which is unlikely,' she added.

'It doesn't tell us who was with her.' Her thoughts flew to the servant Lydia was said to have her eye on.

'Did you see anything of interest, domina?'

When she used her formal title Hildegard knew it was Josiana's way of making amends so she told her about the footprint, and how they had imagined it was left by someone she, Josiana, had met, and how worried she, Hildegard, had been, and no doubt Alaric too, because, though silent, his expression was still grim.

Rather than looking contrite at the confusion she had caused, Josiana seemed engaged by the mention of a print. 'That's interesting,' she mused. 'It wasn't mine. It must have been left earlier.

Maybe even a few days ago. You see, the tide is higher today. Yesterday it would not have reached the level it does today. It increases a little bit every day towards high water as the moon draws it up by some mysterious power before releasing it again until low water – I can tell you more about the moon if you wish?'

'Yes, later perhaps, when other matters are not so urgent.'

'The footprint will have been covered over by now, otherwise I would ask you to show it to me.' As they mounted their horses and made for the gatehouse Josiana said something that made Hildegard pause. 'What was that?'

'I said, I also checked the stables to see if anyone had taken horses out that evening, bearing in mind what they told me about the little stable lad being woken up in the middle of the night. No one had leave to take out a horse but one was found outside its stall next morning. They put its escape down to the activity of hobgoblins,' she added.

'That was probably taken by Lydia to save her from walking,' Alaric said to Hildegard.

'Come,' she replied, 'we must return to Swyne and leave the canons here to search for the obvious culprit, whichever manor he has escaped to.'

# NINETEEN

The rain had abated since yesterday and they made good time on the return journey despite the deepening flood water across the track and it was not yet Tierce when they rode back over the moat at Swyne.

Blanche came to open the gates into the garth at once. 'The lady Prioress is asking after you, Hildegard. I gather you're to go to Meaux without delay.'

'What? Again? What's this about then?'

'Something to do with the lord Abbot de Courcy, I'm told. I'll warn you, he's in a rage. His messenger was terror-stricken!'

'It can't be anything to do with me,' she replied.

'I wouldn't be too sure.' Blanche gave her a sympathetic glance.

Hildegard dismounted and walked wearily over to the Prioress's house to have her instructions confirmed thinking, *What now, what now?*

# TWENTY

The lord abbot kept her waiting in the anteroom to his private chamber long enough for her alarm to grow. His clerk sat with his head down and would not look at her. She rose to her feet and paced about. He knew she was here so why was he keeping her waiting?

She went to sit down again. The clerk still did not look up. He was a new fellow. Young. Probably as wary as she was herself faced with the lord abbot and his moods.

Suddenly the door flew open and there he was.

Her composure fled in an instant. They say sometimes that knees can turn to jelly on meeting the beloved. To her astonishment she felt it happening now. It was inappropriate. She could barely stand. His austere, handsome, arrogant, forbidding, dearly beloved, and, at this moment, plainly enraged features swam before her gaze and she found she was unable even to summon a greeting.

His glance pierced her to the soul, she felt stripped naked. What sin was she supposed to have committed this time?

Without speaking he indicated for her to enter his chamber. As she stumbled past him she imagined he must be able to feel the heat of her desire radiate from every pore of her body to seek communion with him but he brushed on into the chamber and took his place on his elaborate wooden chair and, arranging the folds of his robe with exactitude, glared at her.

Deliberately he has not asked me to be seated, she registered. *How I hate him*, she thought in confusion.

Propping his elbows on the arms of what she saw as a pretentious throne he steepled his fingers and inspected her over them as if she were an exhibit. His expression was black.

'Hubert,' she blurted, 'is something amiss—?'

'Be silent, domina.'

It took her breath away to hear him call her domina. To order her to be silent! How dare he? Something must be very much amiss for him to avoid using her name. To tell her to be silent, she thought again, who did he think he was? She held her tongue.

'Do you carry informality and contempt for my office so far you forget to make obeisance?'

Her lips opened at this astonishing remark. A feeling of weakness swept over her and she allowed herself to crumple to her knees in a billow of linen. She bent her head. 'My lord abbot, I am at fault.'

Has he taken leave of his senses, she wondered, as she knelt in front of him? Even in all this her heart was pounding, aware of loving him, of having missed him in these last few weeks, of yearning for him as if, forgetting her desire, it was now remembered and was sweeping back with greater force.

How could she have forgotten how he made her feel? She had been swept off her feet by him ever since that first meeting long ago when she had come to beg for permission to establish a small house of nuns near Yedingham.

They had regarded each other as contestants even then.

Fiercely confronting each other. Neither willing to yield. And yet both, as she could not help but remember, both desiring to succumb. Only the strictness of the Rule kept them apart.

In a rush of memory she recalled his declaration under the echoing vault of the Minster in Beverley when, unarmed, he had outfaced Sir William, a knight armed to the teeth, and how he had turned to her after William had been defeated and made that declaration of love forbidden. What he suggested then was against all the tenets of their Order. They were young then, perhaps seeing themselves as another Abelard and Eloise. But that was then.

When she risked a glance he was staring hard enough to imprint her in his memory and gave a start when their glances collided as if caught out. He lifted his head to stare at the small gilded cross above his reading stand like somebody calling on it for strength against the devil.

Eventually he intoned, 'Are matters at Swyne so pressing they took you away as soon as you arrived at the gates of Meaux last time you deigned to visit us?'

His words astonished her. He rose abruptly and strode towards her, pulling her to her feet and glowering into her shocked face as he drew her up. Letting go of her as if suddenly aware of what he was doing he stepped back.

Hildegard drew herself up. 'Hubert?'

For a long moment he regarded her without speaking and they squared up like enemies, neither giving quarter.

With an effort she managed, 'It seems I have displeased you. Pray do enlighten me,' adding, for good measure, 'my lord.' He could not mistake the contempt in her voice, surely?

His voice was hoarse. 'Never call me Hubert again. It is not appropriate.'

Her thoughts ran to and fro to make sense of this. Was it something to do with Ulf of Langbarugh, Lord Roger's steward, her childhood friend with whom, it must be admitted, she had broken her vow of celibacy? The only mitigating fact was that Ulf had been at that time condemned to death for a murder he did not commit . . . No, it was too long ago. He could not dredge up that avowed sin again, and penance had been done, she had been absolved, but what other accusation could he throw at her?

'I believe you arrived at the gates of my abbey but declined to enter?' He cleared his throat, and began again. 'You arrived to deposit a stranger who had apparently turned up—' When he waved his arms she admitted that it was so.

'We took pity on him. And allowed him to remain in a chamber in the gatehouse overnight. Safely locked in. There was no impropriety.'

He cut in. 'I would not expect impropriety. And this – he – this stranger no doubt confided in you – telling, mayhap, some fantastic story—?'

When she risked a glance his glance was so intent he seemed alert to every nuance of her expression.

'He told us quite freely that he was being pursued by someone who wished to kill him – and that's why our Prioress decided he would be safer here. And besides, we are nuns, we do not allow men into our enclosure. As you know,' she added.

'What else did he tell you?' His glance was so piercing it was as if he was trying to force words from her.

'Nothing . . . my lord,' she said, to placate him.

'Nothing?'

She was mystified. What was he getting at? 'He claims to be

a musician from the royal court. King Richard fosters music and poetry as against the war-mongering faction of his mercenary uncles. The minstrel, Leonin, so named, fears for his life. That is the sum of what I know. Oh – and that he plays a vielle. And probably has a good voice, good enough to allow him to perform at King Richard's court. May I ask what this has to do with me?'

'Is that all he said?'

When, open-mouthed, she nodded, he turned briskly with a swish of his robes, his sleeve brushing her arm as he went to the door. 'I will enquire further into this. You may leave.'

'But Hubert – my lord, what on earth is this about?'

'Go back to your priory. Stay there until I send for you again. Go! Go!' He made a shooing movement which she found insulting so she stood her ground.

'Is he causing trouble? . . . This story of his, for instance . . . is it true or false?'

'Story?' He looked stunned for a moment then his brow cleared. 'About being pursued?'

'What else?'

His strength seemed to leave him and his voice was scarcely above a whisper. 'Go back to your priory, Hildegard. I will call you in a day or two.'

As she reached the door he said, 'I was sorry to hear that one of your serving-women was murdered. Have they caught the fellow who did it?'

'Not yet.'

'If my monks can help in any way—' He waved a hand and she took it as a sign to leave.

# TWENTY-ONE

Puzzled by Hubert's manner she was making her way to the stables to ask someone to fetch her horse when, emerging from the cloister, a familiar figure appeared. It was one of the monks. Tall and athletic, very much a monk militant, it was her old comrade, Brother Gregory. He saw her at once and came over.

'Hildegard! Well met!' He smiled with his usual beguiling charm.

'Gregory, I am glad to see you of all people. I've just had a most bruising encounter with Hubert—'

Gregory's smile faded. 'In that case spare a moment to sit with me. I'm not surprised you feel bruised. None of us dare go near him. He seems possessed. It's something that minstrel fellow told him. They were in private discussion for some time. Hubert looked pole-axed when he emerged.'

'Can't the minstrel himself shed any light on matters?'

'He's been sworn to secrecy, he tells us, milking his importance for all it's worth. Of course, we pretend indifference. Indeed,' he corrected, 'we are indifferent to gossip but it's the effect on our lord abbot that concerns us.'

'It seems to concern me, I'm afraid, but I'm at a loss to understand why. I wondered if – of course it cannot be anything connected to Ulf—' She glanced at him for reassurance.

'To Sir Ulf of Langbarugh? That affair will never be forgotten, but you are forgiven, Hildegard, you know that.'

'You and Brother Egbert saved my life when that arrow caught me.'

'Praise God and all his angels we were able to help. And Ulf too, a good fellow although he aroused in me powerful feelings I did not want—' He grinned sheepishly. 'I have to admit it was jealousy that consumed me at that time. Even at Beaulieu Abbey I was still in its toils – but I thank you, Hildi, it was my possessiveness, a fault I had to face, and I feel nothing but gratitude that

I was strengthened by the challenge.' He touched her hand. 'You know you will always live in my heart and I hope I in yours – but we have come through it, both of us – have we not?'

They shared smiles of true friendship after the years when their obedience to the strict discipline of the Rule was at risk.

'Dear Gregory, our vows can lead us down some strange paths. To break them can only lead us into hell. But as for Hubert?'

'I'm hoping you might know something to help us men of Meaux to understand him. He confides in no one, not even his confessor. I fear for him.'

'I'm as much in the dark as you.'

'I'm wondering if it's something to do with his allegiance? Some matter at the royal court and the King of France?'

'It may well be.'

'May we make a pact to keep each other informed? It grieves me to see him so distressed. He seems locked in combat with the devil and a hand outstretched may save his soul from hell.'

# TWENTY-TWO

On the short ride back to Swyne she was able to compose her shaken feelings and reorder her thoughts to search out a solution to Hubert's misunderstanding, which it surely was. It was the youthful stranger who had roughed up the sleepy calm of both Meaux and Swyne, as if the murder of Lydia were not enough.

She went in to have a word with the Prioress as soon as she returned.

'Our interview lasted only minutes, my lady. Hubert is in a strange emotional state. I was at a loss to understand it and couldn't help but wonder if I'd done wrong, but then I chanced on Brother Gregory with a similar story to tell.'

The Prioress had no shred of enlightenment to offer. 'We need to send someone down to Westminster to find out more about this minstrel.' She tightened her lips. 'There's something not right there. We may learn something that will surprise us and I wouldn't be surprised if it had something to do with matters at the royal court.' She hesitated, 'If not, then it must be Lydia's murder, as we first imagined.'

'You think he's involved—?'

'Look at it. She was wandering in the woods near this haven they mention. Somehow she was put aboard a boat, if that footprint Alaric told me about means anything and, after being swept downriver by the tide, she pitched up on the mudflats near here. This stranger, Leonin, claims he made the river crossing by boat at about the same time. Where is this boat? Think on it.'

'You believe Leonin and Lydia may have encountered each other and . . .?'

'Keep this thought to yourself until her so-called betrothed is found on his manor and can inform us otherwise.'

'I will do so.'

'Meanwhile we are being warned by Josiana, and some others

who imagine they can predict the weather, to bring in our animals to shelter and make all safe within the priory as if preparing for a siege.' Her eyes gleamed with pleasure. 'We are called to action, Hildegard. Make sure everyone knows what they have to do.'

# TWENTY-THREE

When she mentioned the weather and the imminence of a great flood at the equinox caused by simultaneous torrential rains and a massive spring tide the warning was met with derision, a response Hildegard tended to share.

Josiana was held in respect because of her facility with arithmetic, geometry and other natural sciences, but they judged that this time she had miscalculated, no matter what she said about the old astronomer at Haltemprice agreeing with her.

'Look around you! Look at the skies!'

After the recent rain the sky was the colour of a blackbird's egg. A light breeze almost like early summer rustled through the leaves. The beech trees were a breathtaking shade of gold and were surrounded by a huge crop of beech nuts with swarms of red squirrels busily gathering the harvest before winter. You could not hope for a milder autumn. Even the novices, chores done, were sitting on the outside of the cloister walls to catch the warming rays of the sun and nobody even bothered to reprove them.

Others, more circumspect, went about their allotted chores without complaint, building up the priory's defences, checking and rechecking the food stores down to the last detail.

The drainage ditches were now able to cope with all but the worst imaginable floods. The moat was cleared. The bridge was in good order.

The sheep, far too many to bring under shelter, were herded to higher pasture up beyond the manor lands on the other side of Cottingham and the cattle had already been removed to a couple of distant granges on land never before affected by floods.

Later that week, however, when officials wearing impressive City livery rode in from Wyke, the king's town on the Hull, to make sure the nuns were as safe as they could be, even the naysayers began to take the warnings more seriously. If Hull expected to flood, they themselves, on the Holderness plain, would be right in its path.

The mood began to change again. It became a question of when would the heavens open, not if. The novices were discovered talking worriedly about it among themselves; the nuns, maintaining silence on the matter, walked about with increasing alertness. Over the next few days the atmosphere became febrile.

# TWENTY-FOUR

'I do feel something needs to be done about poor Lydia.' It was Hildegard at Chapter a few days later. She had been brooding about the matter and when there was still no word from Haltemprice concerning the arrest of the chief suspect she felt it was time to call someone to account. The girl could not go unmourned. She was sick of all the doom and gloom about the expected floods as well.

The Prioress was presiding and looked up. 'Continue, Hildegard.'

'In my opinion we need to find out from the Austins whether that fellow who is said to have wanted to wed Lydia has been found and questioned. Why have they not sent word?'

Before any futile gossip could break out she said, 'I am quite willing to ride over there to find out what is happening, before this threatened storm breaks over our heads and makes it impossible.'

A few murmurs followed and everyone looked at everyone else.

'It would only take a few hours,' she added.

'Let's think it over,' the Prioress suggested. 'If this blessed inundation doesn't strike by tomorrow you may go. In my view it is they who should come to us with news if they have any. At least if you went,' she added to Hildegard, 'you would enjoy a respite from this atmosphere. By the way everyone is carrying on you'd think the end of the world was nigh and the river had never burst its banks before. It's water, that's all. Nothing to it. Brace up, everyone! Pray continue!'

With that she swept from the chamber with her clerk running after her and documents flying in all directions to be picked up later by the novices.

# TWENTY-FIVE

When Hildegard came out of Lauds next morning and with no sign of rain she decided she would set off for Haltemprice as soon as she could get a horse saddled up.

Aware that anyone with sharp eyesight might have noticed a small darkening of the sky to the west, she was undeterred, remembering only to take a waterproof for the ride back later in the day, just in case.

The prevailing wind, as they all knew, was easterly. It was as cold as Russia was said to be whence it came. For most of the winter months it scoured the coast but now, at this time of year, the equinoctial gales swept in from the west, out of the great dark ocean beyond Ireland. They were rarely as disagreeable as the Russian easterlies.

The last time anyone could remember a really bad storm was far back in their mothers' days when steeples were brought down, trees uprooted and some glass at York Minster was said to have been smashed to smithereens.

The wind, Hildegard recalled, was the element of air – that element between fire and water, between judgement and redemption.

The idea, if you dwelt on it, could arouse a feeling of disquiet, of impending disaster, of judgements being handed down and severely enforced. With imagination let loose it could even seem as if something was hanging over the priory like a curse.

But this is exactly what it is, she told herself, a judgement on the murderer and on us for failing to bring him to justice. For the sake of the sinner himself, we must pray for the redemption of his soul. First, however, we must identify him and prove his guilt.

Glad to get out of the priory, with such dark thoughts haunting her, it was especially welcome to be on the road in weather as dry and clear today as anyone might wish. Alaric had been as keen to get outside the precinct as she was and so it was with Josiana's dire warnings ringing in their ears, they set out.

Only the small cloud, no more than a smudge on the horizon, could cause disquiet.

# TWENTY-SIX

The first thing to go wrong was when Alaric's horse threw a shoe. Cursing under his breath, he dismounted. 'Nowt to be done,' he muttered. 'I'll have to walk. You go on, domina, if you wish.'

'Nonsense. We started out together. We'll arrive together. It's such a lovely day, we can take as long as we like.'

'That's grand of you,' he replied. 'As it's not above another three miles or thereabouts we'll make short work of it and I'll get it fixed by their blacksmith while you're about your business with the Prior.'

They walked for a while through the woods in friendly silence until they reached a crossroads in a clearing. Alaric became more alert and the horses snorted and shook their heads. She looked round. Everything glistened in the early morning dew. No breeze disturbed the trees.

'Steady, old fellow,' she patted her horse. 'What's wrong with him, Alaric?'

He grinned up at her. 'Nothing, domina, just a wraith bringing unease. The horses always sense when they're passing by the Foul Oak.'

'Why is that?'

'They must know about the many who've been hanged here. Back in the old days they say it was the favourite place for the Norman invaders to hang their enemies after their torturers had done with them. Quiet enough with only the devil watching?' He stopped and gazed up into the gnarled limbs above his head. 'Aye, many a good Saxon met his end here.' He shot her an apologetic glance. 'I brood not on those days, domina, you need not imagine I would join the rebels to lay waste the streets of London to assert our rights as freeborn men. After our defeat last time we will put up with injustice until the right time returns.'

'Are there many who'll rise up against the barons if there is a next time?'

He shifted his glance to the path ahead. 'It'd be to their doom to admit it.' Without another glance he began to walk on.

Hildegard watched him. She could understand that as a Cistercian she might not be trusted.

It was a French Order, that was bad enough, but the Order's wealth, which seemed to accrue to them with little effort beyond a deal of astute planning, was another grievance. The monastics were aliens among a defeated people, even if it had taken place long ago.

Stories still circulated about the heroes who fought the Norman invasion. Hopes of a new leader, a Hereward, an Alfred, another Wat Tyler, still haunted the dreams of the bonded labourers. They would never forget their once free state as long as it remained out of reach.

King Richard knew this as a child. He offered freedom during the Revolt just over ten years ago and only the King's Council, his uncles, the Norman barons, had forced him to withdraw the letters of manumission he had handed out.

Now it was still too soon for an enslaved people to forget their brief taste of freedom.

She led her horse alongside Alaric. 'My great-grandmother was of Viking stock. My great-grandfather was a bonded serf to a Norman overlord on land further north from here. Only the wheel of fortune enabled him to buy his freedom and rise in the hierarchy. My heart still lies with those who are forced to work for their owners' profit and have to bow and scrape to their overlords under alien laws.'

'That's why I'm here beside you, domina. I know your story. I will protect you. For the sake of our grandames who were no doubt neighbours in some long-forgotten Saxon vill – before William's Harrowing of the North burned it to the ground – and salted the earth to infertility – and forced the folk into famine.' He gave her a smile, rueful but complicit. 'The times we live in! We know what it was like then. Now we can only tend our own small plot and do what's right. I'm sure we both agree with that?'

'It's why I joined the Order. It seemed the best way to live, better than swearing obedience to some Norman lordling who would treat a wife as no better than one of his cattle!'

He chuckled at this. 'We all live in hope of a change for the better.'

# TWENTY-SEVEN

It was around midday when they walked into the priory enclosure and almost as expected they found the friars at table. While Alaric went down to the kitchens the Prior himself rose to his feet when Hildegard was ushered in.

'Dear revered sister in Christ,' he greeted her. 'You come about this tragedy to your dear servant Lydia, but I regret to tell you the suspect has vanished without trace. We did our best to apprehend him.'

The story was that Aethelburt had gone over to a place called Kirk Ella, not far away, discovered that the rumour about his grandmother being ill was exaggerated, and then set off back to Haltemprice, all unaware that he was a wanted man.

'So where is he now?' She glanced quickly along the table but it was the familiar small group as before.

'To our mystification he has vanished, as I say. Mayhap he heard the news that he was wanted for murder? Mayhap.' he looked sombre, 'he is guilty and thought it best to defeat his accusers by absconding?'

'Our journey then has been for nothing.'

'But dine with us before returning. I beg you.'

Alaric was treated to food and drink and later looking somewhat bemused brought the horses out for the return journey, his own newly shod.

'Did you not hear any rumour about this fellow's whereabouts, Alaric?'

He shook his head. 'Despite our situation I would tell you. Murder is murder whoever commits it. I would not shield him. But nobody knows anything. Or if they do they're keeping very straight faces. I trust them to give a hint as long as it could not be traced back to them but no,' he shook his head, 'not a whisper.'

'So he's gone to ground. That's an admission of guilt if ever there was one. What's his name again?'

'Aethelburt.'

'A good Saxon name.'

'He was a good Saxon fellow, so I hear. Nobody can believe he would harm anyone, least of all Lydia. They were serious about each other. Lovebirds, somebody called them.'

'I wish he would appear and clear his name if he's innocent. This uncertainty gives the real perpetrator a chance of covering his tracks. By disappearing he'll be called and made outlaw and what good will that do?'

'There's plenty survive in the woods,' he replied shortly.

# TWENTY-EIGHT

They were back at the Foul Oak just as the first spots of rain began to fall. At least this time Alaric was mounted. The horses bristled when they reached the great tree and increased their pace.

Rain began to fall more heavily. They could have returned and sheltered under its wide branches but neither of them was inclined to linger in a place with such a sinister reputation.

They were only a few yards further on when a scuffle in the undergrowth alerted them and three men reared up without warning and before they could urge their horses on ran alongside them, one of them grabbing the reins from Hildegard to drag her horse to a halt and the others surrounding Alaric.

Before she knew what was happening she was being pulling out of the saddle. Lashing out as best she could she fell to the ground with the breath knocked out of her.

It happened so suddenly she could do nothing to resist except slide her knife from her sleeve and turn to face her attacker while still on her knees.

Somewhere close by Alaric gave a shout and she thought she heard the rasp of blades meeting. Still on her knees she managed to wield her own knife as her attacker moved in and taking him by surprise she got it against his throat even as he grappled to wrest it from her but something made her hesitate.

It was a mistake. Even as she wavered he grabbed her wrist and forced the knife from her hand.

'Get up, lady. On your feet.'

When she did so, the better to thwart him, she reached for the bridle and he stepped between her and the horse muttering, 'Not so fast.' Springing at her he managed to twist her arm behind her back and push her across the clearing to where two of them were now holding Alaric with a knife at his throat.

'What do you want?' she demanded, forcing her voice steady

to belie the pounding of her heart. 'We have nothing of value. I'm a nun as you can see and this is my escort.'

'A lot of good he is, nun,' growled one of the men holding him. He was a red-bearded fellow, covered in mud and filth like one living rough for some time.

Rain was rattling through the trees by now, soaking them all, and the ruffian manhandling Hildegard said, 'Get them under them trees. I'm not suffering another drenching like last time.'

With little choice both Hildegard and Alaric were bundled over towards a grove of oaks.

Fully expecting the men to slit their throats she heard Alaric gasp, 'Let her go. You've no argument with her.'

The men gave Hildegard a sneering assessment.

'What's she doing out of her nunnery anyway?' demanded the one with the red beard, truculent and unbending.

Trembling, aware of the knives held at their throats, she croaked, 'I'll tell you if you ask this fellow to loosen his grip. I'm not likely to run anywhere at present, am I?'

'Saucy!' He looked her up and down. 'Are you going to answer my question?'

'I'll tell you then.' Fighting down her fear she looked directly at the fourth fellow, who so far had not uttered a word. 'We're looking for the man who was going to be hand-fast to the maid Lydia at my priory at Swyne. We hope he'll clear his name. There are accusations of murder against him. If he does not come forward with an alibi he will be outlawed.'

Their three captors roared with laughter. 'You mean like us?'

One of them did a little dance in the rain. 'Do we look afeared, lady?'

'It's a grand life,' said red-beard, 'for those of us who don't like Norman law as it now stands.'

She turned to the silent one. 'Are you Aethelburt?'

Taken by surprise he backed off. 'What if I am?'

'If you did not murder Lydia and throw her body in the river, you must say so.'

'How did you know I'm—' He glanced wildly from one to the other.

'You sot-wit,' growled the man grasping Hildegard.

'Now that's sorted what do you want with us?' Alaric demanded, still struggling against his captors.

'We want vittles.'

'Take what we have. It's nothing but a bit of bread and cheese from Haltemprice. You're welcome to it.' Hildegard, breathing a little easier, indicated her saddle bag. 'But to set my mind at rest,' she turned to the fourth man, 'did you harm Lydia?'

He shook his head. He was the youngest of them, no more than twenty, a soft-faced, fair-haired fellow with the beginnings of a beard. 'I would never have harmed a hair on that girl's head,' he announced. 'So help me God. She was my light, my life. And I blame myself for her death. They told me her body had been swept up on the shore downriver. I am grieved to the bottom of my soul. And if I knew who had done such a foul deed I would kill them with my own bare hands and take the consequences believing it a thing well done.'

The other three were solemn at this admission and none of them spoke for a moment.

It was Alaric who broke the silence. 'Well said, man. Nobody at Haltemprice thinks you did it. They tried to cover up for you. So how did it happen? We're at our wits' end to work it out. How did she get into the river?'

Aethelburt, clearly owning the name, shook his head. 'I left her at the gate to the priory where she was bedding down for the night. We wanted a few hours together. It would be well before Lauds when we parted.'

'Was it likely she would later return to the haven – I take it that's where you did your trysting?' Hildegard asked.

'I can't think why she should.'

She had a sudden thought. 'Could she have left something behind and maybe gone back for it?'

The man blinked.

'God in heaven,' he muttered.

Everyone stared at him. His eyelashes, pale and long, glistened with moisture that was caused by other than rain. His cheeks blanched. 'So that's it.'

He closed his eyes for a moment. When he opened them they looked depthless. 'She told me she had left something behind, a kerchief, the blue one I gave her, she thought it right precious, the

silly love. Oh, no,' he moaned and the muscles of his face worked
as he tried to control himself. 'Did she go back for it? She must
have decided to . . .' He lifted his head with a great howl of
anguish. 'I did it! I killed her with that scarf! If I hadn't given it
to her she would never have gone back!' He began to sob with
helpless grief.

'Come on, lad,' said red-beard. 'You don't have eyes in the
back of your head. She should never have gone back by herself.
It was not your fault.'

'She set such store by it,' he told them between gulping breaths
as he tried to control his anguish. 'A nothing, a little scarf, a gift,
only meant for her pleasure. How could I ever guess it would
mean the end of her?'

The knife that was still held at Alaric's throat was slowly
lowered.

Hildegard's captor loosened his grip. She told Aethelburt,
'You've shone a different light on things. I have a better suspect
than you in mind.' She addressed red-beard as he seemed to be
the leader of the group. 'If you let us go free I believe we can
bring her murderer to justice. There is someone far more likely
to have killed her than Aethelburt.'

She wondered if he knew that Lydia had been hit savagely on
the back of the head before being dumped in the river. It had been
enough to kill her instantly. Thinking it kinder not to mention it
at present, she said, 'Your version fits with what we already know.
It absolves you.'

Red-beard glanced at the man holding Hildegard. 'What do you
reckon? Is it a fair bargain? Shall we release them?'

'What do we do if she's lying?'

'I'm a nun!' Hildegard broke in heatedly.

Alaric spat at his feet. 'She's on the level,' he announced.
'Saxon like us, brought by force of circumstances to her present
position, like us,' he added.

Red-beard was still undecided.

'Look,' Hildegard interrupted, 'you wanted food, you've got all
we have. If you want more then come to the priory kitchens and
ask. Tell them Hildegard says so. Better still, go back to Haltemprice
to the Austin friars. They'll feed you, no questions asked. Tell
them you met us and that Aethelburt has proved his innocence to

our satisfaction.' She paused then announced, 'The most likely suspect is now in custody at the abbey of Meaux.'

A moment of surprise followed.

Red-beard gestured to his accomplices. 'Let's risk it. They won't mind if we take their weapons for our trouble.'

Alaric was released and the man holding Hildegard put her knife in his belt along with his own, walked over to the horses and gathered the reins in his hands. 'I'll take these as well, if you don't mind.'

A few moments later the men, two to a horse, vanished into the undergrowth. Hildegard rolled her eyes at Alaric. 'At least we live to enjoy another day.'

Disgruntled at being caught unawares but mildly satisfied that if Aethelburt was on the level the mystery was nearly solved and the killer would be brought to justice, they set off on foot to Swyne, taking rather longer than it had taken to travel in the opposite direction earlier that day.

Alaric looked puzzled. 'So . . . you think it's him, do you? . . . Him in his fancy clothes and embroidered boots.'

# TWENTY-NINE

B y the time they spotted the grey stone buildings on the slope between the trees, the heavens had opened. Hildegard was soaked right through to her undershift. She was sure Alaric was similarly wet despite his leather jerkin although he made no complaint.

They reached the gatehouse and threw themselves under the arch with cries of relief but it afforded little shelter. Wind drove the rain as through a funnel. The moat was already gurgling as it began to fill.

The porteress poked her head out of the lodge then came right out holding a waxed cover over her head.

'Where's your waterproof, domina?'

'It was taken, along with the priory's horses and my knife and the saddle bag containing a few scraps of food.'

'Outlaws?'

She didn't answer. She was angry now they were back in relative safety. To have allowed the men to take what they wanted? Was it fair exchange for the information they had gleaned? It was only circumstantial and could finish up meaning nothing if Aethelburt came to trial. In truth they were back where they started.

Before they parted to rid themselves of their wet garments Alaric stopped at the entrance to the inner close.

'What was this you told them outlaws about the abbey of Meaux?'

'I'm getting out of these wet things then I'm going over there.'

'I'm coming as well. Wait on till I get out of mine and into something dry. I'll bring the horses round to the lodge.' His expression changed. 'That is, if you'll kindly give me permission to accompany you, my lady?'

'Sot-wit. I'd be disappointed if you refused!'

They parted.

\* \* \*

Quickly going to her cell and stripping off she rubbed her body all over with a rough cloth then slid a crisp, dry shift over her head, pulled on her spare habit, knotted her belt, and scuffed about looking for some dry boots. Snatching up her cloak she was soon ready to go but hesitated for a moment. Rather than wait until the Prioress came out of prayers to ask her permission to ride over to Meaux – and no doubt get into a long discussion with her – she found a servant and told her to give a message to the Prioress when she was free.

By the time she went out onto the garth with a borrowed waterproof Alaric was already sheltering in the entrance with two fresh horses saddled and bridled. He began to move off the moment she flung one leg over the horse's back to follow.

The way through the woods to Meaux was studded with deepening puddles as they cantered through the rain and they were soaked and breathless by the time they reached the gatehouse. Tossing the reins to Alaric she set off towards the church. Hubert would be on the point of leaving, the last Office near its end. The monks were already filing out with the Prior in the lead so she stepped into the shadow of the cloisters as they approached.

But there was no sign of Hubert.

As the monks processed by she noticed Brother Gregory and his military-looking companion and guessed it would be Brother Egbert, whom she knew of old. Gregory noticed her at once and Egbert lifted his head in surprise. They broke away from the others and strode over.

Gregory looked worried. 'Back already, Hildegard? Has something happened?'

'Where is Hubert?' she whispered as the rest of the monks filed past.

'In church. He will see no one.'

'He must see me. I believe I know who may have murdered Lydia.'

'He absolutely will not but if you feel strongly about it I'll go and see if I can fetch him.' He went off in his usual brisk manner.

Egbert gave her a quizzical smile. 'You know who the guilty person is? Come with me. We'll wait over by yon wall where we can watch Gregory being pitched out on his ear.'

'Is it as bad as that?' she asked as she followed him to an unobtrusive vantage point.

'It's to do with something happening down in London we believe.' His tone was doubtful as they settled out of the rain in a corner of the north wall. He glanced along the cloister to make sure it was empty. 'The school lads are having lessons inside today,' he remarked. 'We've got the place to ourselves. But listen, he will not speak nor explain. That young fellow, Leonin, is embedded in a small chamber in the abbot's house and we've seen neither hair nor hide of him since that first day when he strutted around looking enigmatic.'

'Is it to do with King Richard?'

'He's safe as far as we know. Gone to Eltham. A courier came down from York yesterday. They get the news there first, of course. No arrays being called. All quiet. He hinted that Richard is thinking of leading an army into Ireland. Some trouble with McMurtagh and his rivals outside the pale. Richard imagines he can call a peace meeting and get it sorted out once and for all. Good luck with that, say I. But it's all we know at present. Nothing bearing on the presence of our fine young visitor.' He raised his eyebrows. 'So?'

'I feel reassured just to know you and Gregory are here,' Hildegard told him. Then she explained what had happened earlier that morning.

'Were you hurt?' He gave her a searching look.

She shook her head. 'They didn't intend to harm us, only to take what they could.'

'As long as it was only food and horses. Where are they going next?'

'I hope Aethelburt will go to the Prior at Haltemprice and explain himself. You should have seen him, Egbert. He was beside himself with grief at losing his girl.'

'As they say also about our dear King Richard. He was distraught at the sudden death of Anne. She did so much good. A great loss to this sorrowful realm. Good Queen Anne, the folk call her.' He glanced towards the church but there was no sign of Gregory or Hubert. 'So what do you think this matter concerning the minstrel is about?' He furrowed his brow.

'He told us he was being pursued by someone who wanted him

silenced. I wanted to ask him what could he, an ordinary minstrel, know that others did not? I wish I'd insisted on an answer.'

'Look, here's Gregory now. Unaccompanied. We told you so.' Egbert rose to his feet and beckoned.

Gregory came over. He was frowning. 'My powers of persuasion have waned,' he announced. 'I couldn't even get near him. His servant refused to allow me into the sanctuary. Hubert was still on his knees, praying, apparently. His confessor was wringing his hands nearby and when I ventured to ask him what was what he simply shook his head. "All will surely be revealed in the fullness of time." He's a very patient fellow,' Gregory added.

'Would that I could achieve the same level of patience.'

'We've done what we can, Gregory. Now Hildegard has something to tell us.'

She explained again what had happened and his reaction was similar to Egbert's. 'Let's hope Aethelburt gets the chance to prove his innocence before they swing him from the nearest tree.' He peered into Hildegard's face. 'But are you seriously suggesting this minstrel is a murderer?'

'It's a fact that at the time Lydia was attacked he was roaming in the woods near by and when he turned up at our gates he was in a terrible panic about something.'

Both men looked serious.

She read their thoughts. 'I know. I have no intention of accusing him until we have some proof one way or the other but we do need answers about what he did after he landed on this side.'

'And about the events that allegedly sent him flying from the royal court,' added Egbert, looking thoughtful.

She mentioned the footprint in the sand for good measure.

With nothing much more she could do now that the matter was shared with her two reliable brothers and, with Hubert's intransigence prevailing, Hildegard prepared to leave.

'I wonder,' she asked as they escorted her across the garth, 'whether I might learn anything if I could speak to Leonin directly?'

'I don't see why you shouldn't try. We'll put your case to Hubert and try to arrange a meeting tomorrow. That might give him time to come to his senses.'

'I could travel over with the priest after mass.'

'We'll see if we can get past Hubert's body servant. He's worse than the most faithful hound,' observed Egbert. 'Which reminds me, Hildegard. Will you come with us to the kennels for a moment?'

Intrigued she accompanied them towards the stable and into the kennel yard.

'Wait here,' Gregory told her.

Egbert seemed to be in on some secret as he adopted an obviously nonchalant air and she believed he would have started whistling to distract her if he had not been conscious of his status among the conversi bustling about within earshot.

In a moment Gregory reappeared. At his heels was an almost full-grown lymer, a tall, sleek hound used for hunting deer. By its lines it looked so familiar Hildegard gave a cry of pleasure.

'So like Duchess!' she exclaimed, referring to her faithful old hound now long gone.

'And so he should be. He's her grandson!' Gregory looked delighted with her reaction. 'I've trained him up so far. The rest is up to you.'

'What?'

'He's a gift from us both.' He included Egbert. 'We know your Prioress allows you to ride out alone wherever you will. Nimrod here will keep you safe.'

Hildegard greeted the animal to show she acknowledged him while preserving his dignity. This was no table dog to be treated as a pet. She flushed with pleasure. 'I'm overwhelmed. When may I take him?'

'Take him now if you wish. You'll find him as intelligent as Duchess and as loyal.'

It looked as if Nimrod understood all this. When it was time to fetch the horses he gave only a swift glance at Gregory to make sure he was expected to follow the nun and then he loped alongside her as she rode out under the gatehouse archway.

Alaric eyed the animal with caution but there was a gleam in his eyes as they set out on the road back to Swyne.

# THIRTY

The Prioress was again standing before her altar and seemed to have regained her customary vigour. Her cat was nowhere in sight. She turned when Hildegard entered.

'I should reprimand you, Hildegard. It is not for you to take matters into your own hands.' She gave her a knowing glance. 'And it's no good trying to look contrite. What possessed you to think he would see you? It's common knowledge he's undergoing some spiritual crisis and will not speak to anyone. Pride, Hildegard. The abbot will be your undoing. I thought you were over all that?'

Uncomfortable with the thought that the Prioress either knew or suspected everything that passed between herself and Hubert she hung her head in genuine shame.

The Prioress relented. 'Get along with you. I will overlook your disobedience this time. I can see there was a pressing reason to ride over to Meaux.' She gave her a straight look. 'Was it concern for Hubert that led you to leave so precipitately?'

'For Hubert?'

'Well?' Her voice softened very slightly.

'That, of course. It's so unlike him and the monks are watching every step he takes. I'm not sure what they expect. It's unprecedented. He's always so firmly in control. But I am more concerned about the minstrel, Leonin, and whether he is other than he seems.'

'If you believe he is a murderer,' the Prioress broke in, coming straight to the point, 'you must fear that Hubert taking such a fellow into his care could be in danger himself?'

'I'm sure Hubert can look after himself.'

'I am not content. If, as you say, he is not in charge of himself what might he not do to put himself in danger? A dagger in the night? What do we know about this interloper? I would not have had him inside our precinct for any reason on earth without finding out more about the circumstances which led him to flee the royal court. Pursued by a killer? Or by the arm of the law? How do we know what he got up to under King Richard's innocent and trusting eyes? Is he a thief? Such luxury there would try a saint with the lure of gold. Did he kill someone down there? What do we know? Nothing. What does Hubert know? Nothing – at least, as far as we have heard he knows nothing. This silence of his involves us all.'

Hildegard knew in her heart she was right. 'Perhaps,' she suggested, 'a message will warn Hubert of our misgivings and how we are being drawn into the matter? A meeting might be proposed as Gregory suggested?'

'It's the least we can do,' agreed the Prioress. 'I'll suggest a meeting and see what he says then.'

# THIRTY-ONE

F eeling more anxious than ever about Hubert and the stranger after her conversation with the Prioress, Hildegard, with spare time before the midday Office, made her way to the kennels ostensibly to see if Nimrod was being properly cared for even though she had only deposited him there a short time ago but in reality to get away to a neutral place where problems did not exist.

The kennel lads were standing round in a group when she appeared in the yard and she hastened over.

One of them, Burthred by name, a child she had known since he first came to them at the age of seven, a scamp with an affinity with animals, glanced up in awe as she appeared.

'He's almost human, domina,' he told her, 'he seems to understand everything we say to him – although he does seem to regard us as his servants.'

'Which is what we are,' one of the lads grinned.

'I'll take him out for exercise now the rain has let up,' she told them. 'He'll need to learn the woods round here.'

Burthred put on a pleading expression. 'I've finished my chores here, domina. I'm sure you'd like me to come with you?' His hopeful little face broke into smiles when she nodded.

'I don't see why not. If you're going to be his chief keeper you may as well start at once. Let's put him through his paces.'

It was while they were out in the woods just over the bridge that she noticed the priest riding out. He would be heading back to Meaux, she assumed, until the evening Office.

Almost immediately, a figure swathed in a black cloak similar to the one Matthew was wearing followed him out. They both had their hoods up and were soon out of sight down the lane. She wondered idly who the second person was but soon forgot about them and became absorbed in Nimrod's explorations.

He was beautiful to watch as he loped gracefully about the clearing and it was clear he wanted nothing more than to be running alongside a horse, matching pace for pace, as they pursued some antlered buck or other. It was what he was bred for and Gregory's training had perfected him in his natural role as a hunting dog. There were still wolves hereabouts and she felt comforted to know she would have protection when she now rode out.

Eventually they heard the priory bell calling them back and made for the bridge. The rain had settled to a dull drizzle but even so the water in the moat had risen almost to the top of the bank. It was fed by the stream that acted as a conduit from one of the canals in the elaborate system put in place long ago when the priory was founded.

Somewhere close by it would link up with the canal feeding Meaux from the River Hull. A bridge built long ago called the Abbot's Bridge linked the precinct with the road leading to the distant port at Wyke from where the demesne exported produce to the Low Countries and on into Bohemia.

Apart from the water in the moat inching upwards, the flood so far was not as bad as Josiana predicted and Hildegard strode back with Burthred and Nimrod at her heels, pleased with both the boy and the hound, if not with matters as they now stood at Meaux.

# THIRTY-TWO

I t was free time in the hours before Vespers when there was a knock at her cell door. 'Who is it?' She had a thin tract open on her reading board but was not really looking at it, thoughts too busy elsewhere to give her sufficient peace of mind to indulge her passion for reading.

It was Josiana who peered round the edge of the door. 'May I have a word, Hildegard?'

'Shall we go down to find some warmth somewhere? It's like an ice box in here. It's always the same at this time of year. No sun.' She got up, glad of the interruption.

'Actually I wanted a word in private. It's the novices.'

'Come in, sit down then. Which ones?'

'Those twins. One of them. Or both, I don't know . . .' She went to sit on the edge of the bed. 'One of them left the precinct after mass this morning. I haven't seen her anywhere about since then. When I asked Bella or the other one, whichever it was, she merely laughed at me. "What's it to you," she demanded in a disagreeable tone. I told her I wasn't being a busybody but with a murderer at large I couldn't help keeping a careful eye on everyone. It's only reasonable, isn't it?'

Hildegard realized she was trying to make amends for her previous indifference to people and their doings. 'It certainly is reasonable. Do you have any idea where the other twin went?'

'Not really. There was some giggling early on when the priest arrived and it was after he went back to Meaux that I realized I hadn't seen them together for a while and I therefore deduced that one of them was missing. I doubt whether anybody else has noticed.'

Hildegard remembered the two riders leaving the precinct earlier. They had not been together. In fact the priest looked unaware that someone was riding along behind him.

'She wouldn't get far if she imagined she was going to follow him to the abbey,' she mused, half to herself.

'What do you mean?'

'I mean I saw someone follow Matthew out. Whoever they were they had their hood up. If it was one of the twins, I wonder what she imagined was going to happen? Did her sister not tell you anything?'

Josiana puffed out her cheeks. 'I can't talk to them. I know it must be my fault. They make me feel ridiculous and – somehow stupid – although I know I'm not. Let them try to understand the workings of an astrolabe! The workings of anything, come to that. It's their manner, as if they know something about us that makes us a laughing stock.' She continued to look troubled. 'The thing is, if one of them did ride to Meaux and was not allowed in she'd be back by now, making some silly joke about the monks, you can be sure of it.'

She got up. 'I just thought I'd let you know. I don't mean to tell tales but we're all nervous while this murdering fellow is still lurking about.' When she reached the door she asked, 'Do you think it was somebody passing through, this killer? Are we getting into a panic over someone who has moved on? Was it Lydia's fate to come across him? Was it her destiny, something observable in the stars at her birth?'

Aware that Josiana would be unlikely to know of her suspicions, Hildegard first reassured her as best she could then added that they could know nothing about the stars or anyone's fate written there until the natural philosophers proved that such a thing was possible.

'As we know nothing at this stage about the real-life murderer we need to be cautious in our speculations. We need evidence. Until we have it's only sensible to look out for our sisters – no matter how careless they are over their own safety. Have you checked the stables to find out who took a horse out earlier?'

'I didn't think of that.'

'Then let's go down and ask them. At least we'll know if it was a servant on a legitimate errand – and if it was one of those twins we'll discover that as well.'

Together they went out, crossed the garth, and entered the sweet hay-scented stable yard. A row of horses looked inquisitively over the tops of the doors then, curiosity satisfied, went on placidly munching. A lad could be heard whistling somewhere further off. It was a peaceful scene, the time of day when most labourers were taking a short rest before the last half of the day with its different duties.

A grizzled old fellow, one of the long-time grooms, was sitting on a barrel in one of the open doorways polishing a piece of leather. He rose hurriedly to his feet when Hildegard appeared.

'Domina,' he touched his forelock, 'what can I do for you?'

'It's this, Jack, please don't get up, it's a question about a couple of horses taken out before midday, one was the priest's horse belonging to Meaux, and the other was—?'

He said at once, 'Aye, it was that there palfrey one of the young ladies took.'

'Was it one of the novices?'

'Aye, is it one or two? Twins are they? I can't tell 'em apart.'

'And did she tell you why she needed to leave the precinct?'

'She did not. She seemed in a bit of a hurry. Did she not have permission?'

'I'm afraid she didn't.'

'I was expecting the horse back in her stall long before this. Where has she likely taken her?'

'I was going to ask you that. It's what we are here to find out.'

'By, the lady Prioress will go spare, a novice taking a horse out without permission! Whatever next?'

'What did she say to you?'

'Only that she needed a horse and she'd take the quiet grey if it was all the same to me. The lad had already saddled up the priest's horse for when he came tearing out of church so I saddled up the grey for her myself. It seemed odd, like, her going out so soon after the priest and alone. I thought maybe she was hoping to ride on to Meaux with him if she wasn't going in a different direction, although where she might be taking herself—' He broke off. 'And not back yet.'

Hildegard found Alaric coming out of one of the barns. When she told him what had happened he suggested sending a few lads out to scour the woods near at hand.

'Maybe we should send one over to Meaux just in case she's still there?' He scratched his head. 'It's difficult to know where to start. She might have had a fall but that grey is as safe as a kitten so it's unlikely. And anyway, old Briquet would find her way back home in that case. Maybe your novice took a short cut and got lost? Leave it with me.'

'I'm sorry to get you out when you're in your rest period.'

'Rubbish. I can rest at night, more's the pity!'

He soon rounded up several riders and although nobody mentioned the fact that she might have fallen into the hands of the murderer they clattered out of the yard without even bothering to saddle the horses. Good riders, it was more natural for them to ride bareback as well as quicker.

'They've lost no time,' Josiana observed as she watched them go. 'Now what? . . . I suppose we simply have to wait and hope.'

'Let's go into the cloister where we can hear when they ride back and you can show me how this astrolabe works while we wait.'

# THIRTY-THREE

When Vespers came round and the riders had still not returned and Hildegard felt she knew everything she was capable of understanding about the planets, she and Josiana followed the others into church and waited for the priest to appear. Sometimes he only conducted the service for Compline, the last Office, if other duties at Meaux prevented him showing for Vespers but most evenings he appeared at Vespers as well. This was not such an occasion. It was left to the sub-Prioress to fill in for him.

Hildegard took the opportunity to glance along the two rows of nuns and the similar number of novices standing behind them. She noticed one of the twins but could not be sure which one. She nudged Josiana. 'Only one, as you observed,' she murmured.

'I think that's Rogella,' she whispered back. 'I don't know by looking at their faces but Rogella is slightly wider in the shoulder, only an infinitesimal amount,' she explained. 'I also wonder if she has better eyesight than Bella. See how she's glancing at that text beside the altar? Bella would have had to stoop to get a better look at it.'

'That's observant of you . . . When this is over, follow me.'

The last amen rose to the stone vault, dwindled and died. Only after a pause did anyone move. A swishing sound like soft thunder rose from the floor as a score of leather-soled boots moved to leave at the same time.

'Come on, she's going on ahead of everyone else.'

Their quarry was already in the porch when they caught up with her. 'A word, Rogella,' Hildegard boldly stated, taking her by the arm.

The girl stopped dead and swivelled with a surprised look on her face. When she saw it was Hildegard she gave a false laugh. 'Don't you mean Bella, domina?'

Hildegard shook her head. 'Let's stay with Rogella for the

moment. I want to ask you something.' She leaned forward to prevent her from slipping away and edged her towards the side of the porch out of the way of those leaving.

The novice gave a giggle. 'I feel as if I'm being kidnapped. Why are you looking at me like that? What do you want?'

'Only the truth. You must be aware that there may be a murderer still at large in the woods and we're naturally worried about your sister. Where is she?'

'She'll be about somewhere. Look, I think that's her over there.' She gestured across the garth but Hildegard gave a short laugh.

'You misjudge us if you think we'll fall for that old trick.' She edged closer. 'Come on, where is she?'

'Find her yourself if you're so concerned.'

'She was last seen leaving the priory without permission at around midday, almost exactly at the same time as the priest set out for Meaux. You know and we know she has not yet returned. So where is she?'

Rogella stared from one to the other. Her expression changed. 'You're trying to scare me now. You think you can frighten me into admitting something.' Despite her words she faltered.

'Look here, Rogella, we only want to help. It's a simple enough question. If you know where she is this matter need go no further. No penance. Nothing. All right?'

Rogella looked hunted and glanced round as if to escape but there was no way out. It was clear both nuns were determined to call her to account. 'Very well,' she muttered. 'It's a fuss about nothing. She was going after the priest and planned to ride with him to Meaux, that's all.'

'Why did she want to go to Meaux?'

'She didn't. She didn't intend to go there. She just wanted a chance to get him alone.' She gave them both a defiant look. 'She knows what she's doing. Does it shock you? We're not all mad enough to want to live a life without men. Do you seriously think we're going to stay here like old maids just because our father tells us to? We hate it here. We want to get away. We have no intention of wasting our lives being nuns. You won't want us here if one of us is with child, will you? And you won't want one without the other.'

Her fists were bunched and she glared as if spoiling for a fight.

She was broad-shouldered as Josiana had pointed out and her rage was suddenly volcanic. With no warning she lashed out at Hildegard intending to claw her down the side of her face but, shocked, Hildegard stepped to one side and grabbed her by the arm. The novice struggled but Hildegard twisted her arm until she yelped with pain.

'Don't be a fool, Rogella. No one would want you to be here under duress.'

'That's not what father says. He says the devil will punish us if we try to leave. He will not listen to reason. He says we have no money. He cannot keep us. When he dies we're done for. Everything goes to our brother and his wife. It's not fair! If we stay here we'll finish up as wizened old crones like half the old hags here, praying and living in fear of hell-fire. It's a living death, a tomb, and we will not stand it!'

'It must be horrible not to have any choice,' Hildegard said, not releasing her grip until the girl calmed down. 'The Prioress will do what she can to persuade your father to see sense. I'm sure he wouldn't want you to be unhappy.'

'Ha! You don't know him!'

'Are you calm now?' Watching her closely she slowly released her. 'All right? Now let's talk. We'll deal with Bella first and then when she returns we'll speak on your behalf if you want us to. Now, tell us, where do you think she is?'

Rogella was unbowed. Rubbing her wrist she said, 'If she's any sense she'll be enjoying that young priest and giving him the time of his life.'

When she abruptly walked off Hildegard put out an arm to stop Josiana going after her. 'She doesn't know anything. But she's worried now. I think we need to make sure she doesn't make things worse.'

Hildegard's concern became clear when, a little later, from the shelter of the lodge, they saw a dark figure flit from one shadow to another across the garth and, apparently assuming she was unseen by anyone, scurry under the arch onto the bridge and into the trees on the other side of the lane.

The light colour of her robe could be glimpsed every now and then as her cloak fell back in her hurry to get away. As soon as it was safe they set off after her. Hildegard had brought Nimrod. He slipped like a guiding wraith ahead of them.

'What is she doing?' Josiana murmured in puzzlement a few moments later. Rogella had reached the beginning of the lane to Meaux but instead of going on she sat down on a log as if to wait for someone.

'It's obvious they've arranged to meet here,' Hildegard said.

'They must have been planning it for ages.'

'That's what all the giggling and sly glances were about.' Josiana sighed. She had recovered from her astonishment at Rogella's outrageous remark about the priest and her twin's intentions. 'It must be unbearable to have no vocation. No wonder they want to escape. I could never see either of them as nuns. They think only of trivial things, who's got the most expensive gown, which shoes are in fashion, who owns the biggest manor, all that sort of stuff. You should have heard them. I feel sorry for them.'

'So Bella must have somehow cozened that young priest – I can't believe how blind I've been.'

'I thought it was all talk. No more than wishful thinking. I don't see how they can have ever got close enough to speak to each other. And he so strict and stern.'

'He's very young.' She frowned. 'I thought he was exactly the sort of fellow Hubert would approve of. He must have believed he could be trusted among the women at Swyne. I thought so too – in fact I still do think so. It's impossible to believe he would betray our trust.'

'I don't think the priest is even aware of them,' Josiana countered. 'Maybe that's why the twins have decided to be more blatant in their pursuit?'

'Both of them?' Hildegard was intrigued by the situation. 'Would he ever know which one he was— Really!'

Josiana looked stunned. 'They would be better off at the royal court where nobody would blink at such a thing.'

Hildegard could see how deeply shocked she was and studied the situation for a moment or two. It did not shock her. In some way, putting their vows aside, it was intriguing what people decided to do. Sometimes there was no predicting them. She asked, 'Are our actions really written in our stars? If so, we can hardly blame them.'

'The great waters are moved by the rhythms of the moon,' Josiana told her. 'Can we say for certain we beings are not moved by other more subtle powers of the planets to do what we do?'

'That means we are never to blame for our actions. It means we never truly have a choice. It means we're driven to do what we do by forces greater than ourselves. This is not what we are encouraged to believe. We're expected to take responsibility and the only way we can achieve redemption is by accepting our part in our transgressions against the Word and making reparation.'

'Yes but—' Josiana began to say, when Hildegard gripped her by the arm.

'See?' she hissed. 'She's getting up. Where's she going?'

It was obvious a few moments later. Rogella slowly started back in the direction of the priory. Her feet dragged and her head was bent. She seemed utterly dejected.

The two nuns waited until she crossed the bridge and disappeared into the enclosure and then, discreetly, calling Nimrod to heel, they followed her in.

# THIRTY-FOUR

N ext day there was a general commotion throughout the enclave when the scandalous news that Bella had absconded broke at last. The search party had returned with no information. Enquiries at Meaux brought the added scandal that the priest had vanished at the same time. No one was slow to put two and two together.

Although urged to pray and generally get on with their duties huddles of gossiping nuns were seen in the warming room when they should not have been there or chatting in the cloisters when they should have been working in silence, until at last the obedientiaries, themselves as eager as everyone else to find out what was happening, made an effort to herd everyone back to work under threat of punishment.

The Prioress was exasperated.

'They are consumed by a kind of madness! . . . First it was an imaginary flood and now it's an imaginary liaison . . .! Get over to Meaux, Hildegard. Take Alaric and that hound of yours and find out what's going on from Matthew about the latter. After that you'd better question this minstrel. You can also tell Hubert I want him over here without delay . . . although perhaps you'll phrase it more tactfully . . . as I know you can.'

# THIRTY-FIVE

'He will not see you.' It was the porter at Meaux. Always friendly to Hildegard he spread his arms to show how helpless he felt. 'He's still on his knees. Nobody can winkle him out of chapel.'

'But what's it all about?' Hildegard demanded in irritation.

'He's been like this for nearly a week.'

'What's it to do with? Doesn't anybody have any idea?'

The porter shook his head. 'You can come in. I'm not stopping you. I'm just warning you not to get your hopes up. If your nuns are taken over by the devil as it seems they are then so are we monks. Nobody knows what to do except pray and call on God for help.'

'And the priest?'

'Missing.'

'What, still?' She told him what she knew.

'Poor fellow. They'll find him in a ditch with his throat cut, mark my words.'

Shaking off this sinister pronouncement, Hildegard led her horse into the garth and looked round for somebody to take it.

Alaric, jumping down, grasped the reins. 'Let me. I'll find out what the lay-brothers are saying among themselves. If anybody knows anything, they will.'

Hildegard set off in the direction of the cloisters hoping to find Gregory or Egbert or some other monk with a cool head but there was no one around other than the one supervising the dole for the beggars at the gate. She had ridden through them with scarcely an acknowledgement just now instead of the usual alms she handed out and now she felt a twinge of guilt and rooted in her scrip for some coins.

The monk waved them away. 'Are you looking for anybody in particular, domina?'

'Would you mind going back in and asking for Gregory or Egbert? I'm sent by the Prioress.'

'The same problem as us,' he remarked. 'Stay there.'

He was back in moments from the monks' private part of the buildings followed by the two militants.

'Has she returned?' Gregory asked at once.

She shook her head. 'Everyone believes they've absconded.'

'I don't believe it,' Egbert broke in. 'Not with Matthew. The lad's as uninterested in the pleasures of this world as you could ever imagine. He sees women as a separate species. He was brought up as an oblate—'

'Everybody changes,' Gregory observed. 'The wonder is how he managed to speak to the novice. Are things so lax at Swyne these days?'

'We don't know how they got together either. The story she told me was that they planned to debauch him, she and her twin. It was a sort of game and a way of escaping the life set out for them as nuns.' She didn't go into more detail.

Gregory and Egbert exchanged knowing glances and Gregory said, 'They'll be far away by now. She must have double-crossed her sister and run off with him!'

She told them she felt so involved in trying to track down Lydia's murderer she had paid scant attention to what was going on in the priory.

'The trail has gone cold, has it?' Egbert scratched his head. 'The killer could have been anybody passing through the woods.'

'I suppose we might never know now, except . . .' She hesitated. 'The reason I came over this morning is to talk to Leonin and then to try to arrange a meeting with Hubert—' Even as she said the words she was reminded of the Prioress's warning that Hubert himself might be in danger.

Before she could share her fear Egbert gave an exaggerated shrug. 'You're too late, Hildegard. Leonin's gone! We've no idea when or why but it's a sure thing he's not here now.'

Gregory cut in. 'Whether Hubert knew he was leaving or he left without his blessing we can't yet tell you. The whole business is shrouded in secrecy.'

'But that's astonishing!' At least it kicked the Prioress's fear for Hubert's safety out of the picture. 'To go off, nobody knows where? Hasn't Hubert made any comment?' When they repeated that he was still refusing to speak to anybody, she reluctantly admitted her own suspicions. 'I've nothing to go on except that it fits with the time when Leonin landed at the haven on the night of the storm. He could easily have attacked Lydia when she went back to look for her kerchief – but why he would do so—' She mentioned the footprint of a man's boot like somebody pushing a boat off that Alaric had found.

Gregory gave a grimace of impatience. 'So Leonin landed, attacked her for some reason, put the body in the boat he'd come over in, then threw her body overboard when he was far enough out?'

'It's a theory,' Egbert said in sceptical tones. 'What was the boatman doing all this time?'

'If our lord abbot will deign to see anyone I'll tell him you're here, Hildi. Wait with Egbert.' He strode off.

'That's a good question, Egbert,' she said after Gregory left. 'What was he doing?'

They exchanged glances. At best it might let Leonin off the hook.

They didn't have to wait long for Gregory to return. He was unaccompanied.

'I couldn't get in again. His servant told me the minstrel left after asking for permission – permission! – to live as a hermit on abbey land.'

'A what?' Egbert raised his eyebrows.

'It seems he felt he needed time away from human beings after what happened to him at the Palace of Sheen. He needs to renew his contact with God in the solitude of the woods. I quote verbatim.'

'How is he going to live?'

'I've no idea. He'll have to build a shelter. Snare rabbits. Lure birds to his traps. I don't know. Perhaps Hubert will see to it that somebody takes him a bowl of pottage now and then. It would be our responsibility. The only boon he asked is to be allowed to live in secrecy.'

'Let's find out more.' Egbert waved for them to stay while he went over to the kitchens. He was back almost at once.

'They can't believe it themselves. The chief kitchener took me to one side. Apparently their instructions are to take a parcel of food once a day and leave it in a certain place for him to pick up.

They got something together for him earlier this morning and somebody rode out to leave it in the chosen place!'

'We'll have to see how this works out.' Gregory gave a mirthless laugh. 'He was an effete-looking fellow. He'll never last out in the woods.'

'And if he did murder Lydia,' Hildegard reminded with renewed alarm, 'now we might never know.'

'He'll simply disappear,' Egbert grimaced. 'If he's got any sense.'

'Is it his idea of penance?' Gregory asked.

'More likely,' suggested Egbert with his usual realism, 'it's a way of dodging the hangman.'

'I can't imagine what's got into Hubert to be so foolhardy.'

Calling Nimrod to heel, Hildegard turned to leave. 'I regret being unable to speak to him. Please tell him I rode over to convey a message from my Prioress, if you will. She requests a formal meeting here at Meaux or at Swyne as soon as he will.'

The monks walked to the gatehouse to see her off. Alaric, like a shadow, emerged with the horses and they rode away with Nimrod forging ahead.

# THIRTY-SIX

Once they were safely out of sight of the abbey Alaric suggested a halt. Thinking it was another thrown shoe she glanced down at his horse but it seemed all right.

He said, 'What it is, domina, is what they told me in the kitchens. About the hermit.'

'The . . .?'

'You heard about that – I noticed your Brother Egbert talking to a kitchener?'

'He told me they were instructed to leave Leonin something to eat—'

'Aye, at a place just up the lane here.' He gave her a look full of significance.

'And?'

'We could leave the track and circle back to catch him in the act. Then you can ask him whatever you like.'

'So I could.' Her lips twitched.

'So are we to lie in wait then and track him back to his hermitage? Maybe we can give Nimrod something to do?'

Her eyes were alight and she was about to agree when two riders appeared up ahead. They were wearing Meaux livery and hailed Alaric like a long-lost friend.

He grinned. 'Have you left something at the Stone?'

'We have. If you're hoping for an extra bite to eat you'd better be quick about it. He'll be ravenous. He can't have eaten since yesterday.'

Alaric glanced at Hildegard. 'Shall we ride on, domina?'

'Indeed we shall.'

The other two continued towards Meaux with shouts of merriment.

Alaric waited until they were out of sight. 'I reckon we should leave the horses and walk the rest of the way. The Stone is just ahead. You might remember it from other times you've passed this way?'

They hobbled the horses in the undergrowth and it was as he said, a stone on the verge put there in ancient days appeared. Instead of a parcel of food lying there they saw only a rind of cheese.

'Quick work.' Alaric unslung his bow. 'He must have been as ravenous as they said. I wonder where he's hiding himself?'

Hildegard stepped clear of the track and went up to the Stone, half-expecting to be hailed by someone, but there was no sound other than the soughing of the trees. Calling Nimrod to attention, she showed him the Stone and let him sniff out a scent. A moment later he gave a joyful bound and set off along a track invisible to human eyes and they followed at a quickening pace deeper into the thicket.

Confident that Alaric was close behind with his bow and arrows Hildegard pushed closely after the hound. If he was on the right trail Leonin had certainly chosen a well-hidden location for his hermitage. Nobody could penetrate such undergrowth without the aid of a hound to help them.

Nimrod disappeared and when she caught up with him he was waiting a short distance ahead. So it went, the lymer pausing every now and then to make sure she was following as the trail wound on through a confusing maze of hawthorns until eventually, for no reason Hildegard could discern, he came to a definite halt. Erect and motionless, ears pricked, an almost inaudible rumble in his throat, he warned of something ahead. She crept forward to part the branches then let out a long breath.

Standing in a small glade was Leonin himself. He had taken off his shirt and hung it on a branch, the better to wield an axe. Obviously in the process of building a shelter, struts of wood lay evenly with their tops resting on a ridge pole. Branches with autumn leaves still attached were strewn over the struts to make the edifice water-tight. He was clearly not as helpless as Gregory had suggested. Every so often he stopped, muscles gleaming, to take a large bite out of a wedge of cheese lying on a tree stump before mopping his brow and returning to his task.

Wondering how to approach she watched for a while, aware that he would not be pleased to learn that his secret hermitage had already been found.

Deciding that the best approach was to be direct and that he could take it as he pleased she sent Nimrod bounding towards him as she stepped from the shelter of the trees.

When he noticed the hound he backed off, swearing, and swinging the axe at it. Hurriedly she called, 'Leonin? It's Hildegard!'

He lowered the axe to the ground. Leaning on the haft, his glance still warily on the large, silent hunting dog, with its formidable jaws, he peered into the shadows beneath the trees.

He stepped forward. 'So, domina, I am discovered so soon!'

'I have no intention of revealing your whereabouts. My hound followed your trail.' She began to walk towards him across the glade. 'It gives me the opportunity to talk to you. I'm happy to see you're recovered from the storm the other night.'

Still carrying the axe he began to approach, taking his time about it, maybe conscious of the lymer following every move he made. The swish of grasses growing high to the knees was the only sound until he came to a halt a few yards away – at a sufficient distance to silence the warning rumble in Nimrod's throat.

'I was hoping to have a word with you and rode over to Meaux this morning only to find you gone.' She was unsure what she was going to say next but there were questions, not the obvious one which would receive short shrift, but other, more general ones, that might throw light on the mystery of his sudden irruption into their lives.

He weighed her words carefully. 'Did they tell you at Meaux that I was here?' he asked. 'Was it the abbot, breaking his promise?'

'Never.' She drew back. 'If he made a promise he would keep it unto death.'

He grinned at her vehemence as if suspecting a trap. 'I see he has his followers even outside his own precinct.'

'Nobody told me where you were – if you really want to know, my hound sensed your presence at the Stone and tracked you from there.'

'My carelessness. I left a piece of cheese rind, didn't I? I half thought the birds might like it. I'm unused to living wild. A royal court is more my milieu.'

'So why did you leave?'

'I mentioned that when I fell through your doors the other night, didn't I?' He gazed off into the woods as if deciding whether to tell her more then said in an unexpectedly humble tone, 'If you will do me a kindness, pray sit with me for a moment.' He indicated a fallen tree with a wide trunk clear of branches. He walked over to it. 'Come. Sit. I've ear-marked this one for visitors.'

'Are you expecting many?'

'In my experience at Sheen the royal hermits had a constant stream of visitors to whom they were delighted to dispense their wisdom in return for mead and other gifts. The woods were alive with hermits. I don't wish to be so visible of course but who knows?'

'You sound as if you doubt their wish for solitude.'

'I doubt everything—' He broke off. 'You're here for a purpose? So tell me, if you will.'

Seated side by side she was aware of the scent of rosemary oil mingling with the sweat of labour. She turned to him. 'I'll not dissemble. You must know your arrival aroused many questions.'

'Go on.'

Picking her words carefully she asked, 'I wonder if there's anybody who can vouch for you when you say you crossed the river from the south bank?'

His reply made her go cold.

'No. No one.' He turned to her. 'For the very good reason I stole a boat. I'm sure somebody will have missed it by now.'

'But you said a boatman brought you over?'

'I'm afraid I lied.'

A silence fell.

Forcing herself to speak she said, 'I ask for Lydia's sake.'

'I see.' He looked away.

'And is that the only lie you've told us?'

Ignoring that, he grimaced. 'Do you know they leave their boats just lying on the bank? Anybody could take them.'

'I expect they believe people are too honest to do so.'

'I had no time to be honest, as you put it. There was a professional killer after me. He's a man who'll stop at nothing to silence me. He's the reason I left the protection of your lord abbot. I would have brought nothing but trouble to him.' He turned to look her full in the face. She could not help but believe him when he said, 'This killer has followed me every step of the way and I believe he is even now close at hand.' He glanced hurriedly over his shoulder. 'You were able to find me with astonishing ease despite the care I took to find this little refuge. It means I shall have to move on. There's no other way to escape his satanic intent.'

'I'm sorry if I've made it difficult.' She realized she meant it. 'This man you fear – he must have reached the haven by boat as well?'

'Close on my heels as ruthlessly as that lymer of yours. But don't ask me to say more. It's too dangerous—' His lips tightened. When she did not respond he added, 'He fears I know something . . . But you must be wondering,' he turned to her, 'what secret can I, an ordinary minstrel, possess?'

'You must know the answer?'

'Know but cannot tell.'

He gazed off into the woods and she read his expression as fear. He was only a half-grown boy and reminded her of her own son as he might be in a few years' time.

'We live quietly here in the Riding—' she began.

'That was my hope and prayer. I misjudged . . .'

A long pause followed. She thought of several lines she could take but none of them seemed right. Rather lamely she said, 'You know that if there is anything we at Swyne can do in the cause of truth or justice we will do our best—'

'There are royal secrets at stake, domina. Not ones for nuns leading a sequestered life in the middle of nowhere – with nothing but the fate of their immortal souls to dwell on.'

She turned to him about to correct this erroneous impression then hesitated. Of course, he would not know of the previous years when she had been at the forefront of matters of state with the regality of King Richard continually threatened by conspiracy. 'We are humble indeed at Swyne,' she returned, staring down at her hands.

He rose to his feet before she could say more and held her glance. 'Maybe you can help me,' he tilted his head and gave a crooked smile. 'You can tell me how far we are from the port where I may take ship to the Low Countries.'

She gave a start. 'Does that mean you're outlawed?'

He shook his head. 'Not yet, not as far as I know. Put simply, I may be safer abroad.'

'Won't your pursuer have thought of that? Won't he even now be making his way to watch the nearest port?'

'I shall have to grow a beard and take my chance in disguise then, won't I?' He gave her a look from beneath his brows. 'Where do you suggest, domina?'

'Not Wyke, or Hull as they're beginning to call it. It'll be too busy with tax-gatherers and other officials.'

'Don't you know of anywhere else? I'm a stranger here. I know of no useful port.' For a moment he looked bereft.

When he began to walk off she shouted, 'Wait!'

He swung back. 'What?'

'When you landed in your stolen boat the other night did you notice anyone else on the riverbank?'

'I fetched up on the mud in the middle of nowhere. Who would I notice?'

'It's odd that a young maid from our priory should have been attacked at about the same time as you made it to this side.'

She noticed his reaction but was forced to continue. 'We cannot understand it. It makes no sense that she should be attacked in such a brutal fashion—'

'So this is what they're saying?'

'It's what I'm saying.'

His eyes narrowed and he took a step towards her. 'I would think you'd be more careful for your own safety than to throw accusations around like that. You needn't spell it out. Say your accusation has hit the mark, what do you think I might do next?'

She tensed.

He took another step towards her. Nimrod growled. 'I think it would be sensible to stop your mouth for a start, domina.' He hefted the axe as if to remind her of it then glanced at Nimrod. 'I even believe in a straight contest I might destroy your pup before it destroyed me. However,' he lowered the axe and offered a smile edged with bitterness, 'I may be a thief of boats, and I may have played one lover off against another at court, and said many a thing that might be construed as lies or, in my estimation, mere embroidery of the banal, but never, never in my wildest imaginings, have I considered murdering anyone. I've felt like it! Who hasn't! But to do it? . . .' He half-turned away. 'I am not a murderer.'

He began to stride swiftly towards the tree stump where he had left his things. Dropping the axe he grabbed his shirt and pulled it rapidly over his head, picked up a bag lying in the grass, and took the vielle from where it was hanging in its leather bag from a branch, then trudged back to her. 'So you advise against going to Wyke?'

'I might suggest Ravenser—' she began, astonished at herself for even this feeble offer of help.

'Where in God's name is that?'

'It's at the end of a long spit of sand at the mouth of the Humber, there's a small town built round the harbour.' She told him this as a warning. 'It's where folk head when they're outlawed—'

'I am not outlawed—'

'Then what happened at Sheen that so burdens you?' Her voice rose. 'If it was within the law why should anyone want to silence you? Why should you flee?' He had given no adequate answer on the question of Lydia but against all reason she longed to believe he was innocent. This other mystery needed an answer.

When he remained silent she demanded, 'Where do you think this will end, Leonin? You cannot run for ever.'

He stared at her, suddenly no more than a boy again. 'I believed I would find sanctuary at the Abbey of Meaux. But even the lord abbot cannot save me. My nemesis pursues me. Wherever I go, whatever I do, he will be there, like a good assassin, binding himself in patience for the opportunity to finish his job. I am too dangerous to be allowed to live.'

'I'm sure Hubert would—'

'Hubert?' His tone was sharp.

'Yes, our lord abbot—'

'Does he allow you to call him Hubert? Not "my lord" not "my lord abbot" – just Hubert?' He turned this idea over in his mind then gave her a quizzical glance that spoke volumes. 'He has been most generous towards me. More than I could ever have imagined. But my predicament is something outside his power.'

Hildegard became aware of a change, something as subtle as a sea-change and she floundered in a perception of what it meant. It held the threat of an enormous wave, engulfing her, dangerous and beyond anything she could know. She blurted, 'Does he know your secret?'

'He knows many secrets. I've overburdened him with secrets.'

'That is not an answer. Is his life now in as much danger as yours?'

'It would be, if anybody else but you and I knew when— Don't you see? That's why I have to leave!' Hefting his bag onto his shoulder, he began to stride away.

She called, 'Are you going to tell me where you're going?' When he gave just one snort of derision she called out, 'What shall I tell him? Ravenser? And then where?'

He ignored her and in a moment had slipped into the thicket and the branches folded behind him. It seemed as if something momentous had happened, giving rise to an emotion she had not expected, a leave-taking, a departure that ended something more profound than she could grasp.

Without noticing she made her way back and once in the cover of the trees saw Alaric jump down from his perch in the branches of an oak.

Still carrying his bow he said, 'So what made him walk off like that?'

'I don't know. Fear that his hermitage has been discovered. And that he has dragged Hubert into the mystery. I think we need to return to Meaux. This time the abbot shall not hide what he knows.'

# THIRTY-SEVEN

Not much later they swept back into the garth at Meaux to everyone's astonishment and several willing hands rushed to help them dismount. Voices clamoured from all sides, 'Why back so soon? Has something happened?'

Leaving Alaric to deal with the questions, Hildegard hurried across the garth towards the abbot's house set apart from the rest of the buildings and pushed past the monk who was in attendance at the doors. Without pausing she stormed down the corridor to Hubert's private chamber causing the young clerk sitting outside to rise in protest as she rapped on it and flung it open.

Hubert was kneeling with his head in his hands in front of his altar. He jerked round when she entered.

'Hubert, I need answers! Who is this fellow you've been harbouring?'

'Who . . .? What . . .? He is . . .' He got to his feet heavily, almost anciently, and collecting himself with a visible effort gave her a shrivelling look. 'He is a young man in distress. Obviously.'

'You believe his story about an assassin?'

'I have no reason not to believe it.' He added with even greater ice, 'Have you good reasons of your own to call him a liar?'

Not even 'domina' this time. She drew herself up. 'I have common sense, which usually holds me in good stead.'

His lips twisted. 'Usually?' He turned back towards his altar. 'I would not trust your common sense on every occasion.'

'How dare you!'

When he turned back his face looked grey. 'Leave me, Hildegard. This is not your business.'

'It is my business when one of our lay-sisters is murdered! We have a duty to them. We cannot sit by as if nothing has happened! What do you think we are? Are we less than human? She was our sister in life. We will not desert her in death. We will not allow her murderer to escape punishment. It is not right! Is that clear?'

'Will you accept my word when you calm down and begin to think with more clarity?'

'What?'

'I wish you to, Hildegard. I wish you to listen to me. I will not command as I know you of old but I wish you to heed what I say. No one can be more concerned about that poor girl's fate than we monks at Meaux but you must believe me, I know that boy did not murder her. I beg you to listen to me and seek elsewhere for her killer.'

'Your faith in him is admirable but we have only his word. I respectfully beg you to consider your own common sense.'

'Deficient as it is, it will have to suffice. Now leave me. I gave instructions to allow no one inside my house. That includes you.'

'Don't blame your clerk, he—'

'I wouldn't dream of it. I know you too well. You could get past a Gorgon with two heads if you chose.'

He turned his back to her. A prayer was audible under his breath. He continued without pause for some moments and she knew it was no use staying to argue. He would not face her.

'Obstinate fool,' she muttered, half-aloud. Was his intransigence because he was in danger too and hoped to deny it? She brushed this thought aside.

It was the minstrel, Leonin, with his tall story, who was at fault. Some scandal at court must have sent him rushing north in the hope that his past would not catch up with him.

Maybe somebody had really followed him, or maybe they had not and it was a delusion arising from his own sense of guilt, or it was a story invented to exact sympathy and protection from someone with the power of an abbot.

Knowing it was irrational she could not help but feel that Leonin was innocent of Lydia's murder. In other respects she reserved judgement. If his plan had been to beg help from Hubert it had gone wrong.

He was in flight once more.

By the time she reached the door Hubert had not come to the end of his prayer and she looked back once, hastily, moved as always by his presence whether turned away from her or not.

With one hand on the door there was ice in her voice when she said, 'My profound apologies for my intrusion. I thought you should know that your protégé is now set on the road to Ravenser, hoping for a ship to take him overseas.'

Hubert did not stir nor falter in his prayer.

She closed the door softly behind her.

# THIRTY-EIGHT

With head bowed she stood for a while in a corner of the precinct until she had recovered enough to face everyone again. Then, asking a passing servant to call Alaric with their horses, she made her way with a heavy heart towards the gatehouse.

Maintaining her silence almost all the way back to Swyne, when she eventually spoke she said to Alaric, 'I made a mess of that, Alaric.'

'The lay-brothers are as much in the dark as we are. Do not blame yourself. This is deeper than we can imagine.'

'But,' she gave a heartfelt sigh and gazed off into the thick belt of trees lining the track, 'will that boy be safe? Distrust him though I did—'

'Did?' He raised one eyebrow.

She returned his glance. 'Can I tell truth from falsehood? There is also the small matter of a footprint too,' she explained. 'Remember that square-toed print you spotted in the sand?'

They rode on a little way until she added, 'His disarming credibility aside – he is wearing court boots, not quite poulaines, but close.'

Alaric weighed this up for a moment then despite her sombre expression threw back his head and roared with laughter. 'So someone else was there at the same time? . . . The minstrel – saved by his fancy boots?'

They were silent all the way back to the gates where they at once re-joined the routine the priory demanded.

# THIRTY-NINE

'I have a mind to send one of our boatmen downriver,' the Prioress announced. Hildegard had told her everything including her flimsy reasons for believing that Leonin was innocent of Lydia's murder and that he had willingly confessed to stealing a boat.

'And what is our boatman to do?' she asked now.

'Well, my dear, it stands to reason doesn't it? The young fellow knows nothing of the terrain round here. How long do you imagine he'll stumble about the woods looking for a way of escape before he lights on the solution of following the estuary down to Ravenser? He asked you the question. You gave him the answer. That's where he'll make for.'

'So?'

'To escape this pursuer he has two choices. He might flee by boat or he might stick to the lanes and maybe purloin a horse. If the former, our boatman will pick up his trail from the rivermen, and if the latter he'll be noticed as soon as he approaches any settlement along the way. People always talk. I'm sure Hubert has thought of this by now and knowing the boy is aiming to flee the realm he'll have stalwarts out on the road already in order to apprehend him. Heavens, a lone stranger striding along the peninsula towards the Roman beacon near Ravenser? May as well take along pipes and tabors!'

'Might he not change his mind about leaving the realm at all?'

'That is a possibility. But did he give you any reason to think so?'

'No, but he may realize it will not be easy to escape and decide to go into hiding again. Or,' she added, 'it may be a clever ruse to put everyone off his trail?'

'We shall have to trust to his lesser cunning than your own, Hildegard.' She paused. 'As for the danger he faces, if this assassin is of flesh and blood, it's obvious, isn't it? We must pray that the speed and skill of our men will locate him first.'

It made her shudder as she left. What the Prioress so clearly implied was that if their men could pick up his trail before he reached Ravenser, then so could an assassin. It would be an all-out race to be first to find him.

# FORTY

S he was hurrying through the north cloister. A cold wind had begun to eddy under the vault.

Josiana was huddled in one of the carrels and when Hildegard swept past she got up and followed her. 'Hildegard! A moment!' She grasped her by the sleeve. 'What of Bella and the priest?'

Hildegard regarded Josiana with a mixture of exasperation and anxiety.

Josiana arched her brows. 'You say the lord abbot did not mention the matter? I'm surprised he has no concern for Matthew's safety.'

'His mind seems taken up with this other business,' Hildegard clipped. 'Affairs of state, if we are to believe Leonin.'

'Does the lord abbot believe his story?' Josiana asked in astonishment.

'That someone really did follow him from Sheen?'

Josiana gave a shiver. 'If it's true – this fellow may be closer than we think!' Doubt flooded her face. 'We only have the minstrel's word that he exists—'

Hildegard was stalled by her response. 'What are you trying to say?'

'Isn't it obvious?'

'Spell it out for me.'

'Surely if this possibly imaginary assassin crossed the river and did for Lydia, a young, innocent woman alone – it begs the question, why would he take time off from his quarry to kill somebody of no importance in passing?'

Hildegard tried to smile but Josiana's expression made her hesitate.

'It is rather hypothetical, Hildegard, I agree,' Josiana hurried on, reading her expression. 'But consider on what grounds it might be likely, if you will.'

'You're asking what's his motive? Why would a professional

assassin pick on Lydia? A whim?' she suggested. 'A lust for killing? Even a moment's thought would warn him that it would inevitably draw attention to himself. I agree. And I suppose you really mean that surely we need to look elsewhere?'

'That seems the most obvious conclusion.'

'Unless the minstrel's story is true?'

'In that case, again, why?'

'What about a case of mistaken identity?'

Josiana nodded. 'I accept that. Imagine what it would have been like in all the rain and wind. It was quite a storm and it came on so quickly. Lydia might have set off after Compline when the rain had abated, but was later caught out when the storm howled in again. It would have been black as pitch. The moon,' she added, 'though near the end of its third quarter, was obscured by thick cloud as we ourselves noticed. It would have been impossible to see anything on the foreshore. A figure in a dark cloak, hood obscuring their face – it might have been a man, a woman, anybody – it could have been someone crossing the river for any of a million reasons. I've been thinking about it and wondering if we're on the wrong track – now I'm confused again. What we lack is proof.'

Hildegard started to hurry on but Josiana put out her hand to detain her. 'And then there's Bella and Matthew. Maybe we're making the same assumption as the lord abbot.'

'Which assumption?'

'That the two events are separate.'

'To bring the two ideas together you must be suggesting that rather than running away together, unlikely in my opinion, something has befallen them . . . something far more sinister?'

'I don't wish to think it but logic draws me towards such an idea,' Josiana replied, still furrowing her brow. 'You must admit it is odd that they should disappear so completely at exactly the time a killer is stalking the woods.'

'Coincidence,' she tried to reassure her. 'They'll turn up with some excuse or other.'

'I understand that someone was sent to Beverley and on to York to find out if they'd been seen and that they drew a blank in both places?'

'They would have been noticed, that's true, especially if they tried to get into York. Ever since the Scots were last raiding down here the posterns are heavily guarded and locked for the night.'

'Where can they be?' Josiana asked fretfully. 'It's my fault for not taking much notice of Bella's sot-wittedness. Twins are said to bring a curse with them.'

'If you're worried about Bella and Matthew I doubt whether an assassin would try his hand against two.'

'That's if they were seen as two. We don't even know whether Bella caught up with Matthew. Maybe they both rode on alone?'

'It has the same flaw as the argument against an assassin murdering Lydia. He would draw attention to himself. Why would he do that? And anyway, Matthew is a priest. There can be no mistaking him.'

'The assassin may not know he murdered the wrong person on the foreshore . . . if an imaginary being can imagine anything,' she finished rather lamely.

'Let's hope that if he is real he doesn't catch up with Leonin before the men pick up his trail and bring him safely back to Meaux.'

'Is that the lord abbot's intention?'

Hildegard gave her a rueful smile. 'That is his hope, it seems.'

'I now know why the superstitious scry to seek the truth. Sometimes it seems the only way.'

With that astonishing remark Josiana released her hold on Hildegard's sleeve and returned to her books.

# FORTY-ONE

A dozen lay-brothers mounted on the best horses in the stables set out from the Priory of Swyne not much later. At the junction where the lane from the priory joined the one from Meaux their numbers were augmented by a band of conversi and a number of choir monks including Gregory and Egbert. The woods on both sides of the foregate resounded to the questing of hounds.

Hildegard did not ride with the men from Swyne. It would have been regarded as unseemly for a nun to set out on a man-hunt. That one of the novices from the priory was being hunted was a side issue. It was the minstrel from the royal court at Sheen who was the primary reason for such a turn-out.

Urging Josiana to ride with her because of her good sense, and with Alaric for his skill with bow and arrow, and Nimrod for his tracking prowess she left Swyne with the Prioress's blessing and tagged on to the band of their own men, meeting the Meaux contingent at the lane end as they came out.

A comrade of Alaric's jostled through the milling horsemen awaiting instructions. 'We're after somebody but don't ask me who it is or how we'll know him. Is it this royal minstrel? Is it Matthew? Is it that scandalous novice from Swyne? Or is it some foreign assassin? Is it one, or two, or four, or some other combination?'

Alaric shook his head.

'Aren't you curious to find out? Come with us?'

'I'm needed here.' The glance he rested on Hildegard held only a tinge of regret.

He was not the only fit young lay-brother to miss all the excitement. Most of the monks who had come out from the cloister to watch their men leave were elderly although not a few longing glances followed them. Gregory and Egbert, of course, were going along, but others, unless proven in youth, horsemanship or other useful assets, were told to stay behind.

Even the beggars at the gate, though most had vanished after receiving their daily dole, had given a thin cheer as the horsemen clattered under the archway and one or two were seen to follow on foot for a little way, although for what purpose no one knew. It was quite a turn-out.

When even the bare echoes of departure faded as the tail end disappeared over the Abbot's Bridge Hildegard turned to her companions, riding slowly on behind.

'So we are agreed?' She called Nimrod to heel. The hound, never far away, loped over. 'Then let us go, my friends. One rule only. We stay together.'

They rode back a little way and when they reached the marker stone where Leonin had picked up his bread and cheese they dismounted and with looped reins followed the lymer on foot down the path he had sniffed out earlier.

On reaching the clearing where the minstrel had started to erect his hermitage they tramped about to have a look round.

It had been pouring with rain since Prime. 'Any scent will have been washed away,' she reminded. 'The men are guessing he's gone on to Ravenser—'

Alaric reassured her. 'Nimrod is a clever fellow, sensitive and resolute, and if there's a hint of a scent he'll sniff it out.'

She led towards the edge of the clearing where Leonin had last been seen shouldering his way between the trees. The lymer nosed about, first following one scent and then another.

He seemed puzzled at first and continually looked at Hildegard for reassurance. 'Yes, boy, search for him, search.'

He snuffled under some roots then changed his mind and trotted more eagerly between banks of gorse, eventually quickening his pace and winding in and out of the trees as if following a clearly marked path. Eventually he led them down a slope and began to lope more confidently through a beech copse where the autumn leaves were still crisp underfoot.

Crossing to the other side without a pause he led them out above a meadow on the riverbank. Something larger than a fox had left a visible trace through a stretch of late blooming yellow mustard, a trail as plain to their eyes as the scent must be to the hound.

In the distance an old lean-to was propped under a gnarled

hawthorn and the lymer bounded over to it with the others right behind him. It faced the estuary. For a moment Hildegard believed they had reached journey's end but when they looked inside the hut was empty. Nimrod circled and ran down onto the sands to stare at the water in puzzlement.

'He was here. He must have stayed overnight.' Hildegard pulled at a beam jutting out of the wattle and daub where something had been hanging, judging by the fresh splinters of wood underneath. 'A place to hang his vielle?'

Josiana came to have a look. 'He might have waited for the tide here. But then, how would that help without a boat?'

'Maybe there was one?' She gestured towards the beach.

Nimrod was pleased to have found the hut although he could not understand why it was so important but he swaggered about for a while before galloping off towards the waterside again.

'This is where the trail goes cold,' observed Josiana as they followed. 'Not even dear Nimrod can track a man across water.'

They clustered on the foreshore in some dismay. 'It was a good guess so far as it went.' Alaric heaved a sigh. 'What do you suggest, domina? Shall we have a look along the bank to see if we can pick up his trail?'

It reminded her of their search for clues at the haven. She felt uneasy. 'I hope he's safe. If he found a boat near the hut . . .'

She turned away again to scan the river where it made a wide and gentle curve downstream to Wyke, faintly visible as an arrangement of roofs and spires and half-built walls. Some distance from the shore several merchant ships, looking like toy boats, swayed at anchor in mid-channel with pennants flapping. A pilot boat slowly made its way to shore.

'It's a treacherous place,' she murmured, 'such tides, such shifting sands. The pilots have to be skilled in order to bring the bigger ships into the estuary.'

'Up past Hedon?'

She glanced at Josiana. 'Are you reading my mind again? I was just going to say—' Turning to Alaric, she asked, 'You know what she means?'

'If he'd got a boat he could come ashore there. Or maybe pick one up?'

'How far to Ravenser from here?'

'It'll be quicker by road,' he pointed out. 'And not beyond the strength or stamina of our horses.'

'We could be waiting for him at Ravenser along with the men from Meaux. Shall we go?'

Hedon was a more ancient port than Wyke, or Hull as it was beginning to be called. Established in the distant past as the first safe haven to greet ships coming over from Scandinavia and the Continent it had thrived on its trade with the rest of the known world for centuries, long before the invasions of Romans and Vikings had used it to settle here.

These days it was less busy, entering a slow decline because of the silting of the harbour, the quayside yearly retreating further and further behind the barrier the tides threw up, with useless sandbars turning the harbourside into land no good for anything, cutting the town off from its life-blood, the ancient river trade.

It had a fine church, however, and its townsfolk in a recent altercation with the monks of Meaux had won a resounding victory. Horse-stealing had been involved, Hildegard remembered, although the event was before her time and the cause ambiguous and no doubt to do with taxes levied by the monks on their leaseholders in the town.

Josiana rarely left the priory but Hildegard and Alaric knew the lanes around the new and more important town that took its name from the River Hull and by the time they left it behind and were approaching Hedon they had talked themselves into believing that this must be the route Leonin had taken. The site of the hut on the foreshore suggested nowhere more likely.

Encouraged by a chance remark from a trader shutting up shop for the afternoon they stopped to put a question or two. He mentioned what he called a fine-looking young stranger, 'with two bags on his back. Bought a pie from me. Likely on his way to take ship to Denmark. We get them all through here.' He glanced at the monastic robes of the two nuns. 'Not in any trouble, I pray?'

'We are friends,' Hildegard told him.

As they rode away she thought it might be true. Leonin was the type to attract friendship. It was what made his story of his life being at stake so difficult to believe. Who could hate him so much and why? It must be someone with access to enough wealth to pay for a professional killer – as well as for the long years of paying a chantry priest to pray for the redemption of his black soul that would lie ahead.

With this chance exchange their only clue, they rode on with greater eagerness, reaching the last vill before the peninsula only to find the contingent in pursuit had been and gone.

'Came past an hour after midday,' an old fellow sitting by the market cross informed them. 'What a to-do! After a young felon, eh? Trespassing on abbey lands? Good luck to you and good luck to your 'orses.'

'Why do you say that?' Hildegard asked, about to ride on.

'You try riding through them sands. That track across the top was washed over during storm t'other night. Gone. It'll have to be trodden through again before you get a horse along there.'

'So what about the folk at Ravenser? Are you saying they're cut off?'

'Aye. Nothing but trouble with them. The bell tower came down as I heard, houses dragged into the sea. It's near its end days is Ravenser. I'd give it ten years, no more than that.' With great satisfaction he predicted that as other coastal settlements had succumbed to the waves, so would all the towns along the estuary, either dragged under the waters by waves as high as houses or shoaled up by the tide into massive sandbanks, depending on where they were sited.

When they left him Alaric rolled his eyes. 'He must think he's safe enough sitting there in the sun. Wait till the Apocalypse. He won't be so smug then. He'll be swallowed into the pit with everybody else.'

'Let's hope our prayers are strong enough to put a stop to that,' murmured Hildegard.

By late afternoon they had reached the beginning of the spit without catching up with the searchers from Meaux. They became strongly aware of the waters on both sides in dangerous proximity as they floundered along the treeless ridge. The sands narrowed to a sea-swept point in the distance, on one side the yellowish tidal flow of the estuary, on the other the incessant pounding of the grey North Sea.

Overhead curlews, caught between two worlds, cried in endless lament. A constant wind whined over the marram grass and it was too easy to believe in local stories about drowned sailors crying forever in the grey green depths for release.

'He must have picked up a horse to get so far ahead,' judged Alaric as they kept up a good pace, 'but the going isn't as bad as that old fellow made out.' The track had already been pounded into some sort of stability under the hooves of those who had preceded them.

Soon the buildings of a settlement came into view. At first it looked like no more than the size of a boulder on the horizon but as they approached it began to assume the form of a vill with a street, a belfry, a quay, with a breakwater jutting out where the sea was already cascading into the deep pool of the harbour.

'England's end,' Alaric murmured. It looked no more than that.

The two groups of horsemen from Swyne and Meaux could be identified even at a distance by the white robes of the Cistercians standing out against the ochre of the lay-brothers' garments. Hildegard even thought she could make out Gregory and Egbert, both men more contained than the others, sitting astride their mounts as immovably as rocks while the others, unused to curbing high-spirited horses set free from their usual confines, jostled skittishly here and there.

As they drew closer she observed that Gregory had already noticed them and after a word to his companion, he broke free from the rabble and cantered towards them along the top of the bank.

'I thought you'd been forbidden to join us?' he asked, with an amused glance when he drew level.

'We were allowed to follow another plan. It's entirely chance that we've fetched up here. It seems we all had the same idea.'

She glanced round but could see no sign of anyone resembling the minstrel. 'Are we on a false trail?'

'We haven't found him, if that's what you mean. He'll have had to talk his way past the customs men, not forgetting the ship-owner who'll want payment over the odds when he sees how desperate he is.'

'You don't seem worried?'

He bent his head close and said to her, 'It's no good giving me

that look, Hildi. I have no more idea than you have where he is.
He hasn't shown up here and, more to the point, neither has anyone
looking like an assassin. We're simply following Hubert's wishes
to bring him back to safety. He could be anywhere. Anywhere but
here.'

She gave him a helpless smile. 'Leonin told me he was going
to the nearest port because he felt he would only be safe across
the sea.'

'Do you believe he's in such danger?'

'He seems to think so.'

'Do you?'

'I have no idea. Sometimes I do. Sometimes not. He's plausible.
I admit I have a sneaking liking for him. There's something familiar
– odd, given that he looks so outlandish.'

Gregory gave her a long look. 'Egbert and I have a theory.'
His horse wheeled, whether by his own control or chance, and
as he was swept away he called, 'We'll talk later. For now, we're
posting men here and the rest of us are returning to Meaux before
nightfall. Maybe we'll meet him on our way back!'

As he re-joined the contingent of monks she called, 'What about
your priest and our novice? Any theories about those two?'

He threw a glinting smile over one shoulder. 'None that I would
besmirch your innocent ears with, Hildi!'

And then he was gone, back into the thick of the melee where
lots were being drawn to see who should be left behind to keep
watch through the night.

With no further reason to linger they were walking their horses
back the way they had arrived, carefully keeping to the track where
the sand was flattened, when they came across a cart with a few
passengers on board. They stopped to have words with them and
while Alaric engaged the driver in conversation Hildegard took a
closer look at the passengers.

He had said, hadn't he, that he would have to adopt a disguise
but nobody on board could have passed as a young minstrel even
in disguise. Nor did anyone look like an assassin.

'So, not seen anyone on the road?' Alaric was asking as she
went back to join him.

'Not us,' the carter replied. 'We came straight on from the last halt without seeing a soul.' He frowned. 'Travellers are put off by these weather warnings. I reckon I'll just make it back inland before it starts. What these poor devils on board a leaky ship will do when the storm hits I've no idea – but don't tell 'em I said that till they've paid me!'

The man cracked his whip and with the lift of a hand urged his team on through the sands.

'Back to Swyne,' Hildegard announced as the cart rolled away. 'We should be in time for Compline.'

# FORTY-TWO

Next morning, between Lauds and Prime, with the rain turning to drizzle and mist spreading a ghostly veil over the woods, some visitors appeared at the gatehouse. The porteress, Blanche, at her duties since coming out of the last Office, peered through the peephole. Two monks on horseback were revealed.

One of them was leading a grey palfrey and when he dismounted he went over and peered back. 'We have a message for your lady Prioress. She's expecting us.'

'You must have left in the dark, Egbert,' countered Blanche with good humour when she recognized him. 'Is that Brother Gregory with you?' She unbolted the double gates to let them into the yard. On a note of alarm she asked, 'And that's Briquet you've brought with you, I doubt not.'

'I'm afraid so.'

'Come in then. You'll find your own way?'

'Visited often enough, my lady porter,' replied Gregory smoothly, 'but without such grim news to impart.'

At the sound of horses two stable lads yawned and stretched their way as if by magic onto the garth. 'You're out early, brothers? I see you've got our old Briquet on a leading rein. Trouble at Meaux?'

'Nothing to spoil your day, you wretches.' Gregory tossed them a few coins. 'Don't forget to water these beasts or they'll have your hands off.'

Relieved of their mounts, the two white-robed Cistercians strode across the garth towards the lodging of the Prioress. Hildegard, crossing in that direction herself, was surprised to see them wearing swords under their cloaks.

She hurried to greet them. 'What's happening?'

'Two riderless horses were caught on the marshes early this morning. The grey belongs to Swyne, we assume? We've just brought her back.'

She glanced at the ill-concealed bulges under their cloaks.

'A precaution,' Gregory admitted, noticing the direction of her gaze. 'We intend to have a thorough look-round on our way back. We're trying to persuade Hubert to call in the Sheriff and his men. It's too much for choir monks to deal with. They're not fighting men. If he calls the Sheriff we plan to join his posse. We have to find this murdering fellow.'

After she took this in she asked, 'So no abbot with you?'

'He's still wrestling with the devil though what the hell – excuse me, domina, *mea culpa* –' Gregory began again, 'why our lord abbot imagines he needs an act of contrition no one can guess. However here we are, his emissaries, to arrange a meeting at Meaux if your Prioress will be kind enough to grace us with—'

A voice cut in, 'She will. Indeed so. And you arrive not before time!'

It was the Prioress herself standing in the porch, having over-heard everything. She came down to meet them and both men knelt at her feet. 'Up off your knees, you fine fellows. You're right welcome. A pity about your futile search yesterday. Are you going to come in to dine with us? It's my guess you came away without breaking your fast. You monks. I know what you're like. Join us, Hildegard. Bring Josiana with you. We have much to discuss.'

# FORTY-THREE

'So yesterday was a fruitless show taking us no further than we already were three days ago? We must ask ourselves, "How did this come about?"'

The Prioress leaned back in a chair of plainer design than that of her counterpart at Meaux and looked from one to the other. Nobody spoke.

'I will tell you then if no one wants to risk their unfounded theories to scrutiny. It was a plan based on fantasy.'

'I have a suggestion, my lady.' Josiana spoke up with some hesitancy but seeing that she was encouraged to continue, said, 'First I acknowledge your point, my lady, this is also an unfounded theory but I have shared it with Hildegard and we could see nothing wrong with it. I'm forced to admit that it is based on supposition and not fact.'

'Go on.'

'I believe, and we agreed, that the minstrel, Leonin, might have met Lydia when he landed on the shore during the storm and it went like this. Mistaking a figure shrouded in a cape to be the man he believes is in pursuit of him he gives him a smash on the back of the head with a stone he picks up from the foreshore. It is thick dark and, too late, he realizes he has killed the wrong person. He therefore drags the body into the water hoping to conceal his crime. Also–' she added with a sudden thought, 'he might feel he wants to hide the truth from himself at having committed such a heinous act as murder . . .'

'Continue.'

'Escaping into the woods to hide in horror at what he has done he comes across our priory and here finds sanctuary. Later, while at Meaux, fearing that his crime is about to be discovered by Hildegard and others, he decides to pass himself off as a hermit and hide a while in the woods until the crime has been forgotten, after which he intends to take ship out of the realm to safety. Our discovery of his secret lair, however, urges him to escape the sooner. By claiming to abjure the realm he'll throw us off his trail and allow him to make good his escape in the opposite direction, maybe to York or to the west. Where he is now,' she finished somewhat lamely, 'is a mystery about which I have no opinion.'

'You're not alone, my dear.' The Prioress gave an ironic glance round. 'Anyone else with a theory, founded on fact or fiction?'

There was a short silence until Gregory said, 'It seems you've taken a logical view, sister.' He inclined his head at Josiana, who lowered her eyes in modesty. 'It does, however, leave the question of the existence of an assassin open to speculation. And of course, the argument works whether he exists or is but a figment of the minstrel's imagination. If he does exist then the minstrel may be innocent of Lydia's murder on the grounds that the argument outlined can be as logically applied to the alleged assassin as to Leonin himself. If this paid killer does not exist, then the minstrel must be our first and I might venture to say our only suspect. Nevertheless, two questions remain: does the alleged assassin exist? And, question the second, innocent or guilty, where is Master Leonin now? He must have left a trace, a track, a clue of some sort.'

Egbert interrupted. 'Our lord abbot happens to believe in the existence of an assassin.'

'Ergo,' Gregory interrupted, 'we must perforce believe in him also and therefore in the likelihood of the minstrel's innocence.'

'Even though it's an assertion founded on the evidence of an unreliable witness?' Hildegard interrupted. 'We only have Leonin's word and it is only too obvious why he might have invented the whole story.' When nobody interrupted she said, 'Further, it fails to shed light on why he claims he had to flee from the court or why he chose here of all places as sanctuary.'

Josiana turned to Hildegard. 'Isn't that what you've been wondering ever since the whole story began?'

'Well, yes. We can't simply accept his word without a shred of evidence. Our feelings are not enough.' For some reason an image of Hubert flashed before her eyes. 'Maybe,' she hurriedly continued, 'he's a traitor to the king? Maybe he's fleeing a charge of treason? Everyone knows how uncertain the king's position is. My point is we do not know. We know nothing about him. We *still*,' she emphasized the word, 'know nothing about him or his purpose.'

'Only one person might know the answer,' the Prioress spoke up. 'Apart from himself. I would hazard a guess that Hubert knows more than he's admitting. That's why he sent you men out from Meaux. Our meeting when it occurs should reveal the truth.'

The Prioress raised both eyebrows.

The two monks stirred and glanced at each other.

'That is why we are here this morning. When the meeting takes place it will be for Hubert to explain his belief in the minstrel's story.'

'And perhaps to share information received from yesterday's courier from the Palace at Sheen—' added Egbert.

'Eltham, don't you mean? I hear King Richard left Sheen in the greatest of misery after the death of his beloved queen and is now nursing his grief at his palace downriver?' She looked puzzled then more briskly asked, 'So Hubert has received information from the royal court?' She sat back. 'We guessed as much. But I assume you know not what?'

Both monks shook their heads.

The Prioress removed her hands from inside her sleeves as if preparing to leave. 'Tomorrow after Tierce I shall set out with an escort for Meaux. Meanwhile, we must keep our eyes and ears open and try to make sense of it all. As for Bella and Matthew, the fact that their two horses were found together suggests that they have absconded as the gossips claim. I wish you good fortune in your search.'

'As we offer prayers for their safety,' Egbert suggested.

'That, of course.' She rose to her feet. 'Thank you, my dearly beloved brothers. You may convey our acceptance of a time and place for our meeting to your lord abbot.'

They all rose as she stalked from the chamber. Hildegard guessed she was going back to her chapel and hesitated. Better to leave her to her thoughts. They might hold different points of view but only time and truth would make sense of such a web.

# FORTY-FOUR

S he was on the point of leaving the refectory towards evening when she heard her name called softly from the darkness of the porch.

'Hildegard!'

Before she could turn somebody stepped in front of her.

With no one around and the last meal cleared long ago, she had stayed to think things through. Now the garth was empty. She gasped as she was pushed hard against the wall and when she managed to focus she saw it was Rogella who had attacked her.

She tried to ward her off. 'Back away! What do you think you're doing?'

'Last time we met you said you would speak for us—'

'I can hardly do that while Bella is still missing—'

'Bella? Are you sure it is her with Matthew?'

'Don't play games. Whichever one of you it is there's nothing I can do at present. But a promise is a promise.'

'It had better be one you keep, *domina*,' the novice said scornfully bringing her face close. 'Otherwise it will be the death of you. And that's *my* promise!'

'What on earth are you saying? Are you threatening me? How dare you—'

The novice suddenly had a knife in her hand and pressed the flat of the blade against the side of Hildegard's neck. It felt like ice.

Through bared teeth she whispered, 'I want Matthew back. Get it? You're supposed to be searching for him. Find her. And then you'll find him. If you have not found them by tomorrow night I shall kill you.'

In a moment she vanished into the shadows and Hildegard blinked as if it was a horrible dream. Such venom. Such spite. Such hatred. What did she mean, she wanted Matthew back?

Her thoughts racing, she gazed into the darkness where the novice had disappeared after her vile threat and pondered the matter.

# FORTY-FIVE

During the night the heavens broke. The rain clouds, threatening for so long, shed their burden at last, stabbing the earth below in a seemingly never-ending cataract. Priory roofs were slicked with water. It brimmed into gutters, swamped the drains and transformed the garth into a shallow lake. It roared through the woods, stripping the last leaves from the branches and dragging them into the mud. Only the heaviest of sleepers managed to ignore the uproar while at window-slits and in doorways anxious, sleepless faces began to appear.

When the bell for Matins tolled its summons through the torrent it was like a haunting from a submerged church under the waves. Everyone was forced to drag themselves forth, heads covered by whatever waterproof they could find, to splash across to the midnight Office.

Mud, instantly hurled up from the pounded garth by the outpour, besmirched the hems of white stamyn robes, and Hildegard, thrusting her feet into sandals, decided it was better to have wet feet easily dried than have to ride over to Meaux next morning in sodden leather boots. She hurried out to join everyone else in the shock and uproar of the deluge.

Lightning split the sky. Thunder crashed. Rain continued to pound the rooftops. Visibility shrank to the hand in front of your face. Utterly drenched, she splashed into the church porch along with the others and, astonished in their half-sleep, everyone gaped back through the lancing rain as others ran to join them.

With no alternative everyone squelched across the puddled floor-tiles into the nave. It swam with water like a bath-house.

The sub-Prioress was conducting things that night and appeared undecided: should she make it short and send them back into the storm and to their beds, or keep them here, with rain drumming like a million tabors on the roof, where at least they would be dry?

Casting a kindly eye over the figures huddled miserable and

wet in front of her she soon sent them out. 'Back to your beds, sisters. Pray God's wrath ends before Lauds.'

Thunder obliterated her words and the wind began to scream fiendishly over the walls and into the sanctuary, whisking round corners and making damp robes flap like wings. The novices, with Rogella prominent among them, ran in a shrieking mob to their dortoir. Returning more quietly to her own chamber near the gatehouse Hildegard stripped and rubbed herself dry.

From there she was almost deafened by the wild thrashing of the trees outside the precinct. It was a continual roar like being at sea in an ill-found cog. It set her worrying about Leonin again and whether he was safe this night and she surprised herself by offering a prayer that it was so.

# FORTY-SIX

Next morning they had to struggle through the devastated woods to Meaux. Hubert appeared at the entrance to the chapter house. His face was white and haggard as he tottered towards them, and Hildegard had to remind herself that this was the lord abbot of Meaux. Normally a tough-looking muscular man in his early forties – and despite the intellectual austerity of his features, at one time a notable swordsman and knight-at-arms – he had always impressed everyone with his vigour.

Now, in the rain-washed light of the nave, he looked almost ethereal and moved towards them fadingly, like a wraith. Astonished by the change in him her mouth dropped open as he drifted towards them.

She was even more alarmed by the change close to. His features had a greyish pallor making his eyes seem to sink deeper and glitter more feverishly in his skull. His cheekbones, angular, somewhat dominant, made him look emaciated when he finally faded to a stop in front of them all.

His glance roamed darkly over the faces turned to him. A discussion about matters involving their two houses seemed beyond his strength.

Hildegard was conscious of the brush of his glance over hers and, without alighting, move on. She thought she saw him stagger when he took another step and his acolytes discreetly lent him their arms. Not quite shaking them away he seemed to brace himself in order to receive an obeisance from the Prioress and her contingent.

With visible effort he intoned, 'Most welcome, my lady. Welcome indeed.'

The Prioress got off her knees first. 'Are you well enough to conduct this business, Hubert? You seem unlike yourself.'

Brushing this aside and despite the effort it seemed to take he waved vaguely towards the open door of the chapter house. 'If you will follow.'

Tall beeswax candles on elegant gold stands were visible inside. The coloured glass in a dozen narrow windows looked almost black because of the overcast skies outside. Rain battered audibly and incessantly against frail depictions of biblical scenes, the nativity, the crucifixion, the heavenly clouds, the praying saints, the ironically appropriate Flood and Ark, as well as angelic choirs, minstrels with their different instruments, all hopefully in harmony as an encouragement to the visitors from Swyne.

As Hildegard drew level with one of the monks stationed at the door she whispered before entering, 'What's the matter with him?'

'He's been fasting and praying for days, domina. Last night I left him at midnight and when I returned before Lauds he was still here on his knees before the altar. See if you nuns can do anything with him. He won't listen to us.'

Perturbed, Hildegard took her place on one of the benches beside Josiana and exchanged glances with her.

Hubert, refusing a seat, was standing with one hand on a lectern as if about to list a catalogue of their sins with suitable penances to follow.

Instead, after glaring darkly round, he drew a breath and in an unexpectedly frail voice said, 'This meeting will be short. As I see it the problem facing us is two-fold. First, at large in our woodland was or is a murderer. Identity unknown. He must be apprehended. And second, missing are three young people, gone who knows where. They must be found for their own safety – if it is not too late.' He hesitated as if expecting an interruption but when no one spoke he announced that he was sending another search party out. 'My men are willing to go out again after Lady Mass to flush out the missing young and deliver them to their rightful places.' He looked directly at the Prioress. 'My lady, we would welcome the assistance of your lay-brothers in the search once again.'

'And you shall have it, my lord abbot. These disappearances concern us as deeply as they concern you.'

He gave a wan smile. 'Maybe so. It is a matter of great urgency.' Turning to address his own monks, sitting like statues ever since the Prioress and her party had entered, he said, 'Is there any disagreement? . . . Anything to contribute?'

Gregory looked as if he was about to get to his feet then changed his mind.

'Very well. I regard this meeting as closed.' He gestured for the Prioress to precede him. It meant that Hildegard held back to allow her to walk ahead and she accidentally collided with Hubert. They both drew back as if stung.

'After you, domina.' He bowed his head as if to a stranger.

Close up she could see how exhausted he looked. Lines of strain deepened the corners of his beloved mouth. 'My lord—' she began but thinking better of it, hurried on.

'Can't you or Egbert have a word with him?' They were sheltering in the cloisters while their horses were being brought out. 'I've never seen him look so terrible. Is he ill?'

'Too much fasting, too little sleep. He's driving himself beyond human limits. What shall we do? Force-feed him? Tie him to his bed and pour a sleeping draught down his throat? There's something tearing him apart.'

Egbert shrugged. 'He's an obstinate devil. It's worse since the courier brought him a message. I thought he intended to tell us this morning what had transpired. It's got to be something to do with what happened in London.'

'It was obviously about Leonin,' Gregory added. 'Information about why he fled the royal court?'

'He won't tell and the courier has left without a word.'

'Doesn't Hubert make confession?' Hildegard asked.

Egbert gave a snort of disgust.

Gregory said, 'Word is he's calling the Sheriff out but so far he hasn't done so.'

Hildegard was dissatisfied with them both.

Surely with five minutes alone she could find out from Hubert what was so profoundly disturbing him? But there was no chance of that now. Even though they had come over from Swyne with the express intention of discovering more he had already returned to his private chapel with orders for no one to be admitted.

'Where are we supposed to hunt for these missing young, as he calls them?'

'Up towards Haltemprice Priory. It's generally agreed those

Austin friars may have heard something since we last spoke to them.'

'They'll all three have fled the Riding long ago,' muttered Egbert, 'for their various no doubt nefarious reasons. Still, it gets us out in the fresh air, doesn't it?' He shrugged a waterproof more ironically over his shoulders. 'I think we're riding over to Swyne first to rouse out your horsemen then we'll comb the woods on the far side of the priory.'

Hildegard had forced aside Rogella's strange animosity while she was on neutral ground at Meaux but before she set out for Swyne the novice's threat came back. It was the swift appearance of her knife that worried her most.

Glad of the short reprieve while safe at Meaux she knew she needed to consider whether to take any precautions. The novice seemed mad. There was no dismissing her venom. Or the knife.

Clearly Rogella felt she had an account to settle.

But now there was something to do first.

# FORTY-SEVEN

That the monks were directing their search in the woods near the Austin priory made Hildegard sceptical. It would be more cunning, as the Prioress might call it, to hide out close to Meaux itself while the searchers looked in the wrong direction.

She wanted to believe Leonin's story, now more than ever, for some reason. It was the hideous idea that they were on a man-hunt.

There was something guileless about him. She could be wrong, she knew that – he could just be a good liar – but then there was the footprint. It didn't have to belong to an assassin, of course, it could have been anyone's. One thing was certain – it did not belong to Leonin.

She couldn't help speculating further. His dark skin suggested – where? Castile? Rome? Or somewhere in the direction of Outremer? Might it have a bearing on his disappearance?

Confused, somewhat fearing the existence of the assassin, she called for Nimrod, and when the others set off for Swyne she swallowed her fears and slipped away down a narrow track beside the walls of the abbey. Eventually she reached the wooden footbridge onto the opposite bank of the canal.

The nuns' house she had opened some years ago had quickly grown out of its cramped quarters, filled by the many children living on abbey lands wanting an education, and they had been forced to move the school to larger premises in Beverley. Some of the boys even went on to the famous Song School, later becoming choristers in prestigious foundations.

Her old building was unoccupied now, silent and shuttered, the garden overgrown. After the bursting of the canal bank the house was up to its windowsills with water. No one could be inside with the pressure of the flood against the door.

Boots slipping in the mire she took the once-familiar path along the top of the bank away from the house. Despite being flattened by the rain the grass showed where someone had walked this way quite recently and her confidence rose.

Glad she had Nimrod beside her, she reached the watermill. After the nuns moved out it had fallen into disuse. The monks had built a bigger one on the river where the more powerful current was better able to turn the massive new waterwheel to supply the needs of the abbey itself as well as the granges.

Usually sluggish the canal came to an end here, fed by a single stream draining from off the marshes. Now it flowed fast over hidden obstacles under the surface, creating whirlpools as it raced to meet the river beyond the lock gates. Someone must have opened them to take some of the pressure off but it did no good now. The mill race was a white foaming torrent. God help anyone who falls in there, she thought.

Overspill from the millpond surged across the path and she had to wade up to her knees in cold slime. Apart from the hiss of the rain again and the occasional creak of the wooden wheel straining against the force of the water, it was eerily quiet.

Nimrod in the manner of his breed loped ahead with scarcely a splash until he came to the door to the mill. It was fastened on the outside by a tattered rope. Bedraggled but still keen he glanced back to wait for instructions.

First she waded round the puddled outside of the building but there was nothing unexpected on the other side. The meadow had already been turned into a lake. The mill itself was half under water where it abutted the canal, and only the landward side stood clear of the flood. By the look of it the timbers would not stand much more, the building was near collapse and the force of the current would soon drag it into the canal.

Deciding not to call out until she knew what lay ahead she paddled back to the door and unknotted the rope, wondering as she edged it open who had tied it so hurriedly.

It was gloomy within. Only a column of light fell from an opening on the upper floor where the miller had once stored his grain. It took a moment to see that the place must have been cleared out long ago. To make sure she opened both doors to let in more light.

As soon as she stepped inside the hissing of the rain was cut off. It made the creaking timbers sound even more dangerous in the echo-chamber housing the grinding mechanism.

She froze.

On the far side where the flood waters were gushing in through cracks in the planking and the gap cut through for the axle she saw a shape. Much like a sack of flour that might have been left behind, but it seemed to move slightly. The fear of rats swept over her.

She forced herself to look more closely and shivered again but for a different reason. There were no rats. It was a human shape.

'Nimrod, heel!' she whispered.

Together they made their way across the canted floor, its timbers sinking with every step, until she was able to stare down at what lay in front of her. Fear gripped her. It was a man after all. A body lying awkwardly half in and half out of the swirling water. He must surely be dead not to move out of it.

Bending down she saw what must be his head wrapped in the folds of a black hood. She stretched out a hand to push the fabric aside and revealed a face. It was mashed up, swollen and distorted by bruises, scarcely human.

One eye opened.

She flinched back.

Recovering, she whispered, 'Matthew? Is this you?'

A moan greeted her remark. Quickly looking him over she saw that his hands were bound in front of him by a length of twine. Hacking quickly with her knife she released them. Instead of moving he lay where he was, oblivious to the rising water. Urging him to get up if he could, she asked, 'Can't you move out of it?'

In reply he moaned again and she thought she saw him give a weak shake of his head.

'Come, try to move. The waters are rising. I don't give much chance for the entire building if it goes on.'

Her words only seemed to make him more resigned.

She spoke more sharply. 'Matthew! . . . It's Hildegard. Can't you get out of the water?'

He made an effort and managed to mutter something about his legs.

She put an ear closer to his lips. 'What's that about your legs?'

'Broken,' his lips scarcely moved. 'Both broken.'

She put her hands under the water up to her elbows. No bonds there. 'I'm going to try to drag you onto the drier part of the floor. Will you grit your teeth for me?'

His lips lifted for a moment and he gave a faint nod. Putting both hands under his armpits she heaved with all her strength and little by little managed to haul his inert body clear of the flood water. Eventually she got him onto the high side of the floor and he sprawled helplessly with water sluicing from his robes. Slowly he began to return from the half-conscious state in which she had found him. His poor face was horribly battered and one eye was swollen shut.

He put out a hand to touch her sleeve as if to catch hold of it then let it drop. It was clear he was in no state to help himself. Deep in his eye was the shadow of some horror.

The rumble of falling timbers alerted her to their immediate danger. 'The building's going to go over,' she told him. 'I'll try to drag you further. Can you find a way to help me?'

He must have understood because when she took hold of him again he began to half crawl using only his arms to claw himself forward, groaning with pain, until at last he collapsed and allowed her to wedge him in the doorway. There was another crash followed by a splash as a different part of the building toppled into the canal.

'If I can get you outside you might be far enough above flood-level to be safe while I fetch help.'

She peered into his face. 'Matthew? Can you hear me?' He seemed to be falling in and out of consciousness. 'Be brave. We will not be defeated by mere water.'

He held onto her sleeve.

'Water means redemption—' As if that was all he needed to say, his eye flickered shut.

# FORTY-EIGHT

Out of breath by the time she crossed over the footbridge and ran all the way back to the gatehouse she hurled herself into the porter's lodge, shouting, 'Fetch help, brother! I've found Matthew. He's unable to walk. Fetch help at once, I beg you!'

The porter didn't waste time asking what had happened. He sent one of the lads to rouse up the conversi, those who were left after the search party had gone out earlier. When he saw men across the garth pouring out of the buildings he turned to her. 'Is he badly hurt?'

'Both legs broken. He was tied by the wrists. Whoever did it intended him to drown – with the watermill as his coffin.'

'Then no mercy to them, God willing.'

It was out of her hands now. She knew she would be in the way if she renegotiated the narrow waterlogged path along the embankment. The men knew where to find him and after assessing the state the priest was in, as she told it, some went ahead and others followed with a stretcher. The infirmarer, warned to receive a man half dead from drowning and with not one but two broken legs, questioned her briefly, concluding by telling her that he would have all remedies prepared.

'You've done your bit, domina. Sleep is best for him now while we have a look at his injuries. Come back tomorrow when the full story may be told from his own lips.'

Hildegard fetched her horse as there was no one else to do it and with Nimrod, royally indifferent to his wetting, they set off for Swyne.

If she was in luck the search party would only now be ready to leave. She urged her mount briskly along the short distance through the woods to find out.

# FORTY-NINE

'Rogella!' She grabbed the novice roughly by the shoulder as soon as she caught up with her. 'Stop what you're doing and come with me!'

'What?'

They were in the garth. It was still pouring down. The search party was about to leave. Hildegard had found her straightaway, giggling and behaving like a sot-wit among some other novices who knew no better. They held capes over their heads as they skittered out of the cloister after their lessons.

'I said, come with me.'

She registered that Hildegard was accompanied by several stern-faced nuns. It slightly took the smile off her face.

'All right, I'll come. But I've no idea what this is about!'

Defiant, fists bunched, the knife at this moment nowhere visible, she managed to give a backward little snigger over her shoulders before being hustled across the garth to the refectory. Waxed cloaks were thrown down in the porch and she was pushed inside and told to sit in a chair.

Hildegard stood over her. 'So what was your plan for Matthew? I want the truth and nothing else.'

'We had no plan.'

'Don't start with a lie or it'll be the worse for you. You boasted to me you and your twin had a plan to lure Matthew away so that she could—' Hildegard searched for an inoffensive way of putting it. 'So that you could find a way of escaping your situation as novices.'

'That was all.' Rogella still looked defiant. Her jaw jutted like that of an insolent child.

'Was it also part of your plan to murder Matthew if he did not agree to be used in such a base manner?'

'Of course not. We well know the penalty for murder. We'd have found another way of getting what we want if he had been so prim as to refuse.'

'Do you know where he is?'

She shook her head.

'Tell me the truth!'

'I am telling you the truth! How should I know where he is? It's up to you to find him if you're as clever as you think you are!'

'You told me you wanted him back. Well, you'd better hand over your knife. I've kept my promise. He is back.'

Rogella looked stunned. 'Where – where is he?'

'Hand it over.'

Reluctantly, having little choice, she did so.

Hildegard put it in her scrip. 'He's in the hospitium at Meaux. Half dead from a beating and a near drowning. And who else is to blame but Bella, with your encouragement?'

'She would never—' A look of uncertainty flitted over her face.

'You disgust me!'

Hildegard walked away for fear she might strike her. The nuns delegated to deal with violence in the priory stepped forward to take the novice into custody.

Hildegard was in a genuine fury. Matthew! How could they? He was the mildest and most honourable young man – a boy, surely no more than twenty-one or two? – strict, yes, but only within the bounds of the Rule. Hildegard wondered what, after incarceration in the priory prison, would happen to Rogella. She would get her way and be thrown out, that was certain. Bella would be the one in real trouble after what she had done.

With the search party already straggling out into the woods, she let them go and instead went in search of Josiana. She had heard all about events at Meaux by the time Hildegard found her in a corner of the cloister.

Her expression was shocked. 'I'm surprised Bella had the strength. How do you think she did it?'

'I don't know.' They talked for a while until Hildegard shook out her sleeves. 'I must go and change out of these wet garments.' About to step outside into the rain again she said, 'How could she break his legs? I still don't understand. I mean, what possessed her to indulge in such cruelty? It may mean he will never walk again.'

'It's a spiteful thing to do.'

'Could she have done it alone?'

Josiana looked doubtful. 'She doesn't seem strong enough—'

'Is it beyond the bounds of possibility that she had someone with her?'

'But who?'

'Or maybe it was someone else altogether, acting alone?'

'In that case where is Bella herself?'

'Maybe she ran away . . .'

Josiana considered this alternative. 'Logically, both are possible.'

'I knew you'd say that.'

It was too soon to admit that she agreed and her anger might be misdirected. But she could not completely reject the idea that it was Bella acting alone until something or someone proved otherwise.

# FIFTY

The single bell tolled across the flooded fields surrounding Swyne. The incessant rain had turned the priory into an island in a grey lake. The lay-brothers returned with faces set hard against failure and the misery of unremitting discomfort at having had to force their horses breast-high through the flood waters for no reward. Despite this they were voluble.

'No sign of poor Lydia's murderer.'

'We quartered the woods to the south of Kirk Ella and some of their men came out to help. To no avail.'

'This endless rain is keeping strangers out of the district.'

'Everyone else is indoors.'

'Nobody has seen neither hide nor hair—'

'Not the novice, not the minstrel, not any assassin neither.'

'That one will've gone to ground. We've no chance of finding him now.'

'Brace up,' someone encouraged. 'The last thing inside the box is hope.'

Matthew's deliverance was the only sign of hope. They expressed wonder that he had been found as well as fear that now the killer was real.

The Prioress stood at the gate. 'Well done, men. Your fortitude is most impressive. Hot mead for you all in your refectory and the kitchens are open to you. Eat what you want.'

Like a crow in her hooded cape, she had braved the garth to meet them with the nonchalance of someone sauntering through an April shower. While flood water licked the tops of her boots she reminded them that the fire was stoked in their hall and they must change at once into dry clothes.

'We don't want you all going down with the rheum,' she finished, splashing away after she had seen them all safely inside the walls.

By tacit agreement no one remarked that they had been sent out on yet another futile search.

\*     \*     \*

Hildegard and Josiana went to sit in the cloisters. They were harried by a blustering wind that swept rain inside in random scuds that made it almost as wet outside as in.

A remark made by one of the men as he squelched past – to the effect that Nimrod would have been a great help as their own hounds were too small to do more than turn into water-dogs and try to grow fins – encouraged Hildegard to reconsider the situation.

'I have an idea,' she told Josiana, 'and I think we are agreed that if the minstrel is in hiding, as a stranger in these parts, he will not have gone far. Are you willing to come out into the wet again and let Nimrod guide us?'

'What do you have in mind?'

'There is, you may remember, a little knoll not far from the haven near Haltemprice Priory. It's very wooded there. Not much good for crops, and the sheep, when they're here, dislike it. But if I were roaming about, looking for somewhere to stay safe above the flood waters and not knowing of anywhere else to hide, it would be a place I would consider.'

'It sounds well thought out, Hildegard. Are we taking anybody else with us?'

'If you mean Alaric, he's being treated for a fever brought on by the drenching he got yesterday. He'll be out and about as soon as ever, but not just yet. I would not want to offend him by finding a substitute so soon. Let's give him chance to get well. Meanwhile I see no reason why we shouldn't go ourselves. We're not help-less.' Not realizing she sounded like the Prioress she added a remark about the times on King's Business when she had been under greater threat than a mere flood could pose.

Josiana got to her feet with a sense of purpose. 'I've been in constant fear of the waters gushing over the land in a huge tidal wave, sweeping all before it, sending folk onto their roof tops and drowning everyone else in their beds, but it's more of a seeping, a creeping, an inch by inch crawling over the flat fields, and in some places it rises no more than ankle-high, thus is the terrain round here. Not pleasant,' she added, 'if you have to find a dry place to sleep but for those of us not living rough it's more of an inconvenience than a threat. A small rise in the ground might be the safe place he would look for.'

'I'm glad you agree.'

'As for the flood, Hildegard, I fear the real problems will come when it recedes.'

She sighed. 'I expect the farmers are going to have a real time of it. Their crops will not grow in mud. The sheep will starve for want of grass.'

Where in the box was hope, Hildegard asked herself.

Arranging a time and place to meet before Vespers, and reminding Josiana to bring her knife for protection, she left to prepare herself.

# FIFTY-ONE

Not much later, they were trudging up the hill through a thicket of wet branches. It was a sinister place, dark with shadows. Josiana was some way off, cursing politely under her breath as she forced a way through the whipping stems and Nimrod had disappeared into a tunnel of hawthorn when Hildegard suddenly froze to a stop.

A voice close by whispered in her ear, 'Are you alone?'

The woods were black under the lowering clouds and glancing nervously ahead she could see no one. She fingered her knife.

The voice came again. 'I'm behind you.'

Jerking round she peered into the darkness and with a shock made out a blur in the undergrowth. Heart in her mouth she gasped, 'Who is it?'

The shape took form and she stepped hastily back. 'You? . . .' She lowered her knife. 'Do you know there's a search party out for you?'

'They think I'm a murderer!' He muttered, 'I've never met the poor girl! I'd never even heard of her until yesterday.'

'Listen – that's not why they're after you—'

Josiana, crashing about among the trees, burst in between them, saying, 'I heard voices— Oh!'

She gaped when she saw Leonin.

At his last gasp, as it seemed, he backed away, asking, 'Where are the others?' He eyed the two nuns with misgivings.

'What others?'

'The huntsmen. They rode straight past without seeing me.' He swayed, about to fall. 'Have you brought them?'

'Look, there's an old watch tower further up. There's more shelter there.' Hildegard gestured towards the top of the slope.

'It's just us.'

'I'm trying to keep above the flood waters,' he began to stammer, 'I found this hillock by accident when the men were out earlier. I heard them riding past. I was lying low and found cover before they could see me. I thought they'd given up when they couldn't find me at Ravenser. They think they're hunting a murderer but it isn't me.' He swayed again and Hildegard took him by one arm.

'Let's find some better shelter. I have bread and cheese in my scrip and it looks as if you might need it. When did you last eat?'

Without answering he allowed her to push him ahead of her through the undergrowth and as it thinned they came out on the rain-swept summit where a ruined wall hinted at the watch tower Hildegard had mentioned.

'It's years since I've been up here,' she remarked, 'but it's better than being in that wood in the rain.'

A wide view over the meandering of the great estuary far below met their gaze as they looked out and they saw the ribbon of water turn to rose in a shaft of light from the westering sun. It lasted no more than a second then the clouds closed in, silvering the scene with more wild gusts.

'We should turn back,' suggested Josiana, 'while we can still see the way.'

Leonin backed off.

'Not me! I would be putting my head in a noose! They think I killed her! I did not do it, Hildegard. Believe me!'

'I do,' she answered simply. With a glance at Josiana she said, 'Illogical though it is, without proof, I'm guided by some other power. I do not believe you did it, Leonin. And neither does Abbot de Courcy. He sent the men out to bring you back to safety.'

Josiana sat down in the shelter of the fallen stones. 'Sit, Leonin. I cannot judge without evidence. Convince me of your story, if you will.'

Finding a seat he made an effort to pull himself together. 'Can you believe that I once wore silks and velvets and walked in marble halls?' He glanced from one to the other. 'Look at me! In my own country I am as nearly a prince as anyone at King Richard's court. Now I'm no more than a walking skeleton of earth and mud. I have returned before my time to the filth from which we are all formed. Bring me my coffin! Inter me! I am finished!'

Hildegard sighed. 'How can that be when we're here, living and breathing and offering help?'

'Angels of mercy? Or devils incarnate here to draw me down to hell?'

'You have no possible reason,' Josiana objected, 'to regard us as devils.'

'Forgive me. My wits are gone. I'm at my end. Tell Abbot Hubert – tell him . . . I would have brought death to him too – I had no choice but to run but I got lost. I've been roaming these woods for an eternity—'

Hildegard put an arm round him, driven by some unexpected emotion, and gave him a hug. He was really little more than a helpless child.

'How old are you, Leonin?'

She opened her bag and offered him some bread and cheese. He fell on it like a wolf, replying through a crammed mouth, 'Nearly seventeen.'

Sixteen then.

'And how long were you at King Richard's court?'

Between mouthfuls he replied, 'A year. I came over with a knight who'd spent many years at Acre, long after its fall.' He stuffed more food into his mouth, swallowed, and continued. 'Because I played and sang well enough, King Richard treated me with extreme kindness. He loves to surround himself with music and laughter.' He bit off more bread and continued, 'A deep melancholy lies in his heart. It darkens his moods though he strives to conquer it. "Death," he once said, "will follow me wherever I go. It strikes at all those I love. Such is my fate, the litany of my beloved friends and allies is now complete with the death of my queen, my angel, my beloved Anne."'

He stopped eating and glanced from one to the other. 'He moved me to tears. He said he could not bear her absence. He said his enemies had snarled at his heels ever since he received the crown. "A nothing, a hollow thing," he told me, "I would not have it but for my holy vow to God and the trust the Blessed Virgin bestowed on me when she gave England into my keeping."'

Leonin looked across the rain-swept meadows like a hunted animal. 'The truth is he believed his enemies would drag the realm into a civil war that would last a hundred years. The land would be laid waste and his people starve if his enemies managed to snatch the crown. It was his by divine right. He was anointed by

God. He could do nothing about that but he vowed to protect England from the monstrous, war-loving barons. He believed they would destroy England to satisfy their own mortal ambitions. It's why they hated him and derided him for making treaties instead of war.'

Hildegard asked gently, 'But why did you yourself flee the court?'

'I overheard something – it made me dangerous to his enemies.'

'And . . .?'

'They feared I would denounce them so I escaped while I could.' He frowned. 'I imagined I would find allies and we might mount a defence against them and would destroy them, Gaunt, Woodstock, and others. And then this, this poor girl, a murder, nothing to do with me – malign fate—'

'But why did you come here?'

He gave a regretful smile. 'I'd heard of Meaux, stories, enough to intrigue me and make me believe I'd be safe until I'd roused the king's allies. I was told it's a place he regarded as loyal to him.'

# FIFTY-TWO

Their garments steamed in front of a roaring fire in the warming room. It had been especially stoked for them by order of the Prioress. Leonin was safely abed in the hospitium, no questions asked, and the priory was asleep in the long silence before midnight brought the nuns forth to pray.

Josiana pulled at the threads of Leonin's story. 'Many places are loyal to the king, so why this one?'

'That is a consideration,' Hildegard agreed. 'He might have chosen somewhere closer to London. But perhaps,' she pondered, 'he feels safer away from the City with its changeable allegiances and its propensity for riot and mayhem.'

'The East Riding is still too close to Lancaster's territory to be safe.'

'But not as far down as this, surely?'

'If you're thinking of the Earl of Northumberland, I would not put my trust in him no matter how deeply he might bow before my throne.'

The flames crackled and spat and the wood shrivelled and fell into the ash.

It was as they hoped when they persuaded Leonin to return with them to the priory. The Prioress hadn't even blinked when they appeared.

'Of course he has sanctuary. The lad must be scared out of his wits. Without evidence there is no question that we would accuse him of murder. Let someone go over to Meaux to tell Hubert. He'll be delighted. That Sheriff has to put in an appearance yet and we'll have to wait to see what he might say, but who else will accuse him? I know of no one. Rumour is not proof of anything.'

So that was that, for the time being.

# FIFTY-THREE

Hildegard, for what was perceived as her closeness to Leonin, was invited to visit him the following day after he had time to recover.

'Poor lad,' agreed the Prioress. 'He has been through it. Let him feel comforted. Maybe later, to reassure ourselves, you might find out if he still wants to stick to this story of what happened after he landed on this side of the Humber.'

Meanwhile, with Matthew found, the searchers shifted their focus to the missing novice. The Sheriff did eventually ride over from York and the two houses of lay-brothers organized by Gregory and Egbert, most nearly looking like something he might wish his own militia to match, were augmented by his hastily scrambled posse of armed townsmen.

'They are but apprentices and merchants' lads,' he was heard to observe, 'and this is but a missing novice, more a concern for the Church than for us. But as we are here now, we will do our best to find her.' Girls were always missing, in his opinion, especially if there was trouble in the offing.

Hildegard's first gently conducted interview with Leonin deepened her concern. He stuck to his story about being pursued by an assassin. Whenever anybody entered the hospitium in a hurry, or whenever there was a sudden loud noise even when it was only the dropping of a metal dish onto the flagstones, he would start up in alarm then sink back with a cry of relief when he saw it was nothing.

'My spirits are sorely shaken, domina. I beg your indulgence. I will feel steadier as time goes on.'

Thinking he might be soothed by the sound of music she asked, 'What happened to your vielle?'

'I left it in safekeeping at Meaux. The rain would have got to it and ruined it. Hubert said he knew of a minstrel from Beverley

who sometimes came over to conduct the choir. He said he could
be trusted to care for it and play it now and then.'

'He must mean Pierrekyn Haverel. He comes over to Swyne to
put our choir through its paces too.'

'It would be something to speak to another musician, no matter
how indifferent,' he made a fretful face and Hildegard was
quick to point out that Pierrekyn was by no means an indifferent
player.

'He was a protégé of King Edward's chief court musician when
he took up a corrody at York,' she explained. 'If he was ambitious
enough he might have been your master at Sheen.'

She changed the subject. The royal court in Edward's days had
been rife with spies and counter-spies, one faction plotting against
another, so nothing had changed there. The king himself had been
a smart intriguer, surviving many plots, with no less than Alice
Perrers, his mistress, shaking things up for her own benefit among
other shifting allegiances and betrayals. Throughout all ran rank
greed for life's material riches. As then so now.

Pierrekyn had not welcomed being taken up by one of
Edward's ex-spies and preferred to remain in Yorkshire at the
Beverley Song School. She decided she would try to get a
message to him. Everyone needed music as things stood. The
flood waters were an insidious presence, seeping into everyday
life, hiding the continuing destruction of the foundations under
a blandly rippling surface, eroding the stones as they eroded
confidence in an end to it.

Several outer buildings in their own domain, barns built in a
hurry, maybe, had tumbled down in the last few days, supports
washed from under them by the pervasive powers of the flood.

'Pierrekyn will cheer us up,' she assured him. 'He can bring
your vielle for you. I expect you'd like to have it back.'

The rain abated and a weak sun appeared. Everyone felt their
spirits rise, hoping a curse had been lifted. During the night,
however, the rains returned more fiercely than ever with thunder
and lightning and the distant roar of the estuary in full spate.

It could be heard from across what had been open pasture and
was now turned by the rain into a treacherous quagmire.

The moon was not quite full, Hildegard noticed. She stood at her window for some time, looking out between the shutters into the thrashing darkness of the woods with her mind on mysteries that would not yield to reason.

Next morning alarming stories were brought in by one of the servants from Meaux who had managed to construct a raft and now hailed them with news about more buildings collapsing.

The disused mill near Meaux, he told them, where Matthew had been trapped, was totally destroyed, the wattle and daub, the planking, the colossal timbers, the smashed wheel itself had been swept wholesale down the canal until the debris formed a barrage and the waters were backed up behind it, inundating the few meadows that remained.

Most tracks between the various habitations were now impassable, he added. They already knew that the moat at Swyne was as wide as a river but to their relief the bridge held although water rose to cover it to a height of eighteen inches.

'No point in crossing to the other side, anyway,' everyone remarked. 'Where would we go in this?'

Boats became a topic of speculation and it was put forward that any man could construct a coracle out of the plentiful supply of broken branches swirling past. It should be possible to fashion something suitable for sculling about the woodland – even, some suggested, taking them as far as the main road between Hull and Beverley. A few optimists set to work and demonstrated the validity of the idea. York, they were told, was now an island, cut off in all directions, and although so far safe within the stout walls, its citizens were trapped.

Not so Swyne, they boasted. Now they could choose to go anywhere if they were desperate enough to take to the waters.

One of these makeshift coracles was eventually manned by a couple of daredevils willing to risk the dangers and paddle over to Meaux to beg for any spare produce the larger establishment possessed.

Before they left Hildegard said, 'You might ask the lord abbot to send a message to Pierrekyn Haverel at Beverley Minster if they have a suitable craft. We would welcome some music here at Swyne.'

They were sent off in the spirit of an unexpected holy day with cheers and a lustily sung Te Deum. The Sacristan folded her arms with satisfaction at the strange sight of the men sculling off between the boles of the trees.

She was even more delighted when they returned in triumph, having piloted themselves back in possession of several dozen eggs from the hens at Meaux, along with other assorted foodstuffs to augment their own supplies together with the bursar's compliments.

A message from the sacristan at Meaux even mentioned Pierrekyn Haverel saying that the abbey choir also needed the solace of song at such a difficult and unprecedented time and that, if possible, they would send either Master Pierrekyn himself in their own boat or at least the precious vielle belonging to the minstrel from Outremer.

Everyone cheered when they heard this whether they liked music or not. Hildegard wondered how it had got about that Leonin came from overseas. There were questions about whether he was a genuine Saracen and carried a scimitar, and intense discussions about what he might prefer to eat and drink. But by and large it meant as much or as little as if he claimed to come from fairyland.

# FIFTY-FOUR

The advantage of all this to-ing and fro-ing was that it became safer to travel between the two places. The waters kept on rising. Even the canals on the other side of Meaux broke their banks but as Josiana had observed, it was not as if it was a great barrage of water sweeping everyone to destruction now that the banks had given way. The waters had spread out until they lay over the flat arable land like nothing more than an enormous puddle, the random presence of dangerous whirlpools caused by obstructions under the surface obvious and easily avoided.

If Hildegard wanted to go to Meaux she could.

She wanted very much to talk to Matthew if he had, as expected, regained his wits. She asked permission. Was given it.

And insisting on taking Nimrod she went down to what they were now beginning to call 'the quay' and organized passage for them both. As she was doing so Alaric, red-nosed and with a scarf knotted at his throat, had emerged from the lay-brothers' quarters and insisted on coming with her.

'Very well, Alaric, so long as you're sure you won't take a turn for the worse?'

'The fresh air will do me good. It'll blow away this miasma then I'll be right as rain.' He grinned. 'If there ever is anything right about rain.'

It took hardly any time for two strong conversi to scull them over to the abbey.

'I'll come in with you if you think that might help?' Alaric offered when they reached the door of the hospitium.

'Maybe he might be more forthcoming if it's only one of us?'

'Let me know. I'll be standing by.' He opened the door for her and she went inside.

# FIFTY-FIVE

M atthew's sick-chamber was unlike Leonin's austere cell. As it was not acceptable to have a male patient in a house of nuns Leonin was lodged at the end of a corridor deep inside the Swyne hospitium. He did not mind being separated from everyone, only relieved not to be sleeping rough any longer. Matthew fared better as she now saw.

He was in a partitioned ward among other monks, all friends and brothers. With a coffered vault and rows of clerestory windows it was light and airy even if the sky outside was grey. The glass rattled with rain at every battering gust but it was warm inside. Orderlies bustled in and out and the infirmarer and his assistants were in constant attendance.

Matthew was sitting up in bed, eyes closed, when Hildegard arrived. He did not stir. Still pale, his legs were encased in the wooden contraption similar to the one at Netley Abbey when Hubert had broken a leg in a fight with New Forest brigands soon after they returned from Avignon.

The thought of Hubert brought bitter-sweet memories of how he had tried to persuade her to consider an outrageous idea which had never come to fruition.

Conscious of his present coldness towards her she doubted whether he remembered what he had asked of her in the heat of the moment. "My dream is to leave the Order for a life with you in the secular world." Events had prevented her from giving him an answer – or burning her boats, as she now saw it.

Her attention returned to Matthew. Evidently asleep, his face bruised and still swollen despite the poultice the infirmarer had applied, he looked peaceful enough.

Something made him abruptly open his good eye. Wincing, he tried a sort of smile. 'They said you would come.'

After a few remarks he muttered, 'I know what you really want to know – it's what happened at the mill and how I came to be in this state?'

When she agreed he replied, 'I cannot accept it even yet. They say the nightmares will stop, that I'll find more ease in my mind as time passes, but I doubt it. I cannot . . . It was unbearable . . . It is too—'

'Only talk if you want to,' she whispered when she saw his distress.

'I must explain because I think you may believe that Bella caused this but she did not except by her presence which she could not help . . .' He took a breath and forced the words out in a hoarse mutter. 'The thing is when we left the path on our way back to Meaux we were waylaid. As I left Swyne she followed me. When she caught up we rode in silence for a while. Then she said she wanted to show me something. She was quite mysterious and because she had been so demure on the ride over I suspected nothing.' He sighed and closed his eyes for a moment. 'When we came to a sheltered grove near the abbey she dismounted saying her horse needed a little rest and then she suggested that we sit down on a bank to let our horses crop the grass before going on. The rain had let up and – *mea culpa, domina*, I was beguiled. I knew I should insist on returning but while we dallied a stranger appeared, asking the way to Meaux. We got to our feet and I was in the middle of telling him when he suddenly drew a knife and held it at Bella's throat. I froze. I never expected it. I was unarmed. I didn't know what to do. He forced me to gather the reins of the horses and follow. All the time he was holding the knife to Bella's throat and she was trembling and stark white with fear. I could do nothing but obey. We must have been near the disused watermill because in moments we were outside it and he pushed her inside and slammed the door behind her then turned to me. That's when I got this.' He raised one hand and let it hover over his swollen eye. 'Before I recovered he grabbed a rope from somewhere and lashed it round my wrists. He knew exactly what he was doing. Then he opened the door and threw me in. I fell and hit my head and remember little after that until I came to sometime later . . . I could hear what he was doing to Bella.' Matthew's voice fell to a whisper. 'In the shadows and with one eye swollen shut I could make nothing out but it was – it needed no imagination to know what he—' He closed his one good eye. 'It was like being in hell.' A tear trickled down his cheek. 'Please forgive me, Lord God, *mea culpa*, forgive me . . .'

She put a hand over his. 'Matthew, you are not to blame—'

'If not I then who? I should have attacked him when he first appeared. I did not think. It was so far outside my thoughts to attack a man . . .'

'Bella was not at the mill when I arrived. So what happened to her?'

He shook his head. 'I know not. I only know that the rain came down in fury and the old building shook. Water surged inside. I lost consciousness with the pain in my legs and when I came round again you were bending over me.' His expression was bleak. 'I know not where she is . . . nor what more he may have done to her.'

They sat in silence for a while and when the infirmarer appeared with a mug of a steaming herbal soporific he indicated with a swift glance towards the door that Hildegard should leave. After placing the mug on a ledge beside Matthew he followed her out.

'I see he has told you what he knows?'

'Nothing yet about the stranger – who he was – what he looked like – and what happened to Bella, which of course he cannot know.'

'Neither can any of us. I fear we will find her body when the floods recede.'

She acknowledged this with a shudder. 'This stranger then . . .? What has he told you about him?'

'Very little. He's too confused. He took more of a battering than he may have admitted to you. The fellow was most brutal judging by the lacerations to every part of the lad's body. He must have been a man-at-arms or similar ilk. The type who can travel anywhere unnoticed because so commonplace.'

'And Matthew had never seen him before?'

'Never. He was quite emphatic.'


Grateful to be returning in a group of men she could trust and with Alaric by her side, Hildegard still felt shaken by the time she alighted from the abbey's boat at Swyne. She went straight along to the hospitium to have a word with Leonin.

'This assassin you mention—' she queried after greetings had been exchanged.

'He does exist. Believe me, domina. I have not invented him, I—'

'Peace. I think he's been sighted at last.' Then she told him what had happened to Matthew after meeting the stranger in the grove.

Leonin tensed himself. 'Are you telling me he's somewhere near?' His glance flew to the single window in his retreat.

'You're safe here. Now we have proof he exists you can be sure we'll soon have him in custody if he's still around.' Before she left she repeated, 'Rest assured, Leonin. You are safe within the confines of our priory.'

# FIFTY-SIX

The beggars were still swarming outside the Meaux gatehouse and a couple of elderly monks were doing their best to share out yesterday's bread and the scrapings from the day's table. Many hands reached out in desperation.

The waters had risen in the night crowding the men into one small area with water lapping at their feet. Out of kindness the porter allowed the destitute band to come in under the shelter of the archway, only beating them back when one or two took advantage of this relaxation of the rules and had the effrontery to step right onto the garth.

'I've told you fellers,' he said, 'keep back or we'll be having the lord abbot coming out to curse you. Back! Here, you! What's your name?' He addressed one of the men who had broken away from the rest and was trying to saunter further into the precinct with an exaggerated air of innocence. 'Come on, feller! Answer me when I ask you a question!'

The beggar gave him a sly glance. 'John,' he retorted unconvincingly when the porter insisted again.

'Well, Master John,' he replied, 'do you understand plain Yorkshire?' The porter, burly, not used to being ignored, lifted his club. 'Back when I say so! And stay back!'

The beggar turned with a glum mutter and, head bent, sidled to the outskirts of the group. Making sure everybody was watching, he unlaced the front of his breeches, took out his member, and pissed long and hard into the flood water. To make sure the porter understood that it was a show of deliberate contempt he glanced back over his shoulder with a leer on his grizzled features as if to say, What are you going to do about that?

The porter scowled in disgust and turned back into the lodge. To Hildegard, waiting inside, he said, 'I hope you didn't see that, domina. Some of them are nothing but animals. I don't hold with feeding them for nowt. They should be set to, to do a day's labour before they put their hands out begging for dole.'

'Is there work for them in the present conditions?'

'There's always work, even the Devil finds work for idle hands and I don't mean thieving and such. They could be set to cleaning out the stables, swabbing down the floor of the refectory, there's always something.' Chuntering somewhat he went back outside, hailed forth by a voice calling his name.

Hildegard heard him reply, 'She's here within, brother.'

Gregory poked his head into the lodge. 'Hildegard?'

'Greetings! You have a message?'

'I do. May we find somewhere to talk?'

# FIFTY-SEVEN

When they were settled in a corner of the guest house she asked, 'Is he the same?'

Gregory shrugged to express bewilderment. He knew what she meant. 'Even he must eventually come to his senses.'

'At least he acknowledged that we found Leonin.'

'And alive, praise be. How is he today?'

'Resting in a private chamber after his ordeal as he calls it, sleeping rough, something he was at pains to tell us he was unused to. There's something else, I forgot a small thing that fits with what Matthew has told us. Remember I mentioned that Alaric found a footprint in the sand we thought might have been left by Lydia's killer?'

He nodded.

'When I saw Leonin I glanced at his boots – they're worn out and much patched by now, of course, but they could never have left such a print. He wears boots in the latest fashion!'

'What? Poulaines?'

His reaction was similar to Alaric's and she said quickly, 'Not quite poulaines.'

Even so he threw his head back. 'Those courtiers!' Then he became serious. 'Of course, it shows that someone else was at the haven. It could have been anybody.'

'He's convinced it's his assassin. Every time there's a sudden noise he jumps like a rabbit.'

'He can't surely imagine the fellow could get inside the priory? Has he really lost his nerve?'

'It seems like it.'

'He needs an infusion of borage. That would stiffen his sinews!'

Hildegard recalled the gift Hubert had folded into her palm soon after they met. The emblem embroidered in one corner of the little square of linen was a branch of borage – 'for courage,' he told her as they parted on separate paths into danger.

'Poor Hubert,' she said now. 'I would have liked to see him. That's why I came over. Is it really out of the question?'

'Still the same. But there is something for you. Come.'

He led her back to the lodge and addressed the porter. 'Brother, they left something here in case anyone came over from Swyne. Can you get it?'

The porter turned to the shelf behind him. It was stacked with bits and pieces of equipment, a broken bridle, one sandal, a pile of vellum, a hood, and something in a leather bag. 'This it?' He handed it over.

Gregory peered inside. 'I used to be able to play one of these long ago in Outremer.' He handed it to her. 'Now you'll have music wherever you go.'

She recognized the bag Leonin's vielle was carried in. 'This is welcome. Everyone's feeling gloomy with the floods still on the rise.'

'If you're going straight back I'll come with you, if I may?'

'I expect you want to meet Leonin?'

'Indeed.'

As they walked over to the postern to let themselves out to where the boats were being moored he said, 'I'm sure there's a lot more you could tell me about him before I see him. I doubt, however, that he's told you why he's on the run from this fellow?'

'He said a little. But he's as obstinate as Hubert. It must be something shameful or otherwise he would wish us to know, to increase his standing with us. As it is he's like a child, cowering under his covers at the thought of bogeymen. He must know he's safe now. Nor need he have fear of censure from us,' she added.

'I expect he needs time. If he's lost his nerve there's little we can do for now.'

# FIFTY-EIGHT

The waters were rising steadily as the Humber, fed from half a dozen tributaries, themselves flooded as rainwater cascaded down from the hills, reached its limits and seeped over the land with nothing to hinder it. As far as the horizon, single dwellings sat in the water, like islands in an expanding lake. The monks had sculled a quickly constructed coracle to one of the distant granges and returned with stories of how the animals that had not been taken up-country were being housed together on their separate islets. Tempers are fraying, they were told.

Gregory handed Hildegard into the wide well-made craft belonging to Meaux leaving the one from Swyne for someone else and they sat side by side as two lay-brothers plied the oars.

'If only people were not suffering,' he remarked as they floated serenely out on the surface of the water, 'this would be idyllic now the rain has stopped.'

Hildegard trailed a hand in the water. 'I wonder how long it's going to last?' She was really wondering how long Hubert was going to finish his self-inflicted penance before he emerged and took control again.

Gregory gave her a penetrating glance as if he read her mind but said nothing.

# FIFTY-NINE

A s they stepped ashore a little while later he put a hand under her elbow. 'We couldn't talk in the boat with those two lads listening in for a bit of gossip but I just want to say, Hildi, I will tell you anything I discover and pass it on to you—'

'And I you, Gregory. You know that.'

'It's difficult. I'm sworn to defend Hubert and I know you would wish me to keep my promise but he believes there is real danger. He was right about the existence of an assassin. If he knows more he will not admit it. I want you to promise not to travel alone until this murderer has been brought in.'

'I'm not planning on going anywhere, Gregory.'

He gazed into her eyes. 'I can believe anything you say when you look at me like that.' His lips tilted. 'Say you promise?'

'I do. I promise.' She gave a small laugh. 'Why so serious, Gregory? Have you heard something we haven't?'

He pressed his lips together. 'Nothing definite. I'd warn you if I had. I'm worried about you, that's all. Stay safe. It's all I wish.'

'I'm not planning on leaving the priory,' she insisted. 'Believe me.'

'But you did go out with only one nun in attendance when you found Leonin. I needn't say how foolhardy I believe it was. What if it had been the murderer who met you in the woods?'

'Perhaps it was foolish. But at least it brought a result!'

He regarded her fondly. 'All right! We failed and you succeeded. But I want to believe your promise not to risk it again. This man is dangerous. We have no idea where he is. We know not for whom he works other than that someone with wealth must have engaged him. He has not finished his task yet. He's a professional. He will not be deterred by what your Prioress will no doubt call "a drop of rain".'

Together they went inside to see Leonin. Hildegard felt sobered by Gregory's words but did not show it.

# SIXTY

Leonin was sitting up in bed. His eyes shone when he saw the bag she held out to him.

'My beloved vielle! . . . My heart is full!' He rapidly slid off the leather covering and drew the instrument forth to cradle it in the cruck of one arm. Then she and Gregory saw that he was weeping. Ashamed to be caught out he wiped the back of one hand over his eyes and bending over the instrument, his face hidden by a lock of hair, began to play.

After a few phrases he murmured, 'This Pierrekyn Haverel you mentioned must have tuned her. She's not as bad as I feared. Dry. Safe. My beauty. I am invincible again!'

After listening to Leonin play a song or two Hildegard left them both. When Gregory emerged a little later, however, he admitted he had failed to persuade him to identify the assassin.

'If he would only confess why he believes a professional killer is on his trail it would give us a clue to the identity of the man who commissioned him. Then we'd know what it all means.'

'We at Swyne fear it's something to do with an insurrection against King Richard.'

His expression darkened.

After a pause he told her that Leonin had told him a little about what made him leave. He had been hustled for safety down the back stairs at Sheen by a couple of courtier friends one night. A gang of armed men had been asking for him and as Leonin's friends didn't like the look of them they told them they would go to fetch him for them. Instead they had warned Leonin, "They're waiting outside. We said we'd fetch you as they'd never find you in the labyrinth of corridors inside the palace. Get to horse. Leave! If they find you, you're a dead man!"'

Leonin admitted to Gregory that he had been in a state of terror ever since. He dared not divulge the truth to anyone until he was sure it could be acted on with no danger either to the king himself or to any of his allies.

The upshot was he had followed his friends' advice, taken a fast horse from the royal stables and ridden for his life. At first he had no idea where to go and then it came to him that north would be the safest direction where he could find sanctuary and later, conscious of the fact that someone was on his trail, he made his escape as complicated as he could. For some time he believed he had shaken his pursuer off. He knew now it was one man, working alone ever since he followed him from the palace. That's what made him convinced it was a paid assassin. And only he knew why.

Gregory told her that when Leonin at last crossed the Humber he thought he was safe. It was the murder of Lydia at the place where he landed that made him suspect that the killer was still on his trail. Why he had killed the girl he had no idea.

Since then he felt eyes watching him. He knew the killer could be hiding in the woods, waiting his chance, and when he found sanctuary in the abbey at Meaux he again thought he was safe. But he feared that the fellow had discovered where he was and he began to believe he would be better in a secret hermitage as he called it and decided to remain there until the assassin concluded that he had escaped elsewhere.

'The rest we know,' was Gregory's only comment as he took his leave.

# SIXTY-ONE

Leonin's hope that his trail had gone cold was as good as any now he was hidden in the labyrinthine corridors of the hospitium at Swyne.

Hildegard had no more doubts after hearing Gregory's version. Her only uncertainty was over what Hubert knew and why he was making a penance out of it. It was as if he feared that Leonin was guilty despite himself, because why should he not give sanctuary to someone who claimed to fear for his life? Whether he knew every in and out, wasn't it his duty to do it, no matter whose hatred Leonin had aroused?

Remembering how Hubert's allegiance to the Crown of England had once before been in doubt at the time when they first encountered each other she now dismissed the suspicion that he had a deeper reason for his actions.

In the past, doubt had arisen because of the Cistercian connection with the mother house at Cîteaux, and hence, possibly, with the French king, Charles VI, with whom England was then openly at war. She pondered the problem with ever-increasing perplexity.

The wars with France had seemed never-ending when the old king, Edward, the third of that name, had laid claim to the throne of France, but as he dwindled towards his dotage aided by his amorous dalliance with Alice Perrers, his martial ambitions that had made him seem like one of the greatest kings England had ever known faded into the past and people began to think of his decades of war-mongering as something iniquitous to a civilized life.

At least, most ordinary people thought so, desiring only peace so they could bring up their children without having to witness the slaughter of kinsfolk and the destruction of their livelihoods.

It was the war party within Richard's court, acquiring their vast wealth from the rich farmlands and constant pillaging in northern France, who wanted that era to continue.

Where did Hubert stand in this? He had given up his own military allegiance for a life dedicated to his Order but what if King Charles instructed his monastics to put themselves on a war footing in order to prepare for an invasion of England again? The chain of French abbeys throughout England and Wales were outside the jurisdiction of the English courts and could offer secure waypoints for an invading army; they could offer provisions, safe houses, they could even offer arms.

Only a handful of years previously the City of London itself had prepared for a siege as the French warships gathered across the Narrow Sea. Bad leadership by the French king had saved England from having to call out the barons and their armies then. Now there was no such call. King Richard abhorred war. He regarded it as barbaric, the last resort of any monarch who aspired to greatness – the first resort of the sweaty barbarians who would rule his court and his realm if he allowed it.

She had not been able to see Hubert giving aid to the French then. The question had been thoroughly discussed at the time of the invasion threat. He had been absolved of treachery towards his host country. It was shown that he was unlikely to betray England at the behest of a strutting monarch across the sea. He was not that sort of man. He would be loyal to the people and place where he lived, to the homeland of his English mother.

But now? Was he being tested again? Was that the source of his retreat from daily life into the isolation of his private chapel?

Much troubled, she threw herself into the daily routine at Swyne. The flood waters inched still higher. There was nothing to be done but defy any sense of foreboding and wait.

# SIXTY-TWO

I t was inescapable. Rogella was in despair. Hildegard had noticed the novice sitting somewhat apart from the others. It would have amounted to nothing if it had been anyone else. Previously, however, she had always been the centre of a noisy undisciplined group, the one to lead the others astray in word if not deed. Now she seemed chastened. She scarcely looked up when anyone spoke to her.

Of course it was better for the peace and order of the priory that she had turned inwards and the novice-mistress, sick and tired of trying to impose discipline on the group, was beginning to feel, erroneously, judged Hildegard, that her tactics had at last got results.

Convinced that she would eventually find herself mistaken, Hildegard blamed herself for hardness of heart in this judgement. Surely it must be frightening not to know what had happened to her twin?

The much-vaunted belief that Bella was too clever to have got herself into serious trouble had worn thin. If she had made her escape from the old mill as was hoped, she would surely have risked returning to the priory by now, or at least, because of the impassable floods, to the abbey, which was closer?

No word had been forthcoming, however, and no clue as to what had happened was found to settle their minds. It was accepted that, like Rogella, her ambition was to escape the life that her father had planned for her and this was the perfect opportunity.

Even so the circumstances were so ambiguous it must only bring fear for her twin's safety.

Gregory, true to his promise to Hildegard to tell her anything new he heard, sent a cryptic message by one of the conversi to the effect that "he cannot remember more."

She took this to mean that Matthew could not remember anything more of that terrible time when Bella had been raped and he had been left to drown.

For certainty's sake the canal and the debris piled up near the lock gates had been thoroughly searched. No body had been discovered. If Bella had escaped from the mill or been abducted, either way it must have been on foot but it fed the hope that she had escaped the dark intentions of her abductor.

Rogella's silence might be rage at finding she had been abandoned while her twin had fled, or it might be due to a paralysing fear about what had happened as the awful truth dawned on her that it was no game and her twin might truly have met an unspeakable fate.

For the hundredth time Hildegard wondered how she might say something reassuring without sounding either patronizing or offering false hope. Rogella, however, gave her no opportunity. She kept her head down. She sat by herself. She spoke only when spoken to. She became a model novice, preparing to make a serious commitment to monastic life. It was unreal and unbelievable.

Hildegard would have felt unsurprised by loud rage, demands to keep up the search for Bella – which they were doing, of course – and heated accusations and curses of a type never usually heard within the precinct. But no, there was only this unnatural silence.

She recalled the knife, the threat, her uneasiness, how she had feared she herself would be attacked when she was least expecting it. Now it seemed inconceivable that this subdued young woman would threaten a nun with a blade.

The third day of this changed mood brought Rogella to Hildegard's side as she crossed to the refectory for the midday repast. 'I beg a word, domina, if I may impose on your kindness.'

Hildegard, prepared for a recurrence of their previous encounter, stopped in her tracks and eyed her warily. At least there were people about this time.

Rogella gave her a demure glance in return. 'I have a boon, domina, if you will graciously allow me to place it before you.'

Wondering what was coming next, she replied, 'You may put a request to me, Rogella, although I cannot say it will be granted before I hear what it is.'

'My gratitude, domina.' To Hildegard's astonishment she gave a slight obeisance. 'It is this. I wish to send word to Matthew to beg his forgiveness for our diabolical intentions towards him. You were right. We should never have entertained such ideas. It was very wrong of us.'

Hildegard gave her a careful glance. There was no sign that the girl was seeking to deceive. 'You may send word, if that is your intention. Our conversi are going over before Nones as usual to see how things are faring at Meaux. Are you thinking of writing something?'

Rogella looked at the ground and didn't answer. Hildegard could not be sure that a tear did not make a glistening trail down her cheek.

'You must be grieving for Bella,' she began. 'Do you feel Matthew may be able to tell you more than we already know? I can confirm that he says he can remember nothing more.'

Rogella lifted her head. 'Just to hear a word,' she breathed. 'Matthew is the last person we know who saw her alive.' She gulped and whispered, 'If only I could speak to him directly . . .'

'That's a question for the Prioress—' Hildegard began.

'Oh but she will listen to you, domina. If you ask her on my behalf . . . I would be for ever in your debt. I know she will listen to you above everyone else.'

She gave her a pleading glance and put her hands together in supplication in such a way that Hildegard imagined she had practised the gesture in front of a looking-glass.

She immediately quashed such a suspicion. 'I can but ask her.'

She changed direction towards the Prioress's house with Rogella's thanks following her.

The Prioress listened carefully. When Hildegard finished, she said, 'You seem to doubt Rogella's sincerity?'

'You know me. I have difficulty in trusting what people say unless it's backed up by action. True, her manner has improved over the last few days – but that may be down to her decision to find a way in to see Matthew.'

'Why should she want to? Is there any other reason why she might wish to see him?'

'I'm not sure . . . It's only something she said earlier . . . It was, "I want Matthew back." It seemed an odd thing to say. I still can't make sense of it.'

'Hm, not much to go on. Charity is a trait we sometimes have to work at.'

'I am no doubt at fault in that respect, my lady.'

The Prioress smiled without censure. 'I'll give permission. Let her go. She will be accompanied by a couple of stout fellows who will not allow her out of their sight. Make sure they understand that. When she arrives she will report to Brother Egbert. Nobody will pull the wool over his eyes, will they?'

'I doubt it.'

'Good, then it's settled. She may leave before Nones and return in time for the next service after that. On no account is she to be late.'

Hildegard made her obeisance and, not fully convinced they were doing the right thing, backed from the chamber.

When she reached the garth Rogella must have been waiting for her because she hurried towards her.

'Domina?'

'You may go.' She gave her the gist of the Prioress's instructions about her escorts.

Without the effusive thanks Hildegard imagined this might elicit, Rogella turned on her heel and hurried off to fetch her cloak.

At once Hildegard went to root out the couple of stalwarts the Prioress had suggested. She found Alaric and asked his advice and soon two no-nonsense conversi appeared, smiling and ready to draw up the coracle they used for these trips.

'Ask for Brother Egbert and no one else,' she instructed. 'The Prioress is most insistent that she is not at any time to be left alone. You must accompany her until she is safely handed over to Brother Egbert. He will bring her back to the quay, where you will be waiting for her.'

Grinning they both told her they understood.

Alaric looked quizzical. 'Shall I go with them, make sure they do as they're told?'

'Don't you trust us, Alaric,' one of them chaffed him, 'we know these novices. What do you think she's going to do? Abscond with one of the monks like her twin?' They both roared with laughter.

Alaric told them, 'It's a prison there, surrounded by water. I hope she's a good swimmer if that's her idea.'

Although he was smiling it was too close to what had been rumoured about Bella to be amusing.

When Rogella herself put in an appearance the men straightened their faces and Hildegard was relieved to see they treated her with the respect due to her as they cast off and set the little craft at liberty over the rain-pocked waters.

'Still no word,' Alaric observed after watching them threading their way along the watery path between the trees.

'It's a bad business. Let's hope she's in hiding somewhere safe.' He turned to go.

Hildegard called him back. 'What does everyone down here think has happened to her?'

'Divided three ways: run off, kept prisoner, or drowned.'

'Taking all three into account it would be best if it were the first.'

'It would. I'll remember her in my prayers tonight.'

Just then the Prioress's servant hurried over with a message.

'My lady Prioress wishes you to accompany Sister Rogella,' she informed her. 'She also wishes for the latest news concerning the lord abbot and his affliction.'

Hildegard's heart gave a leap at the possibility of seeing Hubert. 'Very well.' She glanced after the receding coracle and judged that it was too far off to call it back. 'I'll have to take another boat and ask the fellow in charge to catch up with them.'

# SIXTY-THREE

E nisled in the flood waters the abbey looked weightless. Set on its small hill it rose out of the mist like an enchanted castle in a fable concerning captive princesses and knights errant. The graceful edifice of towers and slanted roofs was doubled in the mirror of the flood, even as rain began to shimmer like a shower of crystal in a dream.

Things soon changed. By the time the coracle scraped onto the patch of dry land on the foregate the showers were a deluge, drenching them to the skin, sending everyone running for shelter. Hildegard pulled up her hood and hurried towards the gatehouse through the usual crowd of ruffians waiting for dole.

One of them stepped abruptly in front of her. Rain ran down his face into a rough beard. Oblivious to it he put out a hand.

'Alms, domina.'

She noticed he wore a ring, a black stone with a gold band across it, quite distinctive, possibly worth something. She glanced up at him. His eyes were hard in expectation.

About to dig into her scrip she felt a hand on her back. It was the Swyne boatman who had sculled the coracle across.

'Let my lady through. Get out of it!' He swept the man aside to give Hildegard free passage. The fellow bunched his fists then thought better of it and turned his back with a sneer.

The lay-brother from Swyne nodded at Hildegard when he saw her safely into the gatehouse before climbing back into his coracle and sculling away.

The porter greeted her with a rueful smile. 'Every man-jack's on edge, domina. The abbey can't take any more inside. It's everybody for themselves. The town boatman won't take passengers who can't pay the fare.' And in the same breath, 'Is it our lord abbot you're here to see?'

'On business for my lady Prioress.'

He cuffed a lad hovering nearby. 'Escort to the abbot's house, jump to it!'

Surprised at how quickly the usually serene atmosphere at
Meaux had become menacing, Hildegard clutched her cape and,
hurrying after her young guide, asked conversationally, 'Those
beggars at the gate, they seem to have set up a camp of sorts.
What do the monks make of them?'

'No time for 'em and nor 'ave I. Worthless villains on the run from
their manors, up to no good. But the lord abbot says we must still
offer them bread and scrapings. "They are lost souls like us," says
he. Anyway, likely they'll be gone as soon as the flood waters go
down.' He grinned, heartless and confident in his own good fortune.

Crossing the garth Hildegard noticed the three from Swyne
making their way to the more distant hospitium to visit Matthew
and decided she would look in on him before she left.

The clerk glanced up as she entered and this time offered a wan
smile. 'To see the lord abbot, domina?'

'On behalf of my Prioress if I may.'

'I'll tell him you're here.'

His smile was presumably meant to convey some meaning but
it meant nothing to Hildegard. Would her name bring an invitation
to enter? Not on previous experience. Last time she had definitely
been consigned to the dog house.

The clerk was some time. She could hear the muttering of voices.

She strove to contain her impatience. She was not here on her
own behalf and hoped he understood that. About to sit down to
prepare for a long wait she glanced up as the door suddenly
opened. Hubert strode forward, reached out and took her by
both hands as she started to kneel. 'Rise. Pray enter, Hildegard.
I beg forgiveness for keeping you waiting.'

The clerk followed him out and with a smirk took up his
station again at the tilted reading stand where he was copying
something.

Confused by the change in Hubert's manner and feeling wary
she followed him in, turning to face him as he closed the door to
show she was ready for any challenge.

To her surprise he was gazing at her with a rather haunted expression. 'I hope those beggars at the gates didn't cause you any trouble?'

'Not really. I had a fellow from the priory with me.'

'Good, good.' He threw her a distracted glance. 'I would not have you accorded less than the honour you are due.' He gave a glance round as if unsure where he was then recalled himself enough to indicate a bench. 'Please, do—'

Amazed at the change in his manner she watched him go to his own chair, the one she privately disparaged as a throne, and throw himself down, robes falling in disarray until he pulled them together and fiddled for a moment with a sleeve caught on the wooden arm.

This was not how she had expected to find him. He was never in confusion over anything.

'So tell me,' he began at last, turning luminous eyes on her, 'what brings you here?'

'The Prioress sent me for two reasons, one, to find out how you are and if you need any help from us, and two, to keep an eye on the twin of the missing novice.'

His eyes darkened. 'Is she still missing?'

'Yes—'

'Then we must expect the worst. It astonishes me that this murdering fellow has not been found despite our efforts.'

'It could be anyone, although a stranger might be noticed.'

'But there are no strangers now the flood has cut us off from the outside world. We are marooned. Both of us. I mean – I at Meaux and you over at . . .' His voice trailed off.

'That makes it worse, somehow.' Trapped. It made her shudder. Deciding to keep to practicalities she kept her voice firm. 'May I ask if Matthew remembers anything more?'

'I believe his story deviates in no way from what he first told our infirmarer. I wondered if anything relevant had been rumoured among your novices – with the greatest respect,' he added uncharacteristically.

'Nothing, my lord. However, I pray you may grant me time to visit him while I'm here?'

'How long do you have permission to stay?'

'Until shortly after Nones.'

'Then you will have time. The twin you mention—?'

'She was being conducted towards the hospitium when I crossed the garth just now. The conversi escorting her have instructions to find Brother Egbert to stay with her until she's ready to be taken back to Swyne.'

'Then maybe I can ask you about Leonin?'

'He's overjoyed at having his vielle sent on. He was quite overwhelmed.'

Hubert's expression softened. 'That is a real delight to me,' he murmured.

Despite this the ice between them, or something like it, remained.

'I suppose there's nothing new to be told about Leonin's flight from Sheen?'

'I trust he will see the sense of speaking out . . .'

When he tailed off Hildegard wondered if she should leave as he seemed to drift into a trance and she waited to see what, if anything, he might add. After a moment or two she began to get up, murmuring something about going to visit Matthew, but he put up a hand.

'The truth is, Hildegard, after several days of meditation I do have something to say to you . . . I . . . not now, not yet . . . not today . . . I beg for more time . . .' He jerked abruptly to his feet. 'Come, let me have a look at my young priest in the hope of giving him encouragement.' As he moved towards the door he added, 'I know full well what it's like to have a broken leg, and to have two of them? Poor fellow, he must feel trapped and useless as I did at Netley Abbey.'

He avoided her glance, no doubt remembering how helpless he had been, unable to move when his life was threatened. Their glances suddenly meshed and Hildegard wondered if he remembered what else had passed between them. A blush warmed her cheeks and she lowered her head. How things had changed. It was impossible to understand him.

Before opening the door Hubert rested one hand briefly on the wall beside her and gazed into her eyes. She was burningly aware how one small movement could bring his hand down and – and the thought must have crossed his own mind at the same moment because he hurriedly stepped back, putting a distance between them, fumbling for the door-ring and dragging the door back with an exaggerated flourish as if to allow some protecting agency to enter from outside.

In the corridor, away from the dangerous intimacy of his private chamber, he smoothed his sleeves as if they were ruffled by a power outside his control. Hildegard stiffened her spine, conscious of his eyes boring into her as he walked behind her towards the double doors onto the open garth.

# SIXTY-FOUR

With the wind battering at the doors rain hurtled inside. Hildegard stepped back. In the short time they had been talking the storm had renewed its fury. The garth was awash, paving stones running with water to make it look like the surface of a lake.

Oblivious to it and already drenched, Hubert leaned towards her. His words were cryptic. 'We shall talk, Hildegard, I promise that. First I must beg your forgiveness. Whatever happens, this is all there is. We two. There is nothing else.'

What on earth could he mean? His lips looked as if they were made to be kissed. Confused, she turned her head away. *I am over all that*, she told herself. *I am over it. I am well over it.*

# SIXTY-FIVE

He matched her step for step as they waded across the garth, and when they slowed with something holding them back from re-entering the world of others they seemed gripped by a spell, by a barrier of ice that could not be melted. The paving stones on the higher ground glistened beneath their feet.

Unable to move away she warned herself, *This is heresy. There are no spells.*

But they were both caught. She could sense that what weakened her resolve to break free was what held him equally in thrall to the same cold power.

Somehow they were outside the doors of the hospitium. Rain streamed down his face as he turned to her. His eyelashes were beaded with drops of moisture.

What would have happened next she could not guess because a monk hurrying out of the building jerked to a halt in the doorway.

He fell to his knees. 'My lord, I am required to summon Brother Egbert but he cannot be found.'

Hubert was jolted back to reality and said with unexpected asperity, 'Have you tried the scriptorium?'

'My lord, how foolish of me. I should have thought of that.' He rose to his feet and, lifting the hem of his robe above the puddles, hurried away.

'Come, Hildegard.' Hubert put a hand on her wrist. 'Let's see what Matthew can tell us.'

She followed him up the stairway to the open hall on the first floor where the infirmarer and his assistants kept their records. The potions they used were arranged in glass demijohns, the liquids like bright jewels where they were lined up on an array of shelves covering the wall.

Several lancets let in enough light to enable the apothecaries to do their work but rain pounded so thunderously against the glass it drowned out all speech. Shadows crawled over the floor tiles like snakes.

Swamping the air was a mingled scent of herbs, familiar ones like thyme, rosemary, mint, borage, tarragon and some less familiar, doubtless from Outremer and further afield, their scent mingling with the sourness of dried nettles hanging from the rafters and with many other plants mingled by the skill and ingenuity of the herberers. It was heady and strange and made them turn to each other as if swept by the same powerful memory.

Hubert opened his lips to say something but was thwarted again when the infirmarer hurried forward. 'My lord,' he bowed his head, 'domina.'

'We wish to see Matthew—'

'My lord, we're honoured, follow me if you will.'

He led them into the labyrinth of corridors until they reached a long ward with partitions at head height separating the patients one from another.

Inside each cubicle was a bed. Bending over a patient with legs encased in a frame, the infirmarer peered closely at the white face on the pillows, 'Are you awake, Matthew?'

The priest moaned something unintelligible and the infirmarer gave him a more intense scrutiny, lifted the lid of his uninjured eye and remarked, 'Odd.' He glanced round. 'Osbert, here a moment. What ails Matthew?'

'Nothing, master, he was sitting up talking last time I looked not more than a few moments since.'

An assistant came over and he too lifted Matthew's eyelid. 'Has he taken something?'

He glanced at the vial on the ledge next to the bed and picked it up. 'Empty?' He glanced hurriedly round. 'How can that be?'

'It was I gave it to him.' From a corner of the cubicle a shrouded figure emerged. It was Rogella. 'Did I do wrong, master?' She turned to the infirmarer. She did not notice the lord abbot and Hildegard hovering in the passage. Hildegard was aware that Hubert had moved further back into the shadows to witness what was happening.

Rogella looked down at the patient then back at the assistant who was standing with his mouth dropping open.

'He begged me so piteously for more, I thought it only kind to let him have it. I pray I have done no harm to him.'

The assistant said nothing at all. Instead he gave a gasp and ran out, dashing between the line of cubicles while the infirmarer took hold of Matthew and hoisted him up to sitting.

'Come on, spit it out.' He glared at Rogella. 'How long ago since you did this?'

'Why, only moments, master—'

'How many "moments" as you call it? Five? Ten? More?'

Rogella gave a piteous wail. 'Oh, what have I done! That I should harm the poor young priest lying there so helpless and begging me for aid. That I should have harmed him! Oh, please tell me he is not harmed—'

She fell to her knees and clutched at the hem of the infirmarer's gown. 'Oh help him, kind master, forgive me if I have transgressed.'

'Get on your feet, you empty-headed child.' He tried to brush her away but she clung on.

Hildegard stepped forward and grasped Rogella by the shoulders. 'Stand up. Stop your noise. Someone has gone to fetch help.' She turned to the infirmarer. 'What was in the vial, master?'

'A concoction to help him sleep, to assuage his pain. An overdose could kill him.' He grabbed hold of an assistant hurrying past.

'It's all right, master. I heard. I'm going to fetch an antidote.'

Hubert revealed his presence by stepping from the shadows.

'How long has she been here?'

'Only a short while. A man from Swyne accompanied her on arrival but left to fetch Brother Egbert as instructed.'

While they were talking Hildegard was watching Rogella. The novice's manner had changed abruptly.

She rose to her feet with something like a smile of triumph. Hildegard pulled her away from the bedside and they glared at each other. When the apothecary and several others turned up Hildegard pushed her outside the cubicle and gripped her fiercely by one arm. 'Why did you do it, Rogella?'

'I told you why. He asked me to. I thought I was helping.' She gave a pert tilt of her head and the smile did not leave her face.

'Don't treat me like a fool. What's it about?'

Rogella's face contorted suddenly with an ambiguous and powerful feeling that was unpleasant to witness. She lifted her chin. 'I told you I wanted him back. Now I've got him. See? She will never get her hands on him again!'

'What?'

'I warned you!'

'If you did it deliberately and he dies you will hang for murder.'

'You'll have to prove it, domina. No one will believe that a young, innocent novice like me would do such a diabolical thing. What a suggestion! They'll see it as you, a wizened up old nun, scheming against her rival for the love of a young priest and spreading lies about her out of spite.' She lowered her voice to a harsh undertone. 'I know which one of us most people will believe. They will hunt you down and burn you as a witch before you can get near the hanging tree!'

'You're mad!'

'Mad for love, nun. What's wrong with that? I made a vow before God. I would allow her to borrow him but afterwards he would be mine!'

'You've tried to kill a man out of *jealousy*?'

'She was always our father's favourite. He can tell the difference between us even if nobody else can. If she had begged him to buy her back from the nunnery he would have done so without hesitation but she fell for Matthew and wanted to stay to be close to him. He had no idea. The lack-wit! But she followed him around like a moon-sick calf and sat right in front of him so he could see her whenever he came over to lead the service. I made her promise to help me escape. Father would never have paid for me to be released from that hell-hole even if I'd pleaded with him on bended knees. But he would do it for *her*! He thought I needed the influence of nuns to save me from damnation! What a sot-wit! I decided that this time it was me who was going to get her own way. *I* would be the one Matthew desired. He would never know the difference! But it was she who would bring him to understand what he could do and what delicious pleasures awaited him! Afterwards he would belong to me. It was my right! It was only fair!'

She swivelled at a sound behind her and in a trice tears filled her eyes as the infirmarer came out to see what was going on.

'Master, my life will be devoted to perpetual penance unto death if I have harmed the dear priest in any way, I promise ye thus.'

She dropped to her knees again and he stared down at her in an attitude of complete bafflement.

# SIXTY-SIX

Matthew was only half-conscious when the apothecaries turned up with the antidote and after they purged him he retched violently into a bucket and the stench of vomit hung heavily in the air.

Orderlies took away several containers of everything he threw up and swilled the foul contents into the drain that ran into the sluice.

When he was thoroughly emptied one assistant held him by the wrist to count the beats of his pulse, another massaged his stomach, a third measured out more purgative just in case, and the infirmarer himself sat by him to observe how he was responding.

Egbert turned up when it was nearly over and was quickly informed of the situation.

He was incensed. 'Why did they not fetch me at once? I could have left my work and got myself here straightaway. Where is she?' He turned and picked out Rogella at once. 'Is this her?'

The abbey bailiff had been called and followed him up, leading two armed men, and they listened while Hildegard told them what had happened.

Rogella stood by, weeping, shaking her head and insisting in pitiful tones, 'No, no, no, it is all lies. I am innocent. Look at me. Do I not look innocent? This nun is lying.'

Hildegard's mouth fell open.

Rogella continued, 'How can I be to blame? I am a scapegoat. It is not my fault. I am Bella. Ask Matthew! The Devil forced me to find a way to save myself. I didn't do it.' And finally, like a refrain she must have repeated all her life, she shouted, 'It's not fair!'

The bailiff looked as if he couldn't believe his ears. 'To harm an innocent priest for nothing but a fol-de-rol of desire?' He looked askance at Rogella and when he got a chance he broke in, 'Did you imagine, girl, in your vanity, you could persuade him to leave the Order?'

Pointing at Hildegard, Rogella lost control. 'It was her! She forced me to do it! She hates him!'

At that point Hubert stepped forward. 'I overheard what you confessed. You are an approver. It is against the law of the realm to accuse an innocent person of a crime they did not commit.' To his bailiff he gave a curt nod. 'Take her away.'

# SIXTY-SEVEN

L eaving Egbert to keep an eye on matters when Rogella had been taken off, Hubert suggested they allow Matthew to rest now he seemed to be out of danger.

As they went downstairs Hildegard said, 'I don't believe she thought any further than getting rid of someone who failed her. Matthew's faith was stronger than she expected.'

'She seems to care nothing for her twin, her own flesh and blood,' Hubert observed in puzzlement.

They reached the outer doors into the garth and were shocked to discover that the storm was more savage than ever.

Wind howled over the buildings like a pack of wolves. Even the water level in the garth had risen since they crossed it and now it resembled a sheet of silver, surging against the walls to create ripples and over-falls. As the double doors of the hospitium were opened wider water swirled in across the tiles. Despite all this, the shock of what had just occurred began to thaw the ice between them.

Hubert took her by the arm. 'You cannot return to your priory in this. I'll tell them to make space for you in the guest house.'

He told someone to fetch a large waterproof and as soon as one arrived he lifted it over their heads and together they stepped outside into the storm. It was strangely intimate underneath the canopy. He whispered, 'Forgive me. I am suffering a deep confusion of the soul.'

# SIXTY-EIGHT

After he left her at the guest house she went into the refectory to find two elderly Benedictine nuns ensconced close to a roaring fire. They were playing chess but offered to stop when Hildegard entered.

She insisted they continue. 'I need to consider everything that has just happened,' she told them. 'I'm feeling rather shocked.' To the inevitable questions she told them only that a young priest had been taken ill and foul play was suspected. Given the worsening weather, she was being allowed to stay overnight. They were sympathetic on both counts.

'We're marooned here by the weather too,' they told her. 'We shall ask a servant to stoke up the fire and bring in another jug of their spiced wine. We'll be dry and comfortable enough here. Fear not.'

Despite the warmth of their words Hildegard felt misgivings. Rogella's blind hatred, strong enough to make her feel no guilt about attempting murder, shocked her deeply. The bailiff would hold her overnight in the abbey prison before taking her by boat to Beverley when the weather allowed. She would be held in custody until the Sheriff could deal with her.

Despite knowing that Rogella was safely locked up she still felt uneasy. The abbey precinct was not the haven of security she had always taken for granted. Outside the walls in the black woods lay a further threat. Her thoughts flew to Leonin and she prayed that he was safe from harm in his sanctuary at Swyne.

And then there was Hubert.

# SIXTY-NINE

Josiana and her fellow astronomer at Haltemprice Priory had predicted catastrophic floods. Hildegard had not forgotten that. She assumed, though, that they would be the result of heavy rain because the Humber, wide and shallow as it was, gave only onto marshland stretching across the Riding, extensive enough to absorb any excess.

The real danger, as she later understood, would come from the big spring tide sweeping unhindered up the estuary and meeting the surge from several already over-flowing rivers – the Don, the Ouse, the Aire and Calder, and other smaller ones, discharging their waters into the estuary from both north and south banks.

The time calculated for this tide was two nights hence, at the full moon.

Hubert was not slow to tell her that his abbey would be as safe as God and man could make it, should the worst happen. He made a point of reassuring her of her safety when he invited her to eat with him. Despite his confidence, the approaching danger as the moon grew larger could not be ignored. That he was secretly worried beneath his bluff assurances was shown by the way he explained in detail how the abbey's defences worked.

'The guest house where you are staying is on the highest part of abbey land within the protection of our outer walls. There is no chance that the waters will ever rise to that extent. Beyond our walls is a well-drained network of ditches and canals. We have our monks of long ago to thank for beginning such work. I'm content to say we have improved it and taken care to build up the dykes too.' He gave a small frown. 'The time of greatest danger is not yet here – but we are prepared, believe me.'

A young monk waited on them but otherwise they were alone.

Candlelight glowed in every nook and on every surface. It shed a soft light over the chamber, picking out the sheen of silver and the sparkle of crystals. Feathers of light brushed Hubert's handsome features as he went on to talk lightly of other topics of shared interest.

She watched him intently and offered appropriate responses but she was not convinced. Despite his efforts he was ill at ease. The wine was good, she noticed, and as always the food was plain but tasty. Even hoping to make up for his previous tainted humour, as it seemed he was trying to do, he did not deviate from the Rule: simple living, Cistercian austerity, nothing to excess – which made his previous behaviour all the more perplexing.

Still wary and as much mystified by his recent hostility as ever, she understood that she was expected to avoid anything that could lead them into forbidden territory. As he went on about the floods and made predictions about the time it might take for things to return to normal, she was haunted by his ambiguous remark that he begged to be forgiven. For what? Arrogance? That had never bothered him before.

Now they both avoided any comment about his penitential excesses of the previous weeks.

It felt awkward. She knew they were skating on thin ice.

The sounds of the monks going about their duties in distant parts of the house might forge the impression that the place had returned to normal. When the attentive young monk came in and out with various additions to the meal and the door closed behind him, Hubert astonished her by saying, 'All we need now is some music.'

Music?

He continued, 'Such a pity Leonin is across the water at Swyne. I hope your Prioress is not incommoded by his presence?'

'She's happy to help,' Hildegard managed to reply. 'He is no bother. He seems content to stay in his chamber away from – from this man he fears.'

Hubert quickly changed the subject. 'The wine,' he told her, 'comes as a gift from an abbey in France for help we gave them when writing up their chronicle recently. It's good to share our knowledge. They are fortunate to have a most skilled illuminator in their scriptorium. Not one of these scribes who travel here, there, and everywhere, but a fellow aged and fixed and happy to remain where he is.'

He recalled one of his own scribes, the old man murdered at

Meaux when they themselves had been in Avignon, and he remarked how he missed his humour and his astonishing skill as well as his endless kindness in small things.

'But his work lives on,' he finished as the young monk attending them re-entered with a message.

'My lord abbot, the bailiff begs me to inform you that he is about to risk it and take his prisoner to Beverley at once. A short break in the rain makes him want to get back before the floods make it impossible.'

'As we're nearly at an end here, we'll come and see him off.' Hubert glanced over the table with its empty platters and raised his eyebrows at Hildegard, 'That is, if you feel so inclined?'

Hildegard rose with alacrity. Fresh air, the company of others – it would prevent the development of any dangerous turn in the conversation as he was clearly not going to explain anything.

Feeling that there was still much to forgive she replied, 'It has been a pleasant evening, my lord, especially in such dire circumstances. My gratitude for the privilege.'

He caught her glance and unexpectedly held it. 'You see,' he murmured so quietly that the monk clearing the table could not hear, 'we can do it. Decorum can be maintained, can it not?'

'Decorum?' She bowed her head as if it was all she wanted. 'Indeed, my lord.'

When she glanced up his head was tilted on one side, his eyes gleaming, the old look lazing over her face that turned her heart upside-down, and said, 'The question, my lady, is one we may both hazard, full of common sense though we both are. It is how long will decorum last?'

Hurriedly allowing the monk to place her cape over her shoulders she barely waited for Hubert to follow before stepping outside into the blustering wind in the garth.

Out here the air was sharp. The moon, bulging almost at its full, was partly concealed behind layers of cloud, its shining rays outlining the darkest of them. The garth itself was as black as a bottomless well.

One of the conversi carried a swinging lantern and by its light led them towards the gatehouse. Hildegard felt only relief to have escaped the very thing she most desired.

# SEVENTY

The large, leather-covered coracle owned by the abbey had been brought round to the foregate by following the line of the moat enclosing the outer wall. It was now beached on a diminishing strip of land closer to the prison where Rogella had been held than the temporary quay down by the lay-brothers' quarters.

A crowd had heard about the novice's departure and gathered in an over-excited mob at the entrance to the abbey.

Faces loomed out of the darkness in the lurid light of the lanterns as they swung to and fro. A few monks genuflected when they noticed their abbot's approach. Outside the gates the habitual beggars, depleted in number, jostled at the water's edge, and a team of conversi looking to offer help where they could forced a path for their abbot.

Hubert had a brief word with the bailiff, gave a glance at the hooded figure in custody, and turned back. He found Hildegard staring in puzzlement at a face in the crowd.

One of the beggars had detached himself from the rest of his fellows and stepped forward with his mouth hanging open. Half covered by a scrap of sacking thrown over his shoulders, he stared at Rogella like a man transfixed by a ghost. He took a step forward as if to put a question but then hesitated.

The bailiff's men handed Rogella into the coracle and took their places on each side of her. Meanwhile the beggar had stumbled forward with the same stunned expression and one hand reaching out. The boatman cast off.

Silence fell as the craft lurched across the watery expanse and disappeared almost at once into the void between the trees bordering the usually well-trodden track to the abbey.

Hildegard was still observing the beggar as he stumbled back to join the rest of the crowd. He did not speak to anyone but merely ducked inside the shelter erected when the flood cut them off.

'Hildegard?' Hubert, oblivious of the glances thrown their way, shook her by one arm. 'Are you all right?'

She came to with a shudder. 'I felt—' She glanced up at him. 'No matter. I'm exhausted by everything – it's been so strange – all that has happened—' She gave a nervous laugh. 'It's making me start at the shadows of shadows!'

'Sleep then. It's what you need. Don't come out for Matins. That's an order!'

He edged her away from the others to say, 'Tomorrow I'll make sure the flood has receded, the sun is shining, and we'll take the hawks out and have a glorious ride in the woods!'

She couldn't help smiling. 'If only!'

'At least stay safe indoors tonight then. I'm told to expect the worst tides yet. Unlike me my astronomers are rarely wrong.'

Walking as far as the doors of the guest house he left with a brief blessing and she trailed back alone up to her empty chamber.

# SEVENTY-ONE

I t seemed as if she had barely fallen asleep when a commotion outside woke her up. The bell for Matins must have been tolling for some time because its deep booming ceased almost as soon as she opened her eyes. But it wasn't that – it was a hubbub out in the garth.

Remembering the turmoil caused by Leonin when he arrived in the dead of night at Swyne she was about to turn over and let the monks deal with it when curiosity got the better of her. More than one man was involved. A chorus of shouts made it sound like a small army thumping their fists on the gates.

Dragging herself from the bed she took a few paces to the window and peered through the shutters. By angling her head she could look down into the garth immediately below.

A lantern above the porch shed a circle of light. A group of conversi armed with clubs tramped past. Flood water still covered the garth to the height of their boots. They began to run in the direction of the gates.

Alarmed, she rammed her feet into her own boots, grabbed a cloak to pull over her robe, checked for her knife, and opened the door. The whole house was asleep. With not a sound darkness closed over her.

Pressing one hand along the wall as a guide she made her way step by step down the unfamiliar stairs, with both arms outstretched, and felt her way towards the shape of the door outlined by a sliver of light from outside. The bolts took an age to find and prise open and all the while the turmoil outside increased.

Shrouded under waterproofs, she let herself into the garth. Once more rain was beginning to patter down. Despite this the garth was busy. It was not only the conversi roused from their prayers, monks carrying flares were swarming from the west door of the church. In the fractured light Gregory and Egbert appeared among them. The familiar shape under Gregory's cloak showed he was carrying a sword. She waded through the increasing flood waters towards them.

Gregory caught hold of her. 'Come no further, Hildegard. There's trouble at the gatehouse. Somebody sounded the alarm just as Matins started!' He splashed up to his knees through the flood water after Egbert.

The shouting increased. Fists hammered against the great wooden doors to demand entry. Peremptory questions were being demanded by the sub-prior of the rowdies he recognized on the other side. Men's voices, surely shouting in terror? She heard the porter calling for calm. Managing to make out a few words she heard the men on the other side continue their shouting to be let in.

A voice was bellowing above the others, 'Save us, brothers! Let us inside! Mercy on us! For the love of God!'

Unable to return to bed until she knew what was going on she approached as close as seemed wise and was drawn into a group of bystanders like herself, trying to find out what was happening without getting in anyone's way.

They heard someone shout, 'We're going to open it! Get your swords at the ready!'

And Gregory countering the command, 'I cannot draw my sword against unarmed men, least of all those roofless fellows on the foregate. Let only one or two of them in and listen to what they have to say!'

The flares flickered garishly over the faces of the monks as they argued what to do but eventually the gate was grudgingly opened just enough to allow several shrouded figures to enter. A row of conversi with clubs at the ready stood behind the unarmed monks and more shouting followed.

A monk waded over to the group Hildegard had joined. 'Did you hear what they're saying? They've seen a headless woman!'

'Sot-wits!' The group roared with laughter. 'Is that what this is all about?'

Hildegard's thoughts immediately flew to Bella. She didn't laugh. Did it mean they had found her body?

She asked, 'May we know where they say they've seen such a thing?'

'Where? That's just it.' Another monk, knee-deep in flood water, gave a derisory guffaw. 'The lack-wits are saying she was floating above the trees! They've all had too much drink. That's my opinion.'

'Let's hope that's all it is.'

It couldn't be Bella. It wasn't a body, floating in the water.

'Worry not, domina,' someone standing next to her said. 'This isn't the first time they've succumbed to mass hallucinations.' He said to the others, 'I'm getting wet out here. This rain is beginning to bucket down. Let the other fellows sort it out. They won't stand for any nonsense. Mark my words,' he added as he waded off, 'tomorrow morning Abbot de Courcy will clear this useless rabble of drunken beggars off our land and restore order. Let's go! Back to Matins!'

He splashed off into the darkness followed by the rest of them to where the church doors stood open allowing the radiance of candle-glow to spill out into the night.

While they were talking the gates were being forced wider by the urgency of the beggars outside.

Hildegard happened to glance towards the guest house and drew in a sharp breath. A man was running in a crouched fashion alongside the wall. She glanced to the now departing monks but nobody else had noticed and when she glanced back there was no sign of any running man.

At the same moment a group of conversi marched up to the spokesman for the beggars, pushing him and his companions back then putting their shoulders to the gates until they were able to force them shut. The beam was dropped back into place. Cheers from those within were countered by jeers from those outside.

As everyone began to return to the church to complete their interrupted service, Gregory came up. 'All over, Hildi. If they're seeing ghosts it means they'll have sore heads in the morning, the superstitious sot-wits! We're going in to Matins. Are you coming?'

'Hubert said I needn't. I—'

'He did, did he?' Gregory gave a jerk of his head and waded off before she could add anything.

Undecided, she stood for a moment as everyone began to disperse. Had she really glimpsed someone running alongside the wall?

There was nothing to see now, no gleam to show where he was, and the nearest large building was away across the garth. Without coming out into the open it was the only place he could have gone.

Reached through a small yard and beyond a stretch of open space was the hospitium. Her heart leaped into her mouth. Was that where he was heading? To where Matthew was lying helplessly in bed?

The more she thought about it the more unlikely it seemed. What she had glimpsed as having the shape of a man must have been a trick of the light. Or maybe it was one of the conversi in the usual dark clothing they wore, definitely not a monk in white, but a lay-brother, yes, hurrying back to where he lived to fetch something, a weapon, maybe, not realizing that the ruckus would soon be over? That would be it. She was as bad as the beggars, imagining things that were not there.

But still the suspicion nagged.

It was his crouching manner, suggesting stealth, and the fact that he was alone, intent on where he was going, that made her wonder about him – if he was not merely a phantasm of the imagination.

It was too late to call Gregory and Egbert back. They had followed everyone else into Matins.

If she wanted to she could run across the garth, the water was not too deep. She could have a quick look in the ward to ensure that Matthew was safe, and return to her bed in less time than it took to sing Salve, Regina.

Resolutely she waded off across the garth as fast as the water would allow.

# SEVENTY-TWO

The yard linking the open stretch in front of the hospitium with the garth was as black as pitch. She could hear water lapping at the walls. With every step a glint of light rippled over the surface, broke into fragments, then dissolved into the darkness.

Whirlpools sent waves bumping against the stone walls before surging back with a force that caused her several mis-steps but when she reached higher ground the waves subsided and the only hazard was mud, skidding under her feet as she made a meandering rush towards the guiding flares shining out from a bracket on the hospitium wall.

She pushed open the great doors into the shadowy vault of the entrance chamber. A lone clerk was sitting on the far side behind a tilted desk with a fat candle beside him. It seemed as bright as the sun and she had to blink to see properly.

The clerk raised his head. 'Is the trouble outside done with?'

She reassured him and after a hasty greeting asked, 'Did someone enter not long ago, brother?'

'Only one of the monks, domina. May I help you?'

She felt a wave of relief. 'A monk, I see. It's only that I would like to look in on Brother Matthew if I may?'

The clerk smiled. 'You may. He wakes and sleeps to his own tides,' he replied, 'much like the waters at present. How is it outside? Raining again?' He glanced at her wet cape dripping onto the tiled floor.

She nodded. 'Still it falls. So I may go up?'

'By all means. Would you like me to show you the way, only I don't like to leave my post—'

'No, you're busy. I know where to find him.'

Hastening along the corridor she ran quietly up the steps into the ward. One or two lights flickered here and there to illuminate the passage between the rows of partitions, otherwise the place lay in a velvety darkness. Counting off the cubicles until she came to the one Matthew occupied she went in.

He was lying as before, legs encased in the wooden contraption, but he opened his eyes at the slight rustle of her robes as she entered. At once he seemed to become fully conscious, his eyes bright and piercing unlike the last time she had seen him.

'I have remembered something, domina – is he still here? I said, "What do you want?" and he just laughed and disappeared!'

'What are you saying, Matthew?' She moved closer.

'I couldn't believe my eyes. I said, "You? What do you want?" I can't move to defend myself and he could see that. I thought he was a monk at first. Then I saw who it was. He laughed when I asked him what he wanted. He said, "I've just had a shock." I said, "If it's a shock for you it's a shock for me as well. What do you want?" Then he gave a cackle and vanished. What do you make of that, domina?'

She went to sit on the edge of his bed. 'Are you still dreaming? Who was it? Who vanished?'

'That stranger I told you about. I did tell you about him, didn't I? How we met him in the grove – yes, yes, of course I told you – you rescued me – the water, it was so cold, you would not believe water could be so – am I awake now? It was like a bad dream. I said, "Have you come to try again?" This time I was ready to throw a glass at him. But he vanished.'

'I think you've been dreaming—'

'He was no dream. I can tell you that! The stink, excuse me, the smell of putrefaction, like a devil from hell, as we might imagine them. You know where they say friars live, don't you? Worse than being there I would imagine!' He wafted the air with one hand. It was true, the smell of putrefaction did seem to drift about but she took it to be no more than usual in a hospitium for the sick and dying.

Matthew leaned forward. 'I asked him, I said, "What do you want?" And he laughed again. So I demanded, "What happened to Bella?" And he said, "Don't ask me, how should I know? She's a witch. They've taken her away." And then he backed out and I heard him hurrying off down the corridor.'

'Matthew, you said when I came in a moment ago that you'd remembered something? Can you recall what it was?'

'Quite surely, domina. I'm clear about it.'

'Would you like to tell me?'

'We were in the grove. Even now I blush to think of it. And this stranger, this same man I've been telling you about, he appeared from out of the bushes giving us both a shock and asking for the abbey and I got to my feet – I regret to say I'd been reclining somewhat at ease beside Bella on the bank of leaves and dreaming of paradise and how it must be akin to this – and, as I got up about to tell him the way, he asked me if a minstrel had visited recently and I said – maybe out of annoyance at being brought back to this world, although I should praise God I was prevented from falling ever deeper into sin – I said, "Who wants to know?" At which he took umbrage. That's when he drew the knife on us and took hold of Bella – and the rest you've heard. Now I'm wondering, how did he know about the minstrel? And now,' his face blanched, 'I have made such a foolish mistake. Twice over, to be honest. Once by my attitude, and again, not realizing what the answer to my question must be: who wants to know? I know now who he must be, this stinking brute of a man, bless his immortal soul. Who else would want to know if the minstrel was here but the assassin who is pursuing him?' Matthew began to cry in silence. Tears tracked down his cheeks. 'I shall mortify myself when I get out of here. I shall mortify my body with whips. He was here, domina, a few moments ago, but why? Where did he come from? . . . Why do you think he came to me? Do you think I'm dreaming? Am I? Maybe I am. Was he a figure out of a nightmare sent to mortify me further?' With tears still trickling down his cheeks he started to mutter a prayer.

Hildegard watched him for a moment or two. Had he been dreaming? He was disturbed in mind. He was not himself. She could see that. Even so, shivers ran up and down her spine.

She went to the opening in the partition and poked her head out. Apart from a few snores and restless turnings in bed the patients were undisturbed. Shadows lay like bars across the floor as far as the wall at the far end.

As she stared, she saw a blur take shape. It slowly resolved into a standing figure. When she blinked it was gone. She caught her breath. Am I dreaming now? she asked herself. A backward glance showed that Matthew was still murmuring a prayer.

With her heart in her mouth she decided to risk it and ran as quietly as she could between the beds to the far end where the figure had been but when she got there she found only a blank wall with off to one side only a small cupboard door.

Striding over to it she pulled it open to discover not a cupboard but a flight of steps leading down. Ducking her head she was about to descend but hesitated. There was no sound. Nothing but a dead silence.

I'm as mad as Matthew, she told herself. Hadn't the clerk in the entrance chamber told her that a monk had entered shortly before she arrived? Now, here she was, running around after shadows with her imagination flying ahead of her reason. Of course it was fantasy to imagine that he was inside the abbey. How could he be? It was the impression of a figure skulking along the wall in the garth that had raised a feeling of disquiet.

She returned between the beds of sleeping patients and only once glanced over her shoulder, back to where the apparition had been standing. There was nothing there.

Matthew was lying as if exhausted.

'Did you go away? And return?' He spoke in a dead sort of voice. 'I thought I'd imagined you. It must be something they made me drink to purge the poison from me. Did we talk? Are you real? I hoped you would come back. I wanted to tell you what happened. I could not keep the disdain from my voice. That was what caused it. If I had answered him with civility maybe he would have left us alone? "Who wants to know?" I demanded. Poor Bella,' he began to weep again. 'I hope she fares well in paradise.'

'Matthew, I'm going to ask the clerk to send one of his assistants to you. He can sit beside you and you can tell him anything you want. This is what the monks are trained to do. I have to go elsewhere now but tomorrow, during daylight hours, I will return. Sleep now if you can, but someone will sit by you.'

'He will have no difficulty in finding me.'

Not knowing whether he meant the assistant or the man who had left him to die at the mill she went down to speak to the clerk.

If they had not insisted on escorting her back to the guest house she might have found an excuse to avoid stepping into the darkness again but fortunately for her self-esteem there was no question that she would not be accompanied by a couple of monks she already knew.

The garth lay like a black lake as they stepped into it then it broke into a million contrary ripples. If anyone had preceded them they would have left a similar trace of their movements on the water, more visible than any footprint in sand.

When the monks heard about Matthew's dream, as they called it, they agreed to have a search for the intruder on their way back but it was clear they only half-believed in a mysterious figure watching from the end of the ward then vanishing.

'Matthew needs rest after being purged and the shock of what happened earlier. We'll make sure he's well attended. In the meantime, worry not, domina. We'll have a look in every nook and cranny on our way back. But it's a fact that if anyone had been this way the waters would not be unruffled.'

They waded away as soon as she was safely inside the building.

When she went up to her chamber she placed a bench across her door. It would not stop anyone from entering but the sound would wake her and give her time to defend herself.

# SEVENTY-THREE

The first thing she noticed was the silence. It was unnerving. On previous mornings the roar of incessant rain sluicing into the gutters greeted everyone. Now a plenitude of blue sky opened and she could see sunlight entering through the slats in the shutters and lying in stripes across her blanket.

When she looked out she saw that the garth was still flooded and a million silver shards danced across its surface.

Guessing it must be late she splashed water from the jug over her face, dragged her robe over her undershift, stamped about in her boots to press the moisture out of them and, grabbing her cloak, removed the bench from the door and hurried down to the refectory. The two Benedictine nuns were playing chess by the fire as if they hadn't moved since the previous evening.

They greeted her with their earlier warmth while still keeping an eye on their opponent's next move.

'What excitement last night, domina. Did you hear? We assume you were out in the thick of it. Prime has been and gone, by the way.' One of them poured a cup of wine from the jug and pushed it over to Hildegard.

She took it and went to sit near the fire and tried to dry her boots by resting them on the edge of the andirons. 'I heard the commotion. Some story about a headless ghost?'

'Oh that, no, that was all made up, it's what happened afterwards.'

'What was that?' She sat up.

'One of the beggars was found in the precinct and a scuffle followed! Luckily no one was hurt and they were able to throw the fellow out. He was last seen trying to find a path round the moat, no doubt hoping to steal a coracle from the lay-brothers where they dock theirs in the open. But if that was his game he would have been sorely disappointed. Somebody gave the alert and they had guards sitting up all night. But he never even showed up and some believe he must have drowned in the attempt while others have decided he managed to wade to his chosen destination, wherever that might be, far from here, we would hope and pray.' She drew a breath. 'My move, I think, my dear.'

She knocked one of the pieces off the board and continued. 'He won't get far while the floods last. He's going to have to swim! They say he's something to do with that minstrel who played for us the night we arrived, do you remember?' She turned to her companion for a moment. 'Most talented. I'm told he was a court musician but was only passing through because the next day he too had disappeared, we know not where, and the beggar, the one we thought was an alms-man who they threw out, said he knew him and was trying to catch up with him to convey a message from his lord if someone would only help him find out where he had gone to.'

'Is that what they say?' Hildegard replied without committing herself. She could guess what sort of message he wanted to convey.

'It seems innocent enough. But that's not all. There's a rumour that the Abbot, dear handsome fellow that he is, has a lady nun as a friend and is sore lovelorn because they cannot be together – you know, because of their vows? We wonder how that might end. It cannot end well because in my opinion both would have to break their vows together. It wouldn't do for one of them to do so and risk hell-fire only to find they were suffering alone. Now, how can you persuade two people to act in concert when they are even forbidden to speak to each other on pain of excommunication?'

'But many conversations are held among the monastics—' Hildegard began.

'Even so, my dear, it is not an easy situation. Far better if they were to eschew the flight of passing fancy and remake their vows to their Order in front of the entire congregation without quibbling. Not that I can see the lord abbot here doing any such thing. He's a most vigorous and practical man. Nor is there anyone less likely than he to give up the prestige of being abbot of Meaux merely for love. I hear the revenues here match their sister house at Fountains! Sheep, of course. You Cistercians were very astute when you decided on sheep. We poor Benedictines have to get by as best we can with our leases and rents. I'm sure there's nothing in the story about the nun,' she added to round things off. 'You know how people talk!'

'It lightened our evening,' said the second Benedictine, who had until now been unable to get a word in. 'We two are chess-mad, a minor sin, I'm sure, but it can become tedious and cannot stand against the more interesting dilemmas of everyday emotional strife indulged in by the laity.' She chuckled. 'We do like to gossip. Pilgrimage is such a pleasure in that way – always someone new to catch our attention. I mean, who would imagine there would be a ghost here at the abbey! The very idea! Of course it's nonsense, but it does add a little salt to life, don't you think?'

'One I would rather do without. I rather fear that sometimes these stories have a basis in fact.' Hildegard regarded the two nuns seriously. 'I myself thought I saw a ghost last night. Of course, on this lovely morning I now realize I was mistaken. Even so, it made my hair stand up at the time.'

They were both avid to hear her story, so she told it to them, adding a few frills, and a more lengthy description of what the ghost had done before vanishing into the wall.

Afterwards she was ashamed.

When Gregory and Egbert turned up at Lady Mass she confessed to them what had happened and what she had told the chess-players.

'But you're not making it up,' intervened Gregory. 'You did see someone, and you felt it looked like a ghost. That is factually true, is it not?'

'And anyway, you look as if you've seen a ghost,' Egbert concluded in a tone that said it clinched the matter.

It was then she told them of her plan.

'Bearing in mind the story the Benedictines told me, it does seem odd that this fellow should simply disappear. Thrown out, they said, if it's the same one. I believe we would be fools not to try to find him.'

'So you believe what Matthew told you? It wasn't merely that you woke him up from a strong dream?'

'I do believe him, yes. He says he recognized him.'

'And you fear this alleged assassin may still be lurking around somewhere?' Gregory frowned.

Ice crawled up her spine. 'Who knows? No one can say for certain where he went.' Shadows seemed to fall darker across the nave where they were talking.

# SEVENTY-FOUR

The plan was simple and obvious. It involved a thorough search of every corner in every building within the purlieu. It involved everyone, the conversi especially as they knew all the places where hobgoblins lurked, and the novice monks and the choir monks all came out and did what they could.

Under a brilliant sky not even the most nervous denizen feared to rattle a broom in every cupboard and corner and under every stair. The result was nothing. He could not be found. No one was lurking within the enclave. There was no assassin, no headless woman. Ghosts did not exist.

As for the beggar who had been thrown out during the night of what was beginning to be called the Riot of the Beggars, he was assumed to have been drowned as no reports had been received of anyone appearing wet and covered in mud as they would be if they had undergone a journey of any sort through the flooded pastures surrounding the abbey.

'That's that,' asserted Egbert. 'It's the last we'll hear of assassins. He'll have given up and moved on.'

Hildegard was not so sure and her uncertainty must have shown on her face.

Sitting later on with the two monks militant within the hortus at the back of the guest house where they could enjoy having dry feet for a while she picked a few sprigs of mint and held them to her nose.

'There really was someone in the hospitium,' she told them. 'The smell, Matthew particularly mentioned it. He likened it to the – the place where friars are said to dwell!'

'You mean in the devil's arse?' Egbert grinned.

She nodded. There was a fresco on one of the walls in a small inner chamber showing just that, a crowd of black-robed friars swarming under his tail while the Devil himself leered and brandished his pitchfork.

'Every other time I've been inside the hospitium it smelled as sweet as you could wish, with sage and mint and such like, and the resin they burn in that little dish with the candle under it.'

'They do make sure it's as pleasant as possible for their patients,' Egbert agreed. 'The devil's arse, though! Is that what Matthew said?'

'Not in so many words but it was what he meant. And it was true, it was a horrible stench. It was like that stink of men-at-arms who never wash and—' She hesitated out of delicacy, but Egbert spoke for her.

'They fill their breeches with shit and don't seem to mind. We came across that sort of thing when we were on the road to Jerusalem. Isn't that so, Gregory?'

'It's something I try to forget,' he replied with a look of distaste.

'But don't you see,' she resumed, 'it means someone did go in to visit Matthew.'

'This elusive assassin?'

'I can only guess. Maybe he heard that Matthew was alive and wanted to find out if it was true?'

'Or,' interjected Gregory, 'maybe he heard about a new patient – and wanted to find out if it was the man he was pursuing?'

'Tracking down his prey . . .?' Egbert sat up. 'You may be right. So what will he do now he knows it was not Leonin?'

'He'll continue his search. He cannot give up.' Hildegard rose to her feet. 'The next place he'll look will be Swyne.' She began to move away. 'I must get back, the nuns must be warned – but for this accursed flood we could be there before Tierce.'

'We can and we will. I'll go and speak to Hubert now.' Gregory stood up as well.

'And I,' added Egbert, 'shall go and commandeer one of the boats. Come on, you two, let's go!'

# SEVENTY-FIVE

B y the time Hildegard had gone up to fetch her things the porter had been told what was happening. He beckoned to her as she came out with her bag.

'Brother Gregory instructed me to beg you to go to the quayside as we're calling it, the one behind the lay-brothers' house. Brother Egbert is holding a boat for you. I hear you're off back to Swyne?'

She agreed she was, asking, 'Brother, you remember the beggar who was leading the others at the gate when they were trying to get in—'

'Because of this headless ghost?'

'Yes, can you tell me when he arrived here?'

'Not above a couple of nights ago. It was shortly after Brother Matthew was brought in with his poor legs broken.'

'Where did he come from?'

'We don't question the beggars. It's our duty to give alms freely, poor devils. Nobody would choose to live in such shame and we see it as kindness not to question them too closely.'

'Did he say anything about himself?'

The porter shook his head. 'He had a lot of opinions. This lord and that lord, the good, the bad. A bit of a troublemaker if you ask me. But saying nothing much about himself.'

'No names?'

'None.'

She took her leave.

When they were being sculled back over the waves sent by a once again strengthening south-westerly she ventured to mention something the two monks might find interesting.

'It may have been tittle-tattle,' she began, 'but one of the Benedictine nuns mentioned that the beggar who broke into the precinct last night was merely trying to convey a message to Leonin from his lord.'

'So how came the fellow to pass for a beggar if he was in the retinue of a lord, manorial or wherever? A retainer mistaken for a beggar must have a lord in poor straits for him to go around like a roofless losel.' Gregory's remark sounded reasonable and as neither monk had anything else to add, the matter was dropped.

Soon they were beaching outside the gates of the priory on a diminishing stretch of the foregate.

# SEVENTY-SIX

F lood water was creeping up the outer walls and soon reached a height of three feet or more. The moat had been brimming over for days. It still felt strange to Hildegard to arrive at Swyne by boat and have to be rowed along a path between trees half their usual height now most of their trunks were underwater. Thankfully the great storm predicted by those said to know about such things had not occurred. On such a bright, cloudless day, it seemed unlikely that it ever would.

Egbert told the lay-brother from Meaux to wait for them in the boat and after they were waved through the lodge gates they splashed across to the precinct.

The Prioress was surprised to see the two monks. 'No change here,' she told them. 'We've been preparing for this much-vaunted inundation but so far our efforts seem superfluous. How are things at Meaux?'

'We've had some excitement,' Gregory explained, rising from his knees and rearranging his robes. He told her everything that had happened and what they imagined about Leonin's pursuer.

'Our purpose here is because Hildegard believes this alleged assassin may have thought it clever to follow him here. It seems a not illogical assumption to us.'

'The lad's safe enough,' the Prioress concluded after listening carefully to the rest of his story. 'But I do wish we could resolve the issue. Leonin plays the dumb ox when it comes to explaining what it's all about. Our courier has left for Sheen. I thought it better that he went there to check out his story about having to flee. Hubert was uncommunicative about his own emissary's report. Frankly I have no wish to harbour a man at risk of being declared outlaw without knowing something of his case. I fear he might be a traitor although my instincts tell me otherwise. Of the fellow allegedly in pursuit I've heard nothing. I'll send someone to question the lay-brothers but I'm sure they would have informed me immediately if he had been sighted trespassing on our land.'

After they left she turned to Hildegard who had been sitting quietly most of the time. She raised her eyebrows. 'So, you believe this fellow Matthew says visited him has made for Swyne?'

'None of the lay-brothers at Meaux had anything to say – no boats were missing as apparently they sat up all night to make sure he did not escape at their expense. They've also searched everywhere. It seems he got away somehow.'

'We have no newcomers. None that have been reported. If he had arrived by boat he would have been seen. There are only a couple of places where he might come ashore. Both our gates are well guarded. Matthew may well have been hallucinating. Everyone here is being turned mad by the unprecedented floods. The prospect of a full moon tomorrow night doesn't help keep them sane.'

'Madness may be a possibility,' Hildegard agreed.

'Judging by your expression you are not convinced?'

'It's more the fact that we simply do not know where this fellow is. Matthew was very convincing. I believe he would swear on the Bible that he was visited by the same man who tied him up and left him to drown. If it is true, he will know what happened to Bella. First he was in one place and now he's in another. But where? People do not disappear.'

'Bella has disappeared as nearly as makes no difference,' the Prioress pointed out. Her face creased with anxiety. 'I cannot believe the dear girl is still missing. Not a sight nor sign of her have we had. Matthew was in a faint and cannot tell us what happened. We must redouble our prayers for her safety.' She turned to her altar but then glanced back as Hildegard prepared to leave. 'If this vanishing man tries to gain entrance to our priory he will regret it. That is my solemn vow.'

# SEVENTY-SEVEN

n some kind of way Hildegard was glad to be back at Swyne. Only now she was safe in her own sanctuary was she aware how much she had been set on edge not only by the fear aroused at Meaux by the rumours of ghosts, headless women and an assassin, but also by the different kind of fear at encountering Hubert and being swept up in something she could not control. Something, she now admitted to herself, she did not want to control. It was back. Her own private madness.

What was it the Benedictines had said to her only this morning? "Such a liaison cannot be. They must renounce it in full view of their brothers and sisters." It was true. Every minute she remained at Meaux she had been aware of Hubert's proximity and how the heat of desire could lead them down to hell.

*Decorum*, she repeated to herself. Yes, that was her watchword for the future.

The next thing was to visit Leonin in his secret chamber. Maybe he would throw light on the situation now he had time to think things over.

Before she had even emptied her boots and placed them with others in the entrance to the hospitium she could hear the lilting melody of a familiar chanson floating on the air. The voice was fine and clear and the vielle that accompanied it was being beautifully played.

One of the orderlies stopped to listen. 'We are blessed,' she announced. 'Every day he sings and plays for us. We're utterly beguiled by the sound.'

'It answers my question about how he is today. Has he said much?'

The orderly shook her head. 'Not a word!' Smiling, she bustled off to her chores.

When Hildegard tapped on the door of his chamber, the music

stopped, there was a scuffling sound and a nervous voice asked, 'Who is it?'

'Hildegard.'

The door opened. 'So happy to see you, domina. I trust you've had an interesting time at Meaux?' He swept it open with a smile. 'Pray enter.'

'So you'd heard nothing of this?' she queried after she told him of the previous night's events.

'We hear nothing on our sequestered isle, nor do I in my lone cell at the heart of the labyrinth.' He gave her an ironic glance. 'I feel I owe you an explanation. It might be safe to tell you something now that the assassin has disappeared.'

He stood up with the vielle still crucked in one arm and walked about as if ordering his words. He turned to her. 'This is for your ears only, domina. May I have your word?'

'Of course.'

'Then you see, it started like this.' He indicated the bench by the window and sat facing her in the embrasure. 'It was when our dearly beloved queen was taken ill.' He paused, moved by the strong emotion sweeping over him. Gaining control he continued, 'We were at Sheen Palace as you know. One minute she was as hale as you or I, and the next day she was dead. You can imagine the shock to us all. The appalling grief. How could it be? Although they muttered about plague no one else went down with it at that time. Only she. There was no sense in it.'

He got up and went to sit on the edge of his bed but got up almost straight away and began to pace the little chamber. 'You can imagine how the king felt? He adored her. She was his light. His life. If he could have died in her place he would have done so without a qualm. She was his protector against all the dirt and slime his barons slung his way. She made everything right in the world. She was the guardian angel of the king and of his realm.'

'I heard he brought down the palace stone by stone with his own bare hands such was the tempest of his grief?'

'He ordered his men to pull it apart. It was of wood, not stone.' Leonin gave a dry smile. 'No doubt one day they'll build it up again in stone but he wanted never to have anyone set foot there again. All was destroyed, all the little follies and pretty arbours, the lawns where he and his courtiers danced, even the wooden footbridge linking the isle to the palace gardens, all destroyed. I sang there for him often. It was a retreat where he could be himself and forget the ugliness of the outside world, a place where his barons, his war-mongering uncles, could not reach him. At least, that is what we all thought.' He pursed his lips and gave her a darting glance. 'I have to tell you this, domina. We believed the king and queen were safe there. But it was not so.'

'What do you mean?'

'This is what I have to tell you. While she lay dying I was playing for her and when they understood that all life had flown and the maids came to lay out the body, I stayed. I felt bereft, quite unable to understand that such a beautiful and kind young woman, our dear Anne, had gone from us for ever. It was impossible to comprehend. Such light, such life! How could it be snuffed out in a moment? As I was sitting grief-stricken in a corner of the chamber after the maids left, someone entered to view the body. It was the Duke of – no, I will not say his name yet, only to say I was stunned to see him of all men and when he spoke to his chamberlain who came with him I was aghast at what he said. I froze in horror.'

Leonin paused then lowered his voice. 'I thought, if he notices me after what he's said, I'm dead. I held my breath. He turned for the door. I thought, he has not noticed me! And out he went. But then, just as I was about to get up, he turned back.

'Our eyes met. His, narrow and vindictive, mine no doubt wide with horror, and without words we both knew what had happened. I thought, he's going to strike me down! His hand moved to his sword. But just then a group of courtiers in mourning appeared in the corridor and he had no choice but to leave the chamber, his glance piercing me as if to remember every lineament of my features.'

Hildegard held her breath. 'And then?'

'That was the night when my friends warned me that some men had arrived, as I told you – they were armed to the teeth and asking for me – assassins, my friends guessed at once – and they urged me to flee, hurrying me secretly down a backstair – and in truth they saved my life—' He glanced round and spread his arms. 'I am saved for this lone cell. But any life is better than none, is it not?' He brushed the back of one hand across his face. 'So that is the reason I fled, on account of something I heard.'

'And the duke who—?'

'No, don't ask me to name him. Not yet. That is information for the king's ears only. Then it will be up to him to wreak vengeance if he will.'

She stayed a while longer but Leonin would add nothing more. She guessed he wanted to retreat into music, the only solace he could rely on.

Now he had admitted a little more, the names of two dukes sprang to mind at once. Neither would cause surprise. Their enmity towards their nephew King Richard was well known. Stories of deliberate insults to him, too persistent not to be based on fact, were plentiful. So what was Leonin's accusation? What exactly had he heard? She went cold at the obvious answer. But would even they dare harm the queen?

# SEVENTY-EIGHT

The astronomers had reached accord in their reckonings. There seemed nothing to do but observe events as they unfolded. The moon was following its orderly path through the mansions of heaven and would soon attain its full size at the expected hour. Nothing could change that.

Already Josiana and her group were meeting in the garth with the hope that the clouds would open like shutters to reveal the constellations and the moon in all its splendour.

Josiana was especially excited by the prospect of getting a good sighting. 'We can only guess what the shapes that make it look like a face can mean. The peasants, bless them, might call it the Man in the Moon, but we want to know more. Are they buildings like ours? Or mountains? Deserts, perhaps. Great oceans? We cannot know. But a learned astronomer in Italy is working on an eye-glass using Magister Bacon's earlier work on the grinding of lenses that, put together, will enhance our observations. Meanwhile we must make do with what we have to aid us. Whatever we discover, we remain in awe at the mystery of the moon's power over the tides – and we're prepared for the worst floods ever to occur in living memory.'

Such was the excitement about what might happen, the mysterious order had gone out, namely that sand must be carted from the riverbank before the expected hour. It was to be heaped on boards above what they guessed could be the new water level. From there it was to be poured into specially stitched bags of sackcloth and then placed in such a way as to line the bottom of all the gates, for the purpose, it was said, of keeping out the water.

Whether the wooden gates would withstand the pressure, no one knew. Some of these sandbags were even propped along the bottom of the doors giving onto the inner garth to prevent further ingress of flood water, although this was thought to be excessively cautious.

The Prioress regarded these precautions with a wry expression. 'I will not have the temerity to say a word against my astronomers. They have studied the matter. This is their conclusion. I will stand by what they say until their folly is clearly demonstrated – or not! After all,' she added in genial tones, 'what do we lose by it? We've seen how Meaux is afflicted. Their garth, as you've experienced yourself, Hildegard, is already little more than a lake since the rains. What will it be like when the rivers spill into the Humber at the same hour as the sea pushes the tide to its highest point of the year? Let them stack up their sandbags. At the very least we'll have one or two fewer rats gaining entrance to our grain stores. It is all to the good.'

No deviation in the strict attendance at the canonical hours demanded by the Rule was even considered. Despite the slow and somewhat malevolent aspect of the rising moon as it waxed in greater visibility with the darkening of the sky, everyone filed into church as obediently as always. The rustle of expectation, however, could not be ignored. Hildegard could only stand on the sidelines as an observer.

Other matters were as important, were they not? The fate of Bella, for one, the safety of Leonin, for another, and the whereabouts of a paid assassin, for a third.

It was fully dark by the time Compline was over. A brief scurry to the warming room, a drink to take up to the dortoir for the night, and the gradual slide into silence before the midnight call to Matins was what many of them looked forward to, but Josiana and her stalwarts on moon watch intended to ignore sleep. They planned to post themselves on the highest place within the precinct – the flat roof of a stores barn – and wait patiently for something, anything, to be revealed.

Hildegard joined them for a time. Her cloak was still damp and she longed to hang it up somewhere to dry. She was thinking about doing so and made a move towards the trapdoor into the barn when Josiana intercepted her.

'Will you come back when you've done that, Hildegard? I would like your opinion on what we observe, if indeed we see anything. As for the rising waters, someone has already gone down to check the sandbags at the main gate and the porteress has been instructed to warn us if the water level rises by any fraction over two inches on the foregate. Someone is also at this very moment checking the back lodge where the lay-sisters are on watch. If all goes well we should be undisturbed in our observations.'

'What do you expect to see tonight?'

'We're not sure. But it's such a huge, important moon this month, we cannot afford to let it go unobserved. You must admit, even if you doubt our expectations, the rain this autumn has been unprecedented. We know the moon exerts an effect on the seas, causing tides to rise and fall, and we fear the joint effect of excessive rainfall and the full moon bringing a massive tide will be a dangerous conjunction. You must agree?'

'I'm guided by you. Nobody round here has experienced such rains before and some are listening to your warning more carefully than others. They see the flood as a judgement on their sins. When you first started to offer warnings based on a series of tables and measurements it was difficult to believe so many acres would be inundated – but you were right.'

'We were mocked, I know,' she shrugged. 'But events proved otherwise. Folk find it hard to believe we can make such predictions. They trust portents more than facts. They feel a magpie in a tree or a murder of crows on the stubble says more about what's going to happen than any careful measurement made by means of an astrolabe.'

'It's no surprise that folk down on the manors are returning in desperation to the rituals of their grandames.'

'They know no better. They believe they can alter the course of nature by spells and incantations.'

'I suspect they're going to be disappointed.'

'We're fortunate to have the advantages of arithmetic, geometry and the writings of the learned Ancients to help us.' Josiana added, 'It would be foolish to disregard what the Greeks discovered. Ptolemy is our guide and we must make sense of the facts and build on what others have proved to be true.' She carried a little book on her belt and indicated it now. 'Here are all the tables needed to determine where the sun and moon rise and set from the equator to the River Don in Russia. It enables us to work out our own calculations. In the northern priory at Tynemouth they send us observations from their own location to supplement our own. As long as we know where we are we can make our calculations from that point and give fair warning to others. With such devastating floods already and now the imminence of the highest tide for some time we owe it to everyone to warn them what to expect. It's only fair, even though they mock and call us witches. It's up to them to heed us or not as they choose. All we can do is work things out to the best of our understanding then warn, watch and wait.'

Their lookout post gave a spectacular view over the whole, flat, inundated, once profitable sheep country stretching as far as the eye could see. The water heaved over it like a living thing.

Somewhere behind a shrug of trees to the west was the small priory of Haltemprice. The market town of Beverley lay to the northwest, like a mere smudge in the distance. Meaux with its towers and steeple was to the north of Swyne, and if they had been able to don wings and fly due east they could have reached the sea and flown across it towards the rising moon. The big threat, the over-brimming waters of the estuary itself, came from the south.

A group of interested nuns were already on the roof when Hildegard went up. It was not yet fully dark and the sun was still sending sheets of gold across the sky as it sank below the horizon. Several nuns knew enough about *scientia* as taught down at the abbey of St Albans to understand the workings Josiana and the Austin canon from Haltemprice Priory had agreed. It had also been corroborated by the monks at Meaux who were no doubt standing on one of their own vantage points this night to see what would happen.

It was a surprise when those with sharp enough eyesight made out a band of what could only be horsemen close to the horizon. They were wading slowly and laboriously through the silken sheen of crimson water that lay between Meaux and Beverley. The white towers of the abbey were visible over the treetops and the huddled roofs of Beverley were a half-imagined blur. The riders were somewhere between the two.

After a moment someone said, 'They're heading this way! They're not going to Meaux after all.'

'Who are they?'

'I can't make out whether they're a band of militia or abbey monks . . . Definitely coming this way though. They're searching for higher ground by the look of it.'

The nuns clustered on the roof amid warnings not to step too close to the edge and watched the approaching riders. They saw them straggle to a halt. Still distant it was impossible not to notice a glint of steel in the fading light. One or two small figures left the main group to cast around in the water then re-joined their companions. Nothing much happened for a while except that the riders did not turn back to Beverley but continued doggedly on what must be the higher ground of the track to Swyne.

One of the nuns sighed. 'It's going to take them an age if they're foolish enough to continue. Why can't they take a boat like every-body else? They'll never make it through all that water. How can they tell how deep it is? It's utter folly. That must be what they're discussing, the lack-wits. One false step and their horses will drown under them.'

The men continued to make slow progress and one by one the nuns turned away to the more pressing matter in hand. The instru-ment for looking at the moon was being passed round. Comments about the nature of the eyes and mouth of the man's face on the moon's silver disc were made, the supposition that they indicated mountain ranges being the most popular.

Hildegard decided there might be time before anything happened to check on the cloak she had left to dry in the warming room.

The fire was well stoked when she went in and she reached up to test the fabric hanging on the rail above it.

'Still damp?' asked a sudden voice behind her.

When she turned there was a hooded, ghost-like figure framed in the doorway.

She gave a start as it stepped forward, pushing back the hood.

'Surprised to see me, domina? I expect everyone was saying, "Poor Bella, we won't be seeing her again."' She chuckled. 'I'm tougher than I look.'

'Bella?' At least it wasn't a ghost. Her face was dead white but she was flesh and blood.

Kicking the door shut behind her she came slowly on into the room saying, 'What a relief to escape from that murdering knave at the mill!'

*It must be Bella*, thought Hildegard uneasily.

She came to warm her hands by the fire, chatting in a cosy manner that belied her words. 'I decided,' she said, 'that I would have to come back to settle a few scores, you know? He can't get away with it, can he?' Her smile revealed long yellow teeth. 'Nor can anyone, with what I've had to put up with!'

*Or is it Rogella?*

'I'm glad to see you safe,' Hildegard managed to say.

'I'm safe all right.' She made a small movement with her fingers inside one of her sleeves. 'But what about you, my dear Hildegard, are you safe, do you think?'

'What do you mean?' Hildegard felt herself freeze. The hairs on her scalp rose. Who was this? The hostility beneath her easy manner was almost palpable.

The garments she wore, those of a novice, were mud-stained, water-stained and marked with something like dried blood and when she reached out to take the kettle off its chain she held it, steaming and bubbling, in one hand as if considering what to do with it.

'A tisane, my dear domina?'

*Bella?*

'Not at the moment—'

'Too many other distractions?' She chuckled again and put the kettle to one side. 'No, "safe" is not the word I would use about your situation at present, my dear.'

*Rogella?*

'Who are you . . .?'

'You see? You don't know who I am!' She gave a trilling laugh. 'I'm Bella. And what a time of it I had at that mill! You wouldn't believe what happened to me.'

*Bella then?*

'Poor Matthew could only lie there like a helpless fly about to be swatted. Was he worth saving, do you think?' She gave a mirthless laugh. 'I think not.'

*Rogella.*

'And, domina, after bringing him back I beg to suggest you've made another mistake. You hope I'm Bella. The good twin who wouldn't harm a fly? And maybe I am!' She gave another trill of laughter.

*No she's not – she's—*

'But what if I'm Rogella?' She lowered her voice. 'What then? What if I'm the bad twin? What if, dear domina, I'm back and bent on revenge?'

'I don't understand you. Whichever twin you are you can have no cause for revenge, you're a free agent, you've caused what happened – or do you believe your actions are directed by the planets? That's debatable, but what is not debatable is how you can have a quarrel with me, or with anyone here—'

'No?' She took a step closer. Then as if without reason she adopted another tack. 'Tell me, has he reappeared yet? After he finished with me he must surely be back on the trail of the so-called royal minstrel. He'll have his nasty little knife well sharpened to deal with him, I don't doubt. Did Matthew tell you what happened? Poor Matthew. He thinks he's safe in his bed at Meaux with his legs trapped inside that wooden box but I can promise you, nobody betrays me. He will not live another moon. How dare he – well, you know what happened. Those gossiping monks were probably only too delighted to spread their lurid descriptions of a novice being raped. It was only what she deserved, they must have said. Did you imagine I would run back to them for safety after that? I've been hiding in the lay-brothers' store-sheds here, living off scraps like a teeny little mouse in my hidey hole.' She chuckled again. 'So now you're sure I'm Bella. Or are you? Which twin do you prefer?' She spread her arms.

'Why did you not return to Swyne at once and let us know you escaped from the mill?'

'And leave Matthew unpunished?'

'Unpunished? Did you tie him up?'

'Don't question me, you nun!' She took a step forward and lowered her voice. 'You have no idea who I am. You're asking yourself, is she the nice twin, the one everybody favours? Or is she the nasty one they all hate for her cruelty to spiders?' She suddenly drew the knife from her sleeve. 'I'm going to show you how cruel I can be when you cross my path. Why didn't you leave him to die? I'm going to carve you, nun, and that abbot will never look at you again. Better, I'm going to bleed you the way you monastics bled me with your rules and your judgements and your penances and your disdain. The things you said to that bailiff!' She stepped closer. 'Nice or nasty, which am I?' Before Hildegard could get to grips with the way her mind flew in one direction and then another, she said, 'If I'm Bella, how can I know what you said about me when you tried to turn the abbot's bailiff against me? I must have been standing right next to you and that means I'm Rogella,' a laugh trilled again, 'but if that's true how can I know what happened at the mill? Answer me that if you're so clever!'

'You know what happened at the mill because you heard Matthew talking about it in the hospitium.'

'That priest! He should have died by the cure I gave him! That would have been comical! And he would have died if you hadn't interfered!'

'Whichever twin you are, I believe you may be genuinely confused about your identity. You happen to have picked up different rumours and now you're trying to piece them together with what you've witnessed. You're trying to make me believe first one thing and then another. You hope to confuse me so you can get the better of me. You think I doubt the evidence of my own eyes? I'm not so persuadable! You are Rogella and I believe you might be mad—'

Before Hildegard could move she saw a flash of silver as the blade came at her. Protected by the speed of her reactions she was in time to duck, then grasp the wrist that held the knife and pull downwards, unbalancing Rogella – or, still in slight doubt, Bella – but before she could do anything else the novice slammed bodily into her, toppling them both into the hearth piled with burning logs.

Flames ignited their robes in an instant. A stench of burning stamyn arose. Hildegard screamed and, struggling against her attacker's dead weight, batted at the flames with her bare hands.

Flames coiled round them as the two women struggled among the burning logs. The novice, instead of rolling away from the fire, seemed oblivious to it and came at Hildegard again while she was struggling to rise to her feet. She was gripping her knife, poised to ram the blade into Hildegard's face, but was suddenly stopped, letting loose a shriek as flames ignited her cloak. The pig fat used to waterproof the cloth burst into flames and towered over her in a column of raging heat.

She attempted to rise, but fell back with another howl as her hair caught fire. Both hands went up to stifle the flames.

At that moment someone opened the door and gave a shout of horror.

It was Josiana. She hurled herself across the room, shouting, 'Away from the fire, Hildegard! Get away!'

Quick-witted enough to notice the knife still gripped in the novice's hand she grabbed her arm and forced it easily from between her fingers to throw it across the room.

Hildegard, scrambling to her feet, kicking away the novice's cloak to free her from its folds then tried to drag her away from the fire.

'It's not fair,' muttered the twin, still struggling as Josiana helped haul her to safety. She lay groaning in a heap of smouldering fabric.

Hildegard gazed at her in astonishment. 'It is Rogella. She must have escaped custody.'

'Probably the men we saw on horseback were the Sheriff and his men looking for her,' Josiana suggested.

Hildegard turned and opened her arms in gratitude. 'Thank heavens you arrived in time!'

With a cry Josiana ran forward and the two nuns embraced.

As it happened, others followed Josiana down from their moon watch and quickly crowded into the warming room, bustling round Rogella who was half-conscious with the pain from her burns. She was frantically trying to pull away the smouldering fabric that was still sending up coils of smoke.

Somebody gripped her hands, warning, 'No, leave it! You'll bring your skin off!'

Snarling she reared up in her smouldering garments, screaming to be let go and trying to force her way towards the door. 'Stop interfering! Get out of my way! I am Bella! I am better than her! I am better than any of you!'

She struggled outside, despite their calls to come back, but her animosity was so overwhelming most of them hung back until someone looked out into the garth saying she was nowhere to be seen.

Josiana observed, 'She will not get far. There is nowhere to run.'

One of the nuns stood in the centre of the room and in tones of fear and dismay announced, 'We came to warn you! The hour has come! The estuary has burst its bounds sending enormous waves thundering towards the priory. We are directly in their path. Now all we can do is pray that our defences withstand the assault!'

# SEVENTY-NINE

Everyone ran up to the lookout on the roof and gazed in alarm at the sight that met them as countless rows of black waves marched towards them across the plain. It was a terrifying sight.

There was no apparent end to them.

It was little solace to see that so far they only ran up to the perimeter of the orchard but the slope on which the priory stood was only shallow and soon the first waves began to surge between the apple trees with unstoppable force.

In the distance as far as the eye could see was nothing but the grey moonlit waters and the dark menace of the oncoming waves.

Barricades against the inundation were hurriedly reinforced. From the stockpile of sandbags more were hurriedly added to the ones stacked across the gates. Shadowy figures filled more bags with sand from the heaps while others hurried back and forth to pile them against the weaker sections of the defences. Soon the waves could be heard battering at the outer walls.

Hildegard hurried down from the roof with Josiana and, about to cross the garth to help secure the gates, they were alerted by a lot of shouts and saw several nuns, robes flying, running towards the strip of dry land where the boats were beached.

Alarmed, Hildegard glanced at Josiana. 'What's happening? Has the wall been breached?'

They changed direction and arrived in the middle of an argument between several nuns standing at the top of the orchard with a figure already knee-deep in the flood. Waves hissed up the slope and surged against everyone's legs.

Josiana put out a hand to grip Hildegard by the sleeve. 'Is that—?'

'Rogella! What's she doing?'

Several figures broke away from the group at the top of the slope and ran into the water as a wave receded but they thought better of it as another one roared up to meet them. The figure standing lower down stumbled with the force of the surge, regained her balance, and continued to wade out towards the moorings. Voices called her back in vain.

They could see her trying to release one of the boats, all the while shouting defiance at the nuns begging her to return to safety. 'You can't stop me!' she was yelling at the chorus of voices. 'Leave me alone! I'll do what I want!'

She was tugging wildly at the boat's mooring and when she loosened it she tried to push the craft onto the water as it drained back over the mud and when the boat bucked in a counter-current bringing it close again she managed to throw herself inside. Grabbing a paddle she began to scull furiously away, shouting about how she would never return.

When she reached deeper water she stood up and yelled, 'I hate you all! I always get the worst of everything! You cannot stop me!'

An extra-large wave scudded the boat briefly towards the shore but then dragged it out again. She emerged on the other side into the flat, shimmering waters that lay behind the crest. Very quickly the flimsy little craft had to rise to meet the next wave. It plunged out of sight down the other side.

Everyone waited to see it emerge but there was nothing except silver, and dark, and silver again, and nothing resembling a boat. They watched and held their breath but the surface of the water was a moving darkness with ripples of silver crossing a void.

Eventually someone dared ask, 'Where is she?'

At once the whispers started, 'Why does she not come up?'

'Can she swim?'

'There's too much undertow. She'll never fight it.'

'She's gone.'

Silence fell as they waited with eyes fixed on where she must surely emerge. Somebody murmured, 'She knew what she was doing. She'll be keeping out of sight to scare us.'

Hildegard and Josiana stood on the water's edge but there was nothing they could do.

'Could she have got away?'

'The horsemen we saw earlier found enough hard ground to stand on,' Josiana pointed out.

'It's difficult to make anything out in all this shifting moonlight.'

They waited to see if they could do anything practical but there was nothing obvious. One or two called her name. A few prayed. Some waded a yard or so into the water as the waves receded but ran back when they hissed after them like snakes up the slope.

Josiana turned to Hildegard. 'The flood may reach equilibrium now the shock of breaching the embankments has taken place. It might find its own level. When the tide ebbs the land could drain back to normal.'

'Do you really think it will?'

She shook her head. 'I think there's too much water coming down from the hills to allow it to drain away yet.'

Hildegard kept scanning the surface. 'There's no sign of her. I wouldn't know where to look – I'd expect to see a shape—' She did not say "body" as that would be too final.

'We must expect the worst,' Josiana agreed with less delicacy.

# EIGHTY

Unsure whether Rogella had made her escape or not, they reluctantly appointed a couple of lay-sisters to keep watch for her and then made their way back to stand guard over the main gates with everyone else as the tide continued to batter them. So far the walls had withstood everything the raging waters could do.

Moment by moment the moon crawled to its zenith. Its light rivalled the sun but the faces of those who glanced up shone like silver, like wraiths, their white robes gleamed.

Time passed, held on a breath.

Everyone fell silent. They did not know what they were waiting for, only that something was coming to fruition, bursting to a climax in some way they could not measure.

Without any particular sign, shadows began at last to reappear in the nooks and crevices in the precinct. First the stone gargoyles standing out in previously unrevealed detail began to shine against the blackness as the sky changed colour. Less drained by brilliance, they became themselves again, sinking paradoxically into chiaroscuro, shadows again drawing a veil over the sharply carved features of griffin, phoenix and devil's minion.

After a little more time passed even the thumping of the waves against the outer walls began to decrease, the fear of an overwhelming inundation began to subside, and the waves weakened and fell back, eventually collapsing and leaving only a harmless lapping at the foundations of the outer wall. Finally they made no sound at all as they were drawn fully away by the ebb.

In the direction of the estuary in the far distance, as tide and tributaries merged, the last sound to be heard was no more than a drifting sigh of waters draining back into the sea.

Movement returned to the garth.

Everyone began to walk about with the awkward gait of people released from a curse.

Some who did not yet know about the ambiguous disappearance

of Rogella smiled without bothering to say much, while others greeted their reprieve with a melancholy awareness of the potency of the moon.

Others yawned and left their posts where nothing but a trickle of water had appeared between the sandbags.

Soon the bell for Lauds began to toll from the high tower. It was a joy to hear. It established the strength of human life against the ferocity of nature.

They had survived.

The power of the moon would threaten over the following nights but it would never be so dangerous again. It was already diminishing and with it the great waters were in retreat.

Men's shouts outside in the woods eventually alerted them to visitors. Recognizing them they hurried to unbar the double doors onto the foregate quay to reveal a wide, shallow-drafted wooden boat about to beach. It contained a party of monks from Meaux.

On hearing their shouts, nuns appeared from the cloisters and hurried to the waterside, Hildegard among them.

The abbot was the first to step over the side onto the temporary quay. He called through the gloaming, 'How fare you here at Swyne, sisters?'

'Safe, my lord abbot. And yourselves?'

'We have survived!'

The abbot made his way at once to Hildegard, saying, 'We feared for you but the boat could not be put to the water because of the strength of the surge. Coming over here just now was like being a leaf wafted over by the zephyrs themselves as the tide ran back into its proper channels.' He added in a lower tone, 'How fare you, my—' He bit off what he had been about to call her and gave her a speaking glance.

'A lot has happened,' she told him.

'We must speak more privately as soon as we can.'

Monks were clustering into the outer garth now the boat was safely beached, forcing them apart.

Everyone was laughing with relief that they had somehow come through the ordeal unscathed.

Hubert took command. 'We observed a band of horsemen apparently riding this way from Beverley and assumed it was the Sheriff with his men. They were too far off for us to identify but we saw them reach the road where it runs along the top of the dyke. Using it is a fair risk. We pray they make it safely.'

'We hope so too, whoever they are.'

'So everyone here is safe within the walls?'

'Only one unaccounted for.' Hildegard told him about Rogella and her disappearance after she took one of the boats from its mooring.

He peered at her. 'I thought I could smell burning. Your sleeve? Are you hurt?'

'The thickness of my garments protected me.'

'Praise God.' He touched her wrist. 'And Rogella? Is there more?'

'We did our best but we lost sight of her in the surge after the tide roared in.' She told him how it had battered at the stone foundations and how they feared the walls would be brought down but they withstood the onslaught, thanks to the masons who built them. 'I doubt whether anyone could have survived it in only a little boat,' she concluded, crossing herself.

'We'll send men out to search for her – when the ebb allows. There's nothing much more to be done beyond what you've already done. When the sun is high enough we'll be able to spot anyone—' He hesitated. 'Anyone trapped in the mud.'

His expression was grim.

'Come to the refectory,' Hildegard invited. 'I'm sure the Prioress will expect us to offer you something for your attendance here.' She sent a servant to inform her of their visitors. 'I know she'll be relieved to hear you're safe,' she told him as they headed towards the guest quarters attached to the gatehouse.

Before they reached the doors the sound of horses was heard in the stables on the other side where guests usually stabled their mounts. 'The Sheriff's men,' Hubert guessed.

Hildegard stared with astonishment when she noticed a tall, rangy, blond-haired knight striding onto the outer garth followed by some men-at-arms. It was Ulf of Langbarugh.

Hubert noticed him at the same moment. Both men came to a halt and eyed each other.

'So those were your armed men we saw heading this way?' Hubert greeted him without a smile.

Hildegard ran forward a pace then, conscious of Hubert's eyes on her, came to a halt, but she could not contain her delight. 'We saw you too! We were on the roof. We were worried when we saw you trying to find a way through the flood waters,' she exclaimed. 'I'd have been even more worried if I'd known it was you—' She couldn't help adding, 'But of course I should have known you'd be one to try to cross on horseback! No wonder you're drenched! How foolhardy you are—' Still unable to keep the smile from her face, she added, 'We were calling you lack-wits and many other uncomplimentary names!'

'York sent messengers to Castle Hutton to tell us the Humber was about to burst its banks. Everybody was standing by to help but we had no idea it was as bad as this. We didn't think we'd reach you—' He took a step and looked as if he was about to sweep her into his arms but she gave him a warning glance.

He looked over her shoulder and noticed Hubert again.

Both men simultaneously took a pace forward. Then Ulf strode decisively to Hubert, made a swift obeisance, then punched the abbot heartily on one arm.

Hubert replied by thumping Ulf on the back. 'Stout fellow,' he said, 'Good man. Thank you for coming. She's quite safe.'

'It was Lord Roger who insisted – but to be honest,' Ulf grinned, 'I'd have come anyway once we heard how bad it was going to be. I should have known you'd both come through.'

'You're fortunate to inhabit a drier, higher part of the county,' Hubert observed. 'Roger's a good fellow for thinking of us.'

'We all think of you – all the time,' Ulf murmured somewhat ambiguously.

The two men turned to where Hildegard was standing. She was looking bemused but showed her delight at having them both safely here. 'I think it's to the refectory for us all, isn't it? We can tell you about how resourceful we've been here at Swyne and how our arithmetical nuns have furthered the story of *scientia*.'

# EIGHTY-ONE

U lf's band of men, wearing the emblem of Roger of Castle Hutton – Hildegard's guardian from the old days when she was a wild girl growing up in the castle – was augmented by the militia of the Sheriff's retinue and both groups now joined the arrivals from Meaux.

With their attendants it made quite a crowd in the guest refectory. The two Benedictine nuns put aside their game of chess and looked on everyone with beaming smiles. Kitchen staff darted in and out with constantly refilled jugs of ale or wine for the abbot and others who wanted it and they somehow produced hot bread to feed everyone with a supply of permitted food even though it was outside the hours.

Sitting at the long table with everyone jostling in together Hildegard was eager to hear Ulf's news from the north. The main event was about Lord Roger's fifth wife who had given birth to another son and, as the Prioress had said a little while ago, despite her youth had managed to tame Roger at long last and bring him to heel.

'He's nothing but a dancing bear!' Ulf exclaimed. 'Absurdly uxorious!' He banged his tankard up and down on the table with hilarity as his men mocked their lord's overthrow by a mere girl, as they saw her. 'Who would have thought the old devil would be defeated by a lass?'

'Time enough for you, Ulf, so don't start crowing yet—' his captain chipped in with a grin. His men, relishing the good ale made by the nuns, agreed with jeers and cheerful warnings about what lay in wait despite Ulf's determination to stay free.

Hubert, strangely, seemed to be enjoying the general mayhem created by the men and Hildegard wondered how he managed to conceal his pleasure in rough banter from his more prim and rigorous monks. He caught her eye and gave her one of his heart-stopping smiles that always swept her into another world where anything could happen.

One of the Sheriff's men leaned between them to pour himself more ale from the jug. As he did so something caught Hildegard's glance but Hubert was starting to tell her about one of his falcons and the moment was lost in the hubbub.

By general consent the men took their ale onto the garth where the rising sun was already turning the puddles to steam. From a high window came the sound of a vielle accompanied by Leonin's pure voice.

'There he is, like a lark singing the new day in,' she remarked.

Hubert looked into her eyes. 'I'm glad you approve.' His expression was sombre. 'We must contrive to meet soon, Hildegard, I need to—'

'If you're sure we can meet with enough decorum?'

'Don't jest. I'm never so happy as when I'm with you . . .' He hesitated before adding, 'Remember I told you I had something to tell you?' When she nodded, he said, 'You may not wish to see me when I tell you what it is.'

She smiled fondly. 'I doubt whether there's anything you could say – unless it was to tell me you're being sent to Cîteaux to run the abbey there!'

'I doubt whether they would ever in any circumstances make me head of the Cistercian Order.' He frowned.

'Do you mind?' she asked, startled that his thoughts might ever turn that way.

He shook his head. 'There's too much I dislike about the Order. I would be a reforming abbot and they would soon drum me out of Cîteaux!' He chuckled. 'My ambitions do not lie within the restrictions of the monastic world.' A slight frown crossed his handsome features. 'I do have ambition, but not in the way the Conclave would approve.'

A man pushing hurriedly out of the refectory between them crossed the yard. He was a stranger and had been the one to reach out for the jug of ale. Hildegard's glance followed him as he turned in the direction of the hospitium and strode briskly towards it.

She glanced at Hubert with a start of alarm. 'Do you know where Leonin is lodged?' She pointed up to the window overlooking the garth where Leonin's song could still be heard.

'Apart from singing is he making himself useful?'

She stared at him in confusion. 'He beguiles everyone with his music—'

'What was he playing just now?' He sang a few bars then stopped when he noticed her expression. 'What's the matter?'

'Hubert! . . . I have had a most terrifying thought! Come – quickly – it's Leonin – we mustn't waste a moment! Follow me!'

She began to run after the man-at-arms who had just walked by and was now entering the building where Leonin was cooped.

# EIGHTY-TWO

S he shouted back over her shoulder as she raced after him, 'Was that one of the Sheriff's men who just crossed the garth?' She had scarcely noticed him nor whether he was attached to one group or another. He could not be one of Ulf's men because they all wore the de Hutton emblem on their tabards. There was no one at that moment to ask and no time for questions.

Hubert was pounding after her. 'What's the alarm for?'

'The fellow in the chain mail? Who is he?'

'Never seen him before—'

'Nor have I. We must stop him getting to Leonin! His life is in danger!'

Without further explanation she reached the hospitium and burst inside with Hubert close at her heels. The desk clerk looked up. 'He's gone up to see him,' he announced. 'Did you send him?'

'In chain mail?'

'Yes—'

'Quickly, Hubert! Stop him!'

Without saying more she hurtled up to the next floor with Hubert in pursuit. Together they trod two at a time to the top where Leonin had his haven, reached the long corridor, stone walls echoing with the sound of steel boots marching ahead, heard them stop followed by a distant slam, and the vielle breaking off in mid-phrase. It ended in a shout then silence.

She was breathless with fear. 'It's the assassin!' she managed to gasp. 'I saw his ring! He was one of the beggars at Meaux. Leonin is trapped!'

Hubert pushed her to one side. 'Let me!'

'Careful!'

'I must save him. He is my son!'

He sprinted down the length of the corridor towards Leonin's cell.

Hildegard faltered.

When Hubert reached the door she saw him put his shoulder to it but it was evidently locked on the inside. Banging with both fists he shouted to have it opened.

Something within crashed to the floor.

'Open up!' Hubert bellowed. He stepped back a few paces then hurled himself at the door like a battering ram but it would not yield.

He turned as Hildegard ran up. 'Is there another way in?'

'Only through the window from the half-roof next door.' As he turned she said, 'Wait, I may possess a key that fits.'

But he had already gone and she heard the noise of shutters being slammed back followed by silence.

Fumbling through the keys in her scrip and aware that many locks in the priory were similar, she tried first one then another until she felt the mechanism turn. She pushed her way inside.

Leonin, still clutching the vielle, was backed into a corner wearing an expression of pure terror as the assassin slowly unsheathed a sword. Before he could drag it free a shape appeared at the window and without pausing Hubert launched himself through the air, knocking the swordsman flying and sending both men crashing to the floor as they grappled for mastery.

The assassin managed to free his sword from the tangle and raised it to slice downwards but it missed as Hubert clawed to get an advantage. The man grasped the sword more firmly and swung it at Hubert's head but he could not have known the abbot had been a knight-at-arms in France and now he was taken by surprise when, robes flying, he rolled out of danger while managing to give his opponent a crushing punch in the face. Momentarily stunned the man brought his sword up again but the sweep of his arm was badly directed and only caused harmless sparks as it hit the paving stones near Hubert's feet as he rolled out of the way.

Nose streaming with blood, the swordsman brought the blade down again and again as Hubert evaded it but when it came down for the third time it pinned the abbot by the sleeve to a nearby wooden bench.

With a roar he ripped his sleeve away leaving it in shreds and, driven by greater fury, managed to grasp his assailant round the throat with both hands. The veins bulged as he increased his pressure.

The assassin retaliated by drawing up a mailed boot and kicking out but despite catching a vicious blow to his thigh Hubert squeezed harder on the man's windpipe until the sword loosened from his grasp and clattered to the floor.

Hildegard came to her senses and grabbed the fallen sword, lifted it, unsure where she was going to strike but Hubert reached in one movement and took it from her grasp.

Choking for breath, eyes blinded by blood, the assassin was on his knees. 'Enough! I yield!'

Hubert growled. 'Get up!'

The fellow was crouching on the floor gasping for air and when he didn't comply at once Hubert prodded him with the sword. 'Get up. Now!'

The man struggled to his feet, rubbing his throat, coughing and knuckling blood from his eyes.

Hubert forced him against the wall with the point of the sword. 'Drop your knife!'

The man pulled a dagger from his belt and threw it at Hubert's feet.

'Is that the only one?'

'Aye.'

'So tell us,' demanded the abbot, 'what's your quarrel with this young minstrel here?'

'I've no quarrel with 'im,' he grunted. 'It's a job, ain't it?'

'Who retains you?'

'It's more than my life's worth to tell you that!'

'At present your life is worth nothing. His name?'

Though at a disadvantage the fellow lifted his chin in defiance.

Hubert poked the point of the sword against his throat in the manner of a man with no qualms about using it. 'His name for the last time.'

With a curse the man spat, 'Woodstock, if you must know. So what are you going to do about that, abbot?'

'I'll show you.' Hubert pierced the mail shirt, hooked the point of the sword into a damaged link and cut it through. Steel rivets scattered to the floor. 'More?' Hubert's expression showed he was in deadly earnest. He pressed the point of the man's own blade into the fabric of his gambeson underneath the mail and tore a hole big enough to pierce the flesh beneath but before doing so he asked, 'Why the boy?'

'Don't ask me.' The man shrugged, eyes darting. 'I do as I'm told. I get paid. End of story. I'm not Woodstock's confessor.'

When Hubert jabbed him as if about to ram the blade between his ribs he put up both hands. 'Hold off! It's a job. He overheard what they'd gone and done. Not worth losing my life over, is it? Live to fight another day, eh?'

'You're an optimist.' Hubert stepped back a pace. There was no doubting that he would use the sword if provoked further.

'Ask him if he murdered Lydia,' Hildegard suggested.

Hubert pressed the sword into his flesh through the gambeson. 'You heard. Answer her.'

'You mean when the boat landed? How was I to know? I thought it was 'im.' He gestured towards Leonin which brought another twist of the sword from Hubert. 'I followed 'im across the water. He thought he'd give me the slip. When I landed somebody was grovelling about in the dark. It was pouring rain again. I couldn't see who it was. I thought, attack first, question later. That's the rule.'

'So you killed an innocent maid and threw her body into the Humber?'

'It wasn't my fault! What would you've done?'

Hubert did not deign to answer.

'And the novice at the mill?' Hildegard asked.

'I didn't do nothing. Tied that priest up. Left 'im. She got away, thought she'd drownded. Then she turns up as a ruddy ghost with the abbey bailiff!'

'My bailiff,' Hubert remarked.

As he edged him further into the corner Leonin had abandoned, the man whined, 'I didn't know you abbots was supposed to fight.'

'If you're working for Woodstock you don't know much about anything.'

For the first time Hubert glanced towards Leonin. 'Did he hurt you?'

'Not me. He nearly damaged my vielle though.'

'Shut that window behind you. Lock it if you can. Then go outside with Hildegard. This fellow is staying here under lock and key until someone fetches the Sheriff and his men. Then they can take him to York and hang him – unless Woodstock cares to redeem him.'

# EIGHTY-THREE

Hildegard turned the key in the lock as they left and when they emerged into the yard and Hubert's story was heard a couple of guards were sent to stand outside the chamber. The Prioress was informed. She ordered her nuns out of harm's way with instructions to clear up after the flood and then to attend the next Office. Order looked as if it was about to be restored.

Ulf announced that he was taking some of his own men up to supplement the guards already there but he came down almost at once. He looked baffled.

'There's a couple of Sheriff's men guarding an empty chamber. What's going on?'

# EIGHTY-FOUR

When more men swarmed up the stairs and into the labyrinth of corridors they confirmed that the chamber was empty. The shutters fixed to the embrasure swung back and forth over the gaping window.

One of Ulf's men leaned out. 'He must have jumped onto that there roof. It's a fair leap. After that, though, he could easily climb over the tops and try to get out over the walls.'

Men from both units rushed down into the garth and were deployed in several directions to see if they could catch sight of him.

Their search was curtailed when one of the nuns coming out of the refectory with a mop and bucket gave a loud shriek. 'Look! Up there on the roof!'

As everyone clustered to see what she was pointing at they were amazed to see the assassin still wearing his tattered mail shirt climb along the guttering of one of the buildings. When he reached the end he jumped across onto the sloping roof of the next one and began to scramble up to the roof ridge. At the top he hesitated as if trying to work out where to go next.

'He's trapped,' somebody observed.

'No, he's not. He can climb over the ridge and slide down the other side onto the wall.'

Someone else said in disbelief, 'He'll never do it. There's a gap on the other side before you get onto the wall.'

Drawn by the sight the watching crowd jostled down the side of the building, still gazing upwards to see what he was going to do.

The mail shirt glinted as he slid down the roof tiles, wedged himself against a piece of masonry and crouched beside it.

'Look, he's going to jump!'

The assassin weighed up the distance and then, with a brutal effort, flung himself onto the next crucked roof, hung on with his bare hands to the ridge and swung there until he got his breath back. Glancing over his shoulder he judged the distance then made another leap, twisting to land in the salient halfway along the wall. From there it would be a straightforward drop into the narrow passage behind the crenellations where he could run out of sight and jump from the wall to the ground outside the enclave.

After this was discussed somebody added, 'Jump down, aye, if there is any ground to jump onto and not merely mud left by the flood.'

'Mud should make a soft landing,' his companion pointed out.

'It's a long drop—'

'He'll get away,' someone murmured.

'He won't. But he's got courage, I'll give him that.'

The story flashed round that this was the man who had pursued Leonin all the way from the Palace of Sheen because of something the minstrel knew which was a royal secret and made him too dangerous to live.

Now they watched with bated breath as the ever more distant figure reappeared in the gaps between the crenellations only to disappear as he ran on.

'There's nothing we can do one way or the other from this distance until we see where he decides to go over the wall,' another voice asserted with some authority.

It was the Sheriff. He was red-faced after learning that the captive had escaped under the noses of his so-called guards. Now he wanted to make amends.

'We'll get the boats out,' he announced, calling up his posse and heading towards the quay.

Hubert had been watching intently and was already turning towards the main gates. Ulf followed.

'We can take the abbey boat and scull round the outside of the walls. The flood water is still deep on the other side. That must be where he's planning on going in. We can catch him there. He has nowhere else to go.'

'Come on.' The two men started to run.

Hildegard stared after them.

Would they be in time to bring the assassin's escape attempt to an end?

More personally, she thought, what on earth had Hubert meant when he said, "He is my son" – Leonin? His *son*?

She looked round for the minstrel to have it either denied or confirmed but he was nowhere to be seen.

# EIGHTY-FIVE

A crowd was already climbing the steps onto the outer wall where they could run single file to the point where their quarry might jump down to make his escape.

When the leaders reached the first turn they gave a shout. 'He's still here!'

It was a false alarm. When they were close enough they saw only his discarded mail shirt. It suggested he was going to try to swim for it.

The ones at the back of the line were peering over the wall as if he might suddenly turn up below them. Instead the boat came into view with Ulf sculling and Hubert standing in the bows to guide him. They were making slow progress. Mud shoaled up underneath the flat bottom and gripped the boat until Ulf was able to pole them off into deeper water.

Men on the walls were shouting down to them. 'He's gone ahead. He's going to jump.'

Hildegard listened to Josiana, who was trying to tell her something. 'What is it?'

'None of the men know about the little snicket down to the orchard,' she said hurriedly. 'Of course the trees are up to their branches in water now but if I wanted to escape I wouldn't jump and break my neck, I'd run down from the wall behind the refectory where nobody would notice me, slip through the door into the snicket then wade round until I could reach the boats—'

'He won't know about the door—'

'We don't know what he'll know. He might have been lurking around wherever he felt like it.' She shivered. 'It's worth a try.'

'Lead on.'

Both nuns hurried across towards the small door set in the wall. It opened into what before the flood was a herb garden with an orchard sloping away close to where Rogella had chosen to make her escape. The boats were tied up just beyond this higher ground.

When they shouldered the door open they saw that the flood

water came only partly up the slope and they were able to scramble over the mud churned up by the previous tide and, by keeping close to the foot of the walls, edge round to where everyone was shouting and pointing.

It was deep viscous mud as they discovered when they tried to leave the drier ground and move away from the walls. Rough stones had broken off under the power of last night's tide, leaving fissures wide enough to be half-filled with rocks thrown in by the waves.

Before they knew what was happening, from the depths of one of these, a figure emerged.

They both stared as if seeing a ghost.

Male or female, it was soaked to the skin, wet garments hung down, ragged and steeped in mud, the boots were split by treading the rough ground, hair hung from under a coif. In the second after they saw each other the expression changed from surprise, to cunning, to rage.

It was Rogella.

There was no doubt this time.

'Get away from me!' She grabbed a hand-size boulder from the debris where she had hidden. 'Come nearer and I'll kill you!'

Her threat echoed strangely against the built-up walls. Above their heads they could hear the onlookers' shouted warnings, their cries as shrill as the distant screeching of gulls.

She aimed the rock. 'Move one inch, either of you, and you're dead!'

The three of them stared at each other.

Then, as one, they gaped in greater amazement as the fellow they thought of as the assassin loomed into view from behind a buttress. He gaped in equal astonishment at the three of them.

Misreading the situation he took a few strides towards Rogella, who was nearest, hooked one arm round her neck, and produced a knife.

'One step closer, you two, and she gets it.'

The shouts of the onlookers on the battlements fell silent. Hildegard and Josiana glanced at each other.

Hildegard turned to face him. 'What do you want?'

'Stay here while I take this one to the boats. When I'm safely on board she can go.'

Hildegard did not believe him. Neither, she suspected, did Rogella because she let out a great howl of protest. His only reaction was to tighten the arm round her neck. Lesson learned, she fell silent, her face twisted with hatred.

She muttered in a low voice which the nuns were just able to hear, 'You filthy, useless losel, so why didn't you finish the job? You didn't even stop that sanctimonious priest. He's lying there at Meaux, laughing at you. You don't frighten me.' She tried to spit.

Surprised at her words he turned her round so he could look into her face.

'Strike me—' His jaw sagged. 'It is you! The one from the mill! The cat with nine lives!'

'You lumbering oaf!' With no fear she taunted, 'Why did you let her go? She's no good to anybody. It was always her! Standing in my light from the day I was born! You useless, lying, strutting cur!' Tears of fury ran down her cheeks.

The fellow lowered his knife, looking bewildered. 'Keep away from me! You must be a ghost! I threw you in the canal when I'd done!' He spun on his heel and, slipping and sliding, ran in a crouch towards the boats.

Hildegard, Josiana and the crowd leaning over the battlements watched in confusion as the man used the knife to hack loose one of the painters. He pushed the boat out, plunging up to his knees in mud and having to drag his feet one by one from its clutches until there was enough water underneath to clamber onboard and stab at the shallows with an oar until he was far enough out to feel the water lift under the keel.

He began to scull into deeper water. His eyes never left Rogella.

Meanwhile, with the idea of escape or pursuit, she was pulling at the rope of another boat with increasing fury.

Josiana watched with an objective eye. 'If she thought for a moment she would know it was a fisherman's knot, easy to undo with one pull.'

Cursing loudly Rogella kicked at the stake holding the boat's painter but to no avail. She turned to the man making slow labour through the shoals and shouted, 'Come back, you! Take me with you!'

He stopped in his exertions and put out a hand as an invitation so, floundering in the mud, she began to slither after him.

He waited until she was almost touching the boat when he began to laugh. Then he sculled away from her as fast as he could.

Furious at being tricked she threw herself full length into the water and began to swim after him. A strong swimmer, she made better speed than he did with his clumsily wielded oar and she was soon grasping the side of the boat with both hands. By now they were out of earshot but something he said encouraged Rogella to climb over the stern and drop down inside.

Able to handle a boat as well as swim she grabbed the oar from him, picked up a second one and began to row vigorously towards the estuary.

The watchers, if they had been listening for it, would have heard the subtle change in the tide in that long moment of mystery when it changes from ebb to flow. It was the sea change. It warns that the waters are returning with all their moon-led force.

# EIGHTY-SIX

Hildegard heard voices behind them and, turning, saw Hubert and Ulf in their unwieldy craft grinding heavily onto the bank. Ulf jumped out at once and Hubert needed no urging to do the same. Together they tried to shift the boat off the mud but it was stuck fast. There was nothing they could do.

On the other side close to the temporary beach where the boats were tied, the Sheriff strode down with his men. They sank up to their knees as they gazed helplessly after the receding boat with their captive in it accompanied by their escaped prisoner back from the dead.

He waded over to join the two men. 'They won't get far.'

Josiana glanced at Hildegard. 'I wonder on what premise he bases that assumption?'

'It seems to me they might get far enough . . . But I still don't see what we can do.'

They went over to hear what the men were discussing only to find they intended to post lookouts to see which way the boat would go, west towards the haven where the Austin friars might be expected to stop them or east, down towards Hull with its river pilots and the port authorities on watch to prevent anyone leaving the realm without paying their tolls.

'They'll soon have the incoming tide to contend with,' Hildegard pointed out. 'I doubt that Rogella will row east.'

The Sheriff said it was a good enough guess to send men in the opposite direction towards Haltemprice Priory, there to rouse the no-good friars to action.

As he sent his men to follow his instructions he told them he would follow after but had something to do first. Then he begged a brief meeting with the Prioress.

She invited Hildegard and Josiana to attend them. 'Don't bother about the mud,' she advised when they all trooped over the tiles into her immaculate private chamber.

First thanking her for the hospitality shown his men the Sheriff told her he had some information for her.

'It's about that novice of yours, the poor unfortunate who was ravished by the fellow we're now pursuing.'

'Yes?' The Prioress gave him a sharp look with her all-seeing eyes.

Shifting somewhat on account of some unconfessed sin, perhaps, he cleared his throat. 'My lady, I have the duty to tell you that the girl has been found and is as safe and well as can be expected. Escaping the clutches of her attacker she managed to struggle on to Beverley where she has an aunt. This aunt, being a strong-minded widow-woman, gave her brother, the girl's father Sir Roger de Campany, a piece of her mind.' He paused to explain, 'I was there and heard every word.'

'Do go on, if you will.'

The Sheriff drew himself up. 'This is it.' In a prim voice slightly higher than usual he said, '"While I respect the Prioress at Swyne,"' he bowed slightly, '"a nun's life isn't for everybody."'

'"You should know that our Bella is not cut out for such a life."'

'"You must buy her back. I shall leave you to grieve by yourself for what you have done to Rogella. You're a cruel man, Roger, and she copied you, knowing no better. She tried her utmost to oust her twin in your heart. But you have no heart and now you'll reap what you sow. I shall keep Bella with me until she has recovered from her ordeal and for as long after that as she wishes. I'm sure that when the time comes my side of the family will put together enough money to give her a suitable dowry, to your shame. Now get off with you. Get yourself into Beverley Minster and pray to St John that you will become a better, kinder man, and I suggest you pray sincerely for the redemption of your eternal soul."' The Sheriff bowed when he finished. In a normal voice he said, 'That's exactly what she said, my lady, not a word of a lie.'

'I congratulate you on the totality of your recall.'

When he left the Prioress remarked to Hildegard, 'Let's hope this aunt, a healer-woman I know and respect, remembers the uses of pennyroyal.'

Hildegard agreed.

# EIGHTY-SEVEN

With the Sheriff's men gone and Ulf preparing to ride back while the tide was still low enough to leave the high road between Swyne and Beverley passable the priory was about to be deserted. And so it would have been, except for the monks from Meaux. And their abbot.

The monks were spending most of their time in the church but Abbot de Courcy left them and sent someone to fetch Hildegard as he wished to speak to her.

'So, Hildegard?' He gave her that dark-eyed look that always made her heart lurch. 'May I ask you to sit with me within the inner garth where we can talk?'

Without replying she made her way to the place where by reason of his authority, the abbot, alone of all men, had access.

'Well, here we are,' he remarked, superfluously, Hildegard thought, as they found seats on the stone bench against the wall of the cloister. 'I'll come to the point. I expect you heard me say that Leonin is my son?'

'I am not hard of hearing, my lord abbot.'

He moved uneasily.

Even as he did so she asked herself why could she not feel this weakness whenever she looked at Ulf? He was a lovable, kind and courageous man with no secrets and she cared for him deeply but it was Hubert, always Hubert, to break her heart.

She blinked and looked away into the distance. The cloisters were empty now. The sound of plainchant could be heard, echoing endlessly in the high vault of the church with a sound as ephemeral and as binding as love.

'Hildegard, we have unfinished business. Will you hear me?'

'Of course.' She drew her glance back to his.

'You look so coldly on me but I deserve it. I cannot hope for redemption. I know you are lost to me.' He bit his lip. 'But I owe you the confession I am about to make.' He knelt at her feet. 'There is more to— It's what happened years ago. My one excuse is that I was a foolish youth with— I was about the same age as Leonin, as it happens.'

He did not look at her as he spoke. 'I was a young knight-at-arms with the Duke of Burgundy, as you know.' His voice dropped. 'We were holding a town near Jerusalem when I met and fell head over heels in love with an older woman, the wife of the Saracen prince with whom our commander was negotiating a treaty.'

He hesitated before managing to overcome the emotion that gripped him. 'After the business was completed over several months of feasting and discussions, our army left and I and my lover parted for ever. I never heard from her again.'

With a guilty look he admitted, 'When Leonin showed up the other day he told me who he was— Heaven help me! I know it's true because of the birthmark on his wrist,' he pushed back his own sleeve to show her a small blemish, 'as well as that he possesses a little jewelled dagger – the very one I gave my lover in a romantic gesture before we parted. He told me she died of the plague when he was three and he was brought up as the ward of Sir John Pembroke, stationed for many years in the garrison near Damascus. Sir John, feeling he would like to return to the land of his birth now old age was approaching, set off with his entire household, including Leonin, who wanted to see his father's country. As fate decreed, Sir John never saw his home-land again. He died in Venice. But as a wealthy man, he made provision for his household including Leonin to return to England, to the new lord Pembroke. It was while being presented at court that Leonin's playing charmed the ear of King Richard. The rest you'll know. But for that terrible revelation beside the deathbed of our beloved Queen Anne he would never have thought of searching me out at Meaux. Only my name, which he well knew, brought information from one of the royal clerks on how to find me. I feel nothing but gratitude that he came to seek me out in his time of need.'

He continued to look at her in such a way that she could not drop her glance. 'So that is my story,' he confessed. 'When Leonin turned up I was in confusion and felt – I felt terrible guilt that I had been so heedless of my lover . . . and our child, so long unrecognized – guilt also that somehow I had deceived you,

Hildegard. If I have, it was by default. I had no knowledge of the truth – but he is too much like me to deny it.'

Striving to come to terms with what he was telling her she gave him a careful look. She longed to reach out to him but there was something else she needed to know first. 'It must be such a shock for you,' she began. 'I'm not surprised you wished to face it alone – but there is one more thing, Hubert. What did Leonin overhear to put him in such fear?'

His expression darkened. 'It was a most evil remark, something he overheard by chance when the duke and his chamberlain went to view the body of the queen. Unaware that Leonin was present, he said, "We've gone too far. We were only meant to provoke another miscarriage, not kill the wench."'

Hildegard gave a gasp of horror. 'What . . .?' She gripped Hubert by the arm. 'Is it true?'

'True enough to send him fleeing for his life.'

'Poor Anne . . . Poor Richard.'

Hubert, still kneeling at her feet, was holding her by the hand and she took courage from its warmth.

'Will the duke be brought to justice?'

'It will not end there,' he reassured her. 'I have already sent a courier back to the king. It will be up to him whether he seeks vengeance or not.'

She gave him a startled glance. 'But what about Leonin? The duke will not call off the hunt?'

'It has been arranged for "Leonin" to disappear. As far as the duke knows, his assassin was killed in a drunken brawl and the courtier he pursued succumbed to the plague. The trail goes cold somewhere in the Midlands. Rest assured, Leonin will not be abandoned. A royal promise is a royal promise.'

He lowered his head, 'Hildegard, there is something more personal I want to ask you – I fear that now is not the time but I must know the truth. I know you will never trust me again and will not care to forgive – but will you at least listen to what I say, even though I fear I already know your answer?'

Wondering what more was coming, she said, 'I will listen, Hubert, I will always listen.'

He spoke hurriedly, prepared for rejection. 'It's to do with what I asked you at Netley Abbey . . .' He took a breath. 'Remember

I asked then whether you would consider leaving the Order to join me in a different enterprise? Events took over and the time never seemed right—'

She held her breath, too surprised to speak. 'I remember Netley.' She saw that he was conscious of her inner struggle. The future hung in the balance. 'I should tell you,' she began hesitantly, 'that the Prioress has greatly honoured me by asking if I will take her place when she eventually enters her final retreat . . .'

Still kneeling, he gripped her tightly by both hands. 'That would be a prestigious position for you. I can easily see you as a Prioress of a wealthy house like this.'

She looked into his eyes and was about to reply when a sudden commotion announced the arrival of Leonin with an entourage of servants. He was in a boisterous mood, he was dressed for travel and hefted one small bag and another larger one containing his vielle over his shoulders.

Hubert jerked to his feet with an expression like the relief of a condemned man given a reprieve. 'So, Leonin, tell me, decision made?' He put his arms around him in a hug then stepped back. 'Are you to Beverley Song School – or have you chosen the royal court and all the dangers and corruption therein?'

Leonin glanced at Hildegard, 'I expect you know my true identity, my lady?'

'I do. I should have guessed. You are so alike.'

'What, I, like this abbot? With my dark skin and black hair?'

'It's more subtle than that – a turn of the head, your direct glance—'

'But he does have a better voice than me,' Hubert broke in. 'But come, Leonin, tell us your choice, north or south?'

'Surely no need to ask, father. Ulf and his men are already in the outer garth ready to escort me safely into Beverley and my new life. I shall glory in being nothing but a humble chorister, noticed by no one!'

Before joining the riders, he turned to Hildegard. 'My father may not have mentioned it but I've been invited to join the Song School by that musician you told me about, Pierrekyn Haverel. I could hope for nothing better. All my cravings for music-making will be satisfied. No one could have offered a more suitable place for me to thrive and grow if they had planned it. I shall astonish you with the beauty of the music I have yet to compose! What's best, I shall be close to my dear father after all these years.'

Ulf led a spare horse for Leonin and when their farewells had faded Hubert turned to Hildegard. He looked touchingly bereft. 'The dear boy, so lately found, so swiftly lost.'

'Not lost. He'll always return now he's found you. Beverley isn't far.'

'So be it.' He watched her with a cautious look and asked, 'As for you . . .?'

She smiled. 'Or do you mean us?'

He stared, halfway between dejection and hope. 'I can never be forgiven,' he murmured.

'Are you sure?'

For a moment he looked astonished then the sorrow was wiped from his face. 'If I dare hope – beloved, I have such plans if you consent – so much to do in this realm of England whether we stay within the Order or not.' His lips trembled with emotion.

'I still remember what you said at Netley,' she admitted. 'You said, "We can live however we choose . . . We serve God by taking hold of life and living to the full."'

'I hesitate to embrace my dreams even now.' He swept her into his arms. 'If we decide to leave we'll have to seek a dispensation from the Pope . . . but maybe you feel you can better fulfil your destiny by becoming Prioress of Swyne . . .? I beg one thing of you, my dearly beloved, that you make no decision in haste. Let's—'

'Let's do what you said then – let's seek the Blessed Isles, to pray, to live, to love?'

He gazed at her in astonishment and delight. 'That was my vow at Netley.' He scooped up both her hands and pressed her fingers one by one to his lips. 'First, we shall seek the help of the saints. We shall go on pilgrimage . . . To St James at Compostela? Or to St Peter in Rome if you prefer?'

'There'll be much to organize!'

'Your Prioress to settle, bags to pack, servants to appoint, horses to hire, and after that—' He pulled her into his arms again. 'If you decide to become Prioress – we shall be together even so, I at Meaux, and you at Swyne.'

'Whatever path we choose, as long as you are by my side nothing will bring me greater happiness.'

# CODA

The floods eventually receded leaving a devastated land behind.

Two men speaking an outlandish dialect crossed from the south bank to the north bank of the estuary. After questioning the canons at Haltemprice Priory – forced to seek refuge in their new tower throughout the inundation – they asked for directions to the Abbey of Meaux. When they arrived they demanded to speak to Abbot de Courcy if he had not already left on pilgrimage as they heard might be his intention, but after some discussion they were ushered in to his presence.

'We have a grievance, my lord,' the leader began. 'Two of our boats went missing before the floods and we believe the thieves fetched up on this side of the water—'

'Say no more. I'm right glad to see you. I believe you saved my son's life by means of your boat. Bursar?' He turned to one of the obedientiaries standing beside him. 'Recompense these men, as we agreed.'

The Bursar fetched a money-bag and thrust it into the boatman's hands.

Feeling the weight of it the man turned to Hubert. 'This is too much, my lord—'

'Nothing is too much for the safety of my son.'

Later, when the first shoots of spring began to push through the mud, some shepherds, bringing the flocks back to their old haunts, saw something shoaled up on a distant bank at low tide that could not be accounted for – and after getting as close as they could they ran back to the priory clamouring that they had found a monster of the deep, safely dead, but still fearsome in aspect.

A more sober-minded and practical group of lay-brothers went out carrying useful tackle to discover what the floods had thrown up.

'It does look a bit like a monster,' observed one of them reasonably, staring down at the thing in the mud when they drew near enough.

'One with two heads – or mayhap two monsters with one head apiece,' suggested another.

When the creature was brought back to the priory and the necessary inspection had taken place it was seen indeed to be two, not monsters but recognizably a human man and woman, locked in what might have been an embrace except for the knife pushed between the ribs of one and the skeletal fingers locked round the throat of the other.

Later, a wrist-chain worn by the woman was recognized by a young bride living in Beverley. It was identical to her own chain, given at birth, one for herself and one for her twin.

That accounted for Rogella.

As for her companion in death, nobody could identify him but logic, as Josiana repeated, led them to hazard a guess at his identity. Nobody had ever known his name and it was thought unwise to send to Woodstock, the king's youngest uncle, to identify him.

Later still, with the king in Ireland, a story that someone had poisoned his beloved queen the previous summer began to circulate. Whether true or not, the general view was that it would be a shocking crime to poison a young queen beloved by so many, a murder most royal and so heinous that if there was justice the poisoner must in time receive just punishment in hell.

And so it proved.

Some three years later Woodstock, the Duke of Gloucester, was imprisoned by his nephew in the English fortress at Calais where he suffered a sudden and violent death. Some claimed it had been secretly ordered by King Richard himself. But that's another story.

# AUTHOR'S NOTE

After twelve books Hildegard's sojourn in the England of Richard II is over. From that first mid-night dream in 2007 about three mysterious characters swapping banter over goblets of Guienne, Hildegard has taken me on an unexpectedly thrilling journey into history. She's urged me to try my hand at glass painting in York, singing plain chant in Salisbury, trying archery in the New Forest and exploring the papal labyrinth in the palace at Avignon, as well as giving me an excuse to hang out with historians and re-enactors, and other passionate followers of strange and personal medieval threads. It has led into archives and libraries too numerous to name. I know I shall always wonder how Hildegard and the Abbot are changing the world and whether she misses Ulf, Roger, the Prioress and the monks militant at the Abbey of Meaux.

For help in bringing these stories to you, I'd like to thank my fabulous editor at Severn House, Rachel Slatter, my eagle-eyed line editor Nicolas Blake, Piers Tilbury for his beautifully sinister covers and editor Sara Porter, Natasha, Mary and the rest of the production team. You're all amazing and a great joy to work with. Thanks to you all for sharing my journey into the dark side of medieval England.

And, readers, if you're still hungry for medieval crime catch up with Brother Chandler in The Broken Kingdom Trilogy and make sure to sign up for my (irregular) newsletters on: www.cassandra-clark.co.uk. Medievalists forever!